where one goes

by B N Toler

WHERE ONE GOES

Cover Design: Cover to Cover Designs
Cover photo: Savage Ultralight
Editor: Eagle Eye Reads
Copy Edit: 77Peaches
Interior Design: Integrity Formatting

For Hannah Graham, Morgan Harrington, Cassandra Morton, and any other woman who has died by the hands of a cruel person.

My heart breaks for you and your families.

May you rest in peace, beautiful girls.

Chapter 1

Charlotte

My grandmother had this saying she'd always tell me when I was down about life. *This too shall pass.* Considering she hung the moon, in my eyes, I believed her. She had a way about her; just being in her presence could right the world in an instant. To this day, I cling to those words, reciting them with every breath I take and release. Sometimes that's all we really have to get us through the hard times. Something as empty and useless as words can be what keeps us treading water in the raging and unforgiving river that is life. And that is exactly what they've been for me. Words have been the fine threads that have tied me to this world, forbidding me to disappear when every instinct in my body is telling me to end it.

To just let go.

"Here." My thoughts are interrupted as Casey speaks, pointing to an overpass just off the highway in Charlottesville, VA. It's been three hours since our last stop and night has fallen, hiding the colorful mountain sides covered with bouts of fall. I pull over my Toyota 4Runner a few feet off the road into the grass just before we reach the bridge. I'm exhausted. Not just physically, but in every way possible. This trip has taken days, exhausted my dwindling funds, and brought me closer to darker thoughts than ever before.

"He left me under the bridge, in the area covered with brush. But it doesn't look like me anymore," she warns, and I give her the most sympathetic smile I can muster up. I'd love to touch her, comfort her with some physical gesture—like a hug.

But I can't touch the dead.

I can only see them and speak to them.

"Casey, I . . ."

"You don't have to go look," she interrupts, "but you said you needed to, to be sure this was real." This is true. I did say that. After all, if I'm going to tip the police off about a dead body, I need to know for sure it's actually there.

It's raining heavily and I stare wearily ahead as the rain beats loudly against my SUV and windshield. I'm wearing my rain parka, well, my brother, Axel's, but it became mine when he passed away six years ago—back when the world tilted on its axis and sent me reeling into the oblivion.

Leaning over, I click open my glove box and grab the blue flashlight from inside. I haven't used it in years, and I'm praying the damn batteries still work. "I'll be right back." I sigh and pull the hood of my jacket over my head before climbing out of the SUV and nearly falling on my ass on the slick grass. I should've known it would come to this. I knew it was only a matter of time before a soul would find me and ask me to reveal where their body had been left after a cruel murder. Nothing happens as I click the flashlight on, but after beating it against the palm of my hand several times, light begins to flicker, albeit very limited light, but I'll take it. The ground dips where it meets the bridge and overlooks a steep hill. There's a creek at the bottom, and it appears the level of the water is higher than usual, so I meticulously crawl down, hoping I won't slide into it. The rain is unforgiving, pelting down on me with hard, cold pricks along my skin. The universe is always against me. Clear skies might have made seeing my first murdered body a little less traumatic—not much, but a little.

At the bottom, I stand, feeling uneasy. The water reaches my knees, seeping into my rain boots, filling them instantly. Scanning the area with my extremely dim flashlight, I immediately see the pile of vegetation Casey described against the pillar closest to me. Taking a deep breath, I swallow back the bile rising in my throat and put a hand to my chest, as if it might somehow calm my thundering heart. It takes me ten steps to reach the surrounding shrubland. As I stand frozen, I take another deep breath.

"Come on, Charlotte. Just do it," I will myself. With a trembling hand, I reach out and grab some of the wet shrub and pull it back. Casey's killer didn't do a very good job of hiding her. As soon as I pull the debris back, her skull is in full view, with what little is left of her blonde hair matted to it. I let the shrub go and stumble back, losing my balance and falling into the water, losing my flashlight as I land. The light immediately flickers out, and I fumble blindly in the dark murky water for it, but after several minutes I realize it's gone. Standing up, I close my eyes, praying I won't get sick. It's the last thing Casey needs to see right now.

Crawling back up the hill to the SUV, I lean on my hood to remove my boots and dump out the water in them, before putting them back on. When I climb back inside, Casey watches me, but says nothing as I stare straight ahead, lost in thought. Casey found me just outside of Vermont at a restaurant her parents and sister were eating at. The moment I looked at her, she knew I could see her even though she was dead. When the dead appear to me, there's no weird sound or blurred image. A warning sign of some sort would be lovely, but it's not a luxury afforded to me. They look like everyone else. It's only when they see me notice them that I figure out they're dead.

"What now, Casey?"

She gently pushes her blonde hair behind her ear. She was a beautiful girl—the kind that couldn't help but be noticed by every man she crossed. Luckily, the dead appear to me as they looked in their everyday life; not how they looked when they passed. "Now you call the police," she says, simply.

"And say what exactly? They might think I was involved in your murder somehow."

"Make an anonymous report."

"What about the guy that killed you? Don't you want them to find him?"

"They will. In time. There are other things more important."

I start my SUV and let it rest idly for a minute, cranking the heat up to full blast. "And this is it? This is what you need to cross over?"

"My mother and father can't move on until they know what happened to me. Once they know I'm dead, for sure, they can mourn and move on. Not knowing is destroying them, and my little sister is falling apart. I can't leave until I know they'll be okay."

"Okay." I nod and put the SUV in drive. I'm soaked to the bone, freezing, but the sooner I report this, the sooner Casey can be at peace, and I can be alone. Although, my alone time is always brief. There's always a soul, everywhere I go, in need of closure, needing to settle some form of unfinished business.

Casey was killed by a guy she met at a bar her junior year in college. She didn't notice he followed her when she left the bar by herself. It upsets me to rehash all the details; frankly, I wish *I* didn't know them. Some things are just too hard to imagine. Her last moments in this world were the things nightmares are made of. But her family has been unable to let go, therefore *she* hasn't been able to let go.

"Thank you for this, Char. I know you consider your gift to see the dead a curse, but you've given me peace."

I don't respond. I know I'm giving her peace of mind, like I have others before her, but their peace costs me my own. This 'gift,' as she called it, has cost me any semblance of normalcy; it's cost me my family, my friends, and my hope. We pull into a gas station just off the highway. I grab my backpack from the backseat and pull out a notebook and pen.

There's a body off of Highway 501 under the Ukon Bridge.

The note is short and sweet. No need to get too in-depth. I take out an envelope and write down the detective's name in charge of her case and the address Casey recites for me. Once that's done, the letter is sealed, and I place a stamp on it. We head into town and find the nearest post office, where I drop the letter in the box.

Casey lets out an audible sigh, filled with what I can only describe as relief. "I'll go see them one last time, and then I can go."

"Good luck, Casey," I offer; I don't know what else to say. What else could I say? *Safe travels? Send a postcard?*

"Thank you," she says, softly. Then, she disappears.

chapter 2

Charlotte

I drive for hours after Casey disappears. At least it feels like hours. I have no map or plans of where I'm going, but I go anyway. My life has become one huge uncertainty.

My SUV revs at a good speed as it climbs the mountain's roads, winding around perilous curves, driving me further into the darkness—literally and figuratively speaking. I've never seen night as dark as it is here in the mountains. It's almost consuming, and oddly, it doesn't bother me. It's funny how the mind works sometimes. I've spent the last six years scared and alone. Not scared of the dead, ironically, but scared my life belonged to them, that I will never have it back. But tonight, I made a decision. Tonight, I will take my life back. I will have control. A numbness settles over me, and my mind is blank. And that's how I know I've made the right decision. When my 4Runner begins to sputter, the motor working overtime around the remaining gas fumes, I steer it toward the side of the road. I have a hundred dollars to my name hidden in my glove box, but I don't need money where I'm going. Whoever finds the SUV first can have it. Leaving the headlights on, I walk, shivering, numb to my soul with a darkness I can't find my way out of. This isn't a life—it's a nightmare. A never-ending torment of death and servitude. And the pain has become too much to bear.

I don't meander far when I find myself on a bridge where a large river runs underneath it; the water is raging, angry with all the rain. Walking to the middle, I let my hand glide along the wet railing and stare down at the water, wondering what it would be like to jump in, to let the water drag me down and take me away from this life—this nightmare.

This too shall pass, I repeat to myself over and over, but the words have lost their magic, and their hold on me. Maybe all of this time I've thought of those words as my lifeline when really, all they've been is a weight shackled to my ankle, slowly dragging me under, keeping me from finding real peace. This will never pass. I will always belong to the dead and because of that, I will never truly live.

It's time to just let go.

Ike

Being in limbo sucks. All you do is watch your loved ones suffer and have no ability to help them. My parents seem to be okay, for the most part. My little brother, too. But it's George I worry about. Most siblings are close, but being twins creates a bond normal siblings could never understand. We'd been best friends since day one.

And now, I'm dead.

"Yes, Ma. I'll be home Sunday for dinner." He pauses. "No, I'm not drunk," George assures my mother over the phone. He isn't lying. He's not drunk—not yet anyway.

"No, Ma! He's just a fucking drug addict high on cocaine!" I shout, even though neither of them can hear me. It's a good thing, too; if she ever heard me drop the f-bomb, she'd whip my ass.

I can't hear what my mother is saying to George from the other end, but I can hear her muffled cries over the phone. "I know, Ma. I miss him, too." He covers his eyes with his free hand, a pained expression taking hold of his features.

"Shit, George," I breathe. I hate seeing him like this.

"I gotta go, Ma. I love you." He hits end on the screen of his cell and plops down on the sofa. The glass coffee table in front of him is covered with white residue, a bag of coke, his wallet, and empty beer bottles. George leans forward and picks up a framed photo of me in uniform, from the day I graduated from basic training. He stares at the photo for a long moment before setting it down gently. Sliding off the sofa onto his knees, he pulls his license from his wallet. Within seconds, he's separating a rock of coke into three small lines. After putting his license back in his wallet, he takes a dollar bill out and rolls it tightly, then uses it to snort the first line.

"George!" I yell. "Jesus, man. Why are you doing this to yourself?" But it's pointless because he can't hear my words of concern.

I can't watch anymore. Besides, I know that whore, Misty, is on her way over and seeing him with her disgusts me. My brother is obviously a mess, mourning my loss, and she's taking full advantage of it, bringing him drugs, snorting them with him as long as he's paying, and then they fuck, even though she has a boyfriend who would beat the shit out of George if he ever found out.

I vanish and reappear about half a mile from Anioch Bridge, just outside of town. George and I used to come here when we were kids and we'd fish; those are some of my favorite memories. As I walk toward the bridge in the blackness of the night, I hear the water from the Jackson River raging. The rain has been heavy here the last few days, and the water levels are high. I envy the river. It moves, flows, and keeps going. Unlike me. I'm stuck, trapped by my own need to fix something I can do nothing about.

I died almost ten months ago, and that whole 'white light' people talk about is bullshit. At first, I didn't realize I was dead. Actually, I thought I was dreaming; somehow I was home with my mother and father, but when I tried to speak to them, they didn't hear me or even respond. It didn't take long before they received the call notifying them I'd been killed by an IED in Afghanistan.

Shock was all I felt as everyone fell apart with the news. At that point, I thought it was a nightmare; I'd wake up at any moment next to my buddy, Sniper, in our barracks and we'd bullshit about one thing or another. But that never happened. Instead, I've been forced to watch my family mourn my passing, unable to offer them any comfort. George has been spiraling out of control since I died, and I can't bear to see him like this. I know, without a doubt, he's what's anchoring me here, keeping me from moving on to whatever lies ahead.

"This is hell," I mumble to myself. So lost in my own thoughts, I don't notice the faint light ahead until I'm just about to step onto the bridge.

"I'm sorry, Grandma. I'm sorry, Axel. I'm sorry I'm not stronger." My thoughts are interrupted when I hear a woman crying. My eyes whip toward the sound of her voice; a thin woman wearing a rain parka that's way too big, her dark hair plastered to her head as the rain beats down on her. Water drips from the tip of her nose. She's standing on the railing of the bridge, sobbing loudly. I'm frozen in place, unsure of how to react, but when her sobs suddenly cease and she lifts her head, my breath hitches. Before, her emotion showed her uncertainty about killing herself. Now, her expression is void, as if she's decided something. She inhales deeply as she comes to terms with her decision and what she's about to do. And I'm certain she's going to jump.

"Don't!" I shout as I run toward her, even though I know she can't hear me, but I can't help my reaction. When her head jerks toward me at the sound of my voice, I nearly fall on my ass in shock. Her dark eyes meet mine and she tenses. *She heard me.*

"Go away!" she shouts back. I stare up at her, my eyes wide and mouth hanging open. She sees me! She can hear me! "Just go away!" she shouts again, wiping her nose with the sleeve of her jacket.

"You can see me?" I shake my head in disbelief.

She clenches her eyes closed and groans. "You're dead." It's not a question, but more of a statement. The rain stops and silence falls between us.

"You can really see me?" I ask again, convinced I'm going mad.

"Dead and stupid," she mumbles. "Obviously I can see and hear you."

"But . . . how?"

She turns away from me, and I stare at her profile as she clenches her eyes closed again. "Go away. I can't help you. I'm done helping the dead. Just leave me alone." She stares down at the water, her gaze lingering longingly.

Shit. She's going to jump. "Listen. What's your name?"

"My name doesn't matter."

"It matters to me," I argue. "My name is Ike. Ike McDermott. Please, just come down. Let's talk about this."

"Why?" She laughs hysterically, but it just sounds cryptic. "So I can help you settle your unfinished business so you can cross over? Well, guess what, *Ike?*" she says, bitterly. "I have nothing. I have one hundred dollars to my name, my vehicle is out of gas, I have no friends or family to help me, and it's all because of *your* kind. Because the dead won't let me be!" Her voice shakes with emotion as angry tears fill her eyes.

I rub my head as I struggle for the right words. She can see dead people. Although it seems like a plus for me, it probably has a lot of downfalls for her. She's obviously alone in the world. My gaze meets hers again and I ask, "What if I can help you with all of that? Well . . . most of it. What if *we* make a deal?"

"A deal?"

"I'll introduce you to some nice people, help you get a job, a place to stay, and you . . . you can help me settle things." She stares down at the water and shakes her head, dismissing me. "Listen, I don't know you or what you've been through, but I know I'd give anything to still be alive right now, no matter what." Tears stream down her face, and I think my words have gotten through to her. "Don't waste what so many of us never got the chance to have," I plead.

She continues to stare down at the water, her sniffles the only sound to break the silence, when she shakes her head and slides down the railing back to the road of the bridge. "You people won't let me be. I can't even kill myself!" she groans as she tromps in the opposite direction toward her sport utility vehicle.

"Where are you going?" I yell as I jog to catch up to her. My mind is on overload. She can see me and speak to me. I've been dead for months with only myself to talk to. This is incredible!

"My 4Runner is this way," she mumbles, stating the obvious, as she shivers.

"Well, if you need gas, the closest station is this way." I jab my thumb over my shoulder. "The Mercers own it. They're nice people. They'll help you out."

She stops and faces me for a moment, and her face is turned in such a way that the lights from her vehicle show me her gray eyes and they nearly take my breath away. It's hard to explain why the pain in her gaze seems so beautiful. She looks like a wild creature, a being meant to be free and roaming, that's somehow been entrapped. Her dark hair is wet and stuck to her face, and I so badly want to reach out and slide it back to see all of her. Our gazes remain locked for a long while when her almost blue lips tremble. She's freezing.

"We have to get you warm. Let me help you . . ." I let my last word trail off, hinting I'd like her to tell me her name.

She takes a deep breath and sighs. "Charlotte," she says, quietly. "But people call me Char." *Charlotte.* I smile softly at her name. It's pretty, like her.

"Okay, Charlotte. Do you have some dry clothes to bring with you?"

"In the truck." She jogs ahead of me and opens her back driver's side door, climbing in. Moments later she comes out with a backpack and a small duffel bag. After turning off her headlights, she shuts the door as the rain begins to come down hard again. She looks up to the sky, letting the rain pelt her face roughly. Her free hand comes up, and she jabs her middle finger up to the dark abyss, and I chuckle. I want to cover her, carry her bags, but . . . I can't.

With a huff, she passes by me, and I quickly join her. "I'm sorry I can't help you carry those."

She snickers softly. "I'm sorry you can't either." She pauses for a beat before adding, "I mean, I'm sorry you can't carry them because you're not alive." Her words hang heavily in the air as the rain beats down on us. "How'd you go?"

I shove my hands in my pockets and sigh. "IED. Afghanistan."

"Shit," she sighs. "I'm sorry."

"Well, if I was going to go . . ." My sentence trails off, and she gives me a nod of understanding. Death sucks. No ifs, ands, or buts about it. But at least I died a noble death. There are worse ways to go.

"So, where are you taking me?"

"You don't know where you are?" I feign disbelief.

She smiles timidly. "I didn't care where I was going. I planned to drive until my SUV ran out of gas and . . . well . . . you foiled the rest of it."

"Can't say I'm sorry about that," I answer honestly. "Is it really that bad?"

The rain abruptly stops again, as if God himself flipped an off switch, and we both stop and look up. After a moment, she starts walking again and I follow, the sounds of her boots making squishing noises to break the quiet. "Every day of my life for the last six years has been spent with the dead. I have no friends—the ones I had all think I went crazy, my parents didn't know what to do with me, so they just pretended like I wasn't there, and forget about a boyfriend. So you see, I have nothing but death. My life is settling the dead's business so they can cross over, and dammit, I'm tired."

She looks it, too. Her pale face and sunken eyes tell a story of a hard life. "We can help each other, Charlotte. This is a good place. You'll like it here."

"And where is here?"

"This is Warm Springs. It's a little town inside Bath County."

"Warm Springs?"

"Yeah. Where one goes to rejuvenate," I say in my best radio announcer voice. "Jefferson Pools? Never heard of them?"

"Nope," she answers.

"They're special springs . . . they stay warm all year round. General Robert E. Lee and Thomas Jefferson frequented them."

"Is that so?" she asks dryly, clearly unimpressed.

"Anyway," I continue. "You're in a good place."

"Am I still in Virginia?"

"Yes."

"And how exactly do you think you can help me?"

"You need a place to rest. You need a job. I can help you with that."

"How so? You're dead." She points out the obvious.

I stop in my tracks. "I am? Are you serious?" I feign shock and she rolls her eyes, the ghost of a smile playing on the corners of her lips. We start walking again, and I answer her question. "I know the people of this town. What they like and dislike. I can help you make nice with them."

"And what would you like in return?"

George flashes through my mind, and I feel that weight settle on my chest. "I have a brother who's having a hard time."

"Unfinished business," she mutters and lets out an audible sigh.

"Look, I know you're tired of helping people like me, but I'm different. I want to help you, too. If I can help you, will you help me?"

"I guess I don't have a choice," she mumbles and shrugs, adjusting her bags to get a better hold. "You have a deal."

Chapter 4

Charlotte

It's funny how your plans can change so drastically within the span of minutes. My life was ending forty minutes ago. I was certain of it. But then Ike shows up and derails my plans. I suppose his words are what brought me back.

"Listen, I don't know you or what you've been through, but I know I'd give anything to still be alive right now, no matter what."

Suicide is selfish. It's a complete slap in the face to anyone who has died and wanted to live. So with great trepidation, the tall built man brought me back to my senses. Now, I'm standing just outside *Mercer's Stop and Go* with him by my side. The store is aged, the lit signs looking as if they were made decades ago.

"It looks like Mr. Mercer is working tonight. He's real friendly. Just go in, and tell him you broke down. He'll help you out." He gives me a crooked smile; I gather that's his way of encouraging me. He's handsome, very broad and muscular, and maybe six feet tall, but his smile is his best feature.

I take a deep breath, and as I near the door, I catch a glimpse of myself in the reflection of the window. My dark hair is matted to my head, and my clothes hang heavily on me. I look like Raggedy Anne's cousin. I look like hell.

"He's going to think I'm a fucking crack head," I say, as I run my fingers through my wet, tangled hair. "Look at me."

Ike laughs and his bright smile warms my heart. "No, he won't. This town has a lot of good people, Charlotte. The Mercers being some of the best. Trust me."

"Okay," I huff as I push the door open and enter. An older gentleman, with thick, gray brows and kind eyes, greets me with a concerned look.

"You look a mess, child. Are you okay?" he asks as he rounds the counter and approaches me.

"Yes, sir. My SUV broke down about two miles back, and I had to walk in the rain."

"My lord, you'll be lucky if you don't catch your death." He shakes his head, sincere concern etched across his face. "I can get your SUV looked at in the morning. There's a motel about four miles down we can get you checked in to for the night. I'll drive you there myself." He quickly sets about putting his jacket on and hanging a *Be Back in 10* sign on the door just before ushering me out and locking up.

"That is so kind of you," I mumble through my shock. Who the hell offers a complete stranger—one that looks like they're on drugs—a ride in the middle of the night? Mr. Mercer simply smiles and nods as we walk to the side of the building.

I'm surprised when he leads me to a Ford Highboy and opens the passenger door for me. *What a sweet old man,* I think to myself. Once he gets in and starts the truck, he cranks the heat up and I couldn't be more grateful. As we drive, Ike is to my left, sitting between us, although, of course, Mr. Mercer can't see him. "Okie from Muskogee" by *Merle Haggard* plays softly on the radio, and I cringe at how fitting it is.

"I'm Bill Mercer, by the way." He nods his head at me. It occurs to me he thinks I've just gotten in his vehicle and don't know his name. I should've introduced myself, but Ike had already told me his name. I'm so tired, I'm not thinking straight.

"Charlotte," I respond. "But most people call me Char."

"Where are you from, Char?"

"Born and raised in Oklahoma."

"Hey . . . you're an Okie," he says as his face lights up with another smile. "The song," he points out.

I smile. "I was just thinking that."

"You're a long way from home," he adds and shoots me a concerned look.

"You're telling me," I agree.

We reach the Warm Springs Motel and Mr. Mercer ushers me inside the office with a neon sign lit above flashing: VACANCY.

"Hey, Bill. How are ya?" a large and robust woman with fire engine red hair and lots of purple eye shadow asks as she stands from her recliner in front of a flat screen television.

"Ginger, this is Charlotte, but she likes to be called Char."

"Well hello, Char," Ginger greets and offers me a friendly smile amidst her chubby cheeks. "You look like you've had a rough night."

I shrug and give her a shy smile. "You could say that."

"Nothing a hot shower won't fix," Ike jibes, but I ignore him. It took me years of practice to learn to ignore the dead and not respond to them in front of other people. Even a glance in their direction can make other people think I'm odd.

"Well, a room is forty dollars a night, but you'll have cable, and the hot water is great."

Forty dollars? That's cheap as hell. I drop my bags to the floor and begin opening my backpack, the thought of a hot shower and a warm bed making me quiver, when I realize I left my money in the glove box of my truck. *Shit!* My face flames red as I stand and pick my bags up. "I'm so sorry I wasted your time, Mr. Mercer, but I left my money in my truck. I'll just go back to it and crash there tonight." Humiliation surges through me as I glance at Ike who closes his eyes, realizing how embarrassed I am.

"Nonsense, child." Mr. Mercer waves at me. "I'll pay. You can pay me back some other time when you get your money."

"I can't accept that, sir." I shake my head vehemently. I don't want handouts.

"Why not?" Ike asks, with his arms extended. "You're freezing and need rest!" Again, I ignore him, which is hard when his body language and tone are so animated.

"Sweetheart, you need rest. If you run off tomorrow and don't pay me, forty dollars won't end my life. At least I'll know you had a safe night's rest. It would put my mind at ease." Mr. Mercer stares down at me softly as he hands Ginger the cash. I hate the pity in his eyes. I probably look like a homeless drifter—which I guess, technically, I am.

"Then here," I say, as I unhook my necklace with the silver cross. I haven't taken it off in years. "Take this and hold onto it so you know I'll return. That's one of my most prized possessions, and I would never leave it behind. But please don't sell it. I'll have your money tomorrow."

Mr. Mercer takes the cross in his hand, a gentle smile playing on his lips. "You have my word." With that, he heads to the door and before he exits, he says, "Good night, Char."

"Thank you, Mr. Mercer. You are very kind." I nod.

"Well hon, I have a room ready for you," Ginger says, as she rounds the counter.

"Big surprise. She only has one other occupant," Ike snorts, and I have to fight not to smile.

Ginger leads me to room thirteen, which is the farthest room from her office. I guess she likes her privacy. "Now, you be sure to lock your door when I leave, and if you need anything just dial zero on the phone and it'll send you to me."

"Thank you, ma'am." I smile appreciatively.

"When is the last time you ate, hon? You look like a light breeze would just blow you right over. I made fried chicken for dinner and have a few pieces left over. I could warm them up for you."

"You are so kind, but I think a hot shower and a nice bed is what I really need right now. Thank you, though." I nod.

"Okay, dear. Night." Once she closes the door, I plop back on the bed. Ike takes a seat in the yellow, pleather arm chair by the door.

"Is this the only motel in town?"

He laughs. "Well, this county has a shit-ton of bed and breakfasts and there's also *The Plantation,* which is pretty much your rich people resort. This motel is lower scale, obviously, but in the next few weeks I have no doubt she'll be at maximum occupancy."

"Why's that?"

"Because fall is our tourist season. People come from all over to enjoy the springs and see the leaves change," he explains. As I listen to him, I shiver, still cold and wet in my drenched clothes.

"You need to get out of those clothes and take a hot shower," Ike observes.

"Yes, mother," I sigh loudly before standing. I stare at him a moment and he just stares back.

"Are you planning on giving me some privacy?"

"Don't mind me. I'm dead." He beams a perfect grin that makes my belly flutter.

"I'm not undressing in front of you, soldier boy," I inform him.

"A fallen soldier, dead and in limbo, can't even get a little peek? That's just cruel, Charlotte," he jests, clenching his eyes closed in mock pain.

I can't help laughing a little as I start digging through my bag and warn, "You better not watch me in the shower, either."

He laughs loudly. His laugh is so rich and deep, it makes me laugh some more. "Come on. What good is being dead if I can't watch a girl shower without her knowing?"

"But I would know," I remind him. "Shit!" I groan as I dump my clothes on the bed.

"What's wrong?"

"All of my shit is soaked," I whine.

"You've got a dirty little mouth on you," he remarks with a smirk.

"And?"

"I like it," he shrugs.

"Guess I'm sleeping naked tonight," I sigh.

"There is a god," Ike stares up at the ceiling, hands clasped in praise.

"You're not sleeping here," I point out.

"It was worth a try," he huffs in defeat. As I head toward the bathroom, I turn and see Ike staring at the floor. "You okay?"

His gaze meets mine and he shakes his head. "You don't know what it's like to walk around for months and months and have no one see you or hear you." He's not the first dead person to tell me this. I try to sympathize and remember that every time I get frustrated about a new soul popping up, but it's hard sometimes.

We stare at each other a long while before he stands. "I'm going to go check on my brother and let you have a bit of peace. I'll be back before you wake up." His dog tags jingle as he stands.

"Okay," I swallow, oddly saddened that he's leaving. Normally, this would be a time of celebration. Alone time. But for some reason, I want to get to know him. He's the first soul I've met that's actually put me first. "I'll see you in the morning."

"Good night, Charlotte," he offers, and then he vanishes.

Ike

I check on George. He's passed out with Misty by his side, her tits out for the world to see. But he's breathing. That's been my biggest fear; that he will kill himself by overdosing. In the ten months since I passed, George has lost a lot of weight and looks half-dead himself. He blames himself for my death, like he could've stopped me from joining the military, or if he'd been there, he could've saved me. Joining was my choice. It's what I wanted and I have no regrets, except for what my death is doing to him.

But there is hope now. There is Charlotte. The wild and beautiful creature may just be the answer. But she needs saving, too, that I can see. To think, if I had been just a few minutes later appearing on that bridge, I may have never met her. I only need to figure out how I can help her while she helps George. I'll need to figure out how to save her, and my brother, from killing themselves.

It's nine in the morning and Charlotte is still sleeping. She looks different with dry hair in the light of day. Her dark hair is shiny and soft, fanned out over the pillows. Her lips are now pink, not blue as they were last night. She's on her stomach, the blanket just barely covering her ass. Her skin looks so smooth and creamy, I'd give anything to touch it. I know I shouldn't be staring at her like this, but I can't help it. I may be dead, but I'm still a man—I like to look at beautiful women.

I have to get her up. She needs to get to her truck, and we need to get her a job immediately.

"Wake up! Wake up! Wake up!" I yell, and clap my hands in front of her face. She jolts up, her eyes frantic. I get a great shot of her breasts, *and dear God, they are beautiful*, I mean, call me an asshole, but I have no shame in staring at her before she jerks the blanket up, covering herself. Man, I miss the feel of a woman. Their softness, their warmness.

"I'm going to kill you!" she shouts.

"Little late for that, babe," I reply and jerk my chin. She tosses a pillow at me. It goes right through me and lands on the floor.

I yawn. "Ouch."

"Don't wake me up like that ever again!" she shouts. "I don't have any clothes on!"

"Really? I hadn't noticed," I mock confusion.

"Asshole!"

"My, my, we're grumpy in the morning," I chuckle as she stands, wrapping the blanket around her. The dead can still get hard-ons. I have to turn from her, so she doesn't see mine as I mentally lick her long, lean body. *Damn!*

She grabs her bag and scurries into the bathroom, slamming the door behind her. Apparently, mornings are not her forte. When she exits the bathroom, she's wearing worn jeans with holes all over and a black tank top. Her dark hair is down and she's put on a little makeup. Although she still looks tired and frail, she looks refreshed, and that makes me happy. I don't know her well, but I hope when all is said and done, I can help *her* find some happiness.

"How much did you see?" she asks as she zips her backpack up.

"Not much." I shrug and she sighs with relief. "Just your breasts," I add nonchalantly, and she throws a hair brush at me, which zips right through me and hits the wall.

"Thought we already established that won't work."

"You suck," she huffs and flings her backpack over her shoulder.

"They were really nice, Charlotte." I compliment her and she blushes, but she can't help but smile.

"You're lucky my gift is limited to seeing and hearing you. If I could touch you, you'd be talking in soprano right now."

I laugh as she opens the door and slams it in my face. I materialize beside her, outside, and we head to the front office to check her out, but Ginger just smiles and shakes her head.

"Apparently, Mr. Mercer went home and told Mrs. Mercer about you; she came in first thing this morning and paid for your room until Sunday."

"What?" Charlotte stares at the woman like she's grown an extra head.

"She left this for you, too." Ginger hands her a Ziploc bag with Charlotte's necklace in it.

"Why would they do this for me?" Charlotte asks, but instead of looking at Ginger, she looks at me.

"I think you remind them of their daughter. She died over a decade ago," Ginger says, before she smiles, sadly.

Charlotte lets out a deep sigh, and I see how this news affects her. Her gray eyes stare down as she takes in the information. "Thank you, Ginger."

"Oh, and here." Ginger sets a brown paper bag on the counter. "These are my homemade blueberry muffins. You need to eat, girly. Put a little meat on those bones. That's what men 'round here like on a woman."

"I like big butts and I cannot lie." I rap like Sir Mix A-Lot and thrust my hips. I see a ghost of a smile on her lips, and I know she wants to laugh at me.

Charlotte smiles at Ginger and takes the bag. "You're too kind. Thank you so much."

"I'll see you later, hon. Oh, and Mrs. Mercer, I call her Susan, said Mr. Mercer had your truck towed in this morning to their gas station. They filled it up and brought it here. She said it's parked around the side of the motel."

Charlotte looks right at me. Something I noticed she rarely does in front of other people. "I told you they were nice people," I shrug. "Come on."

"Thank you, Ginger." Charlotte waves before we exit.

"What is this place? Fucking Mayberry? Why is everyone so freaking nice?"

"Not everyone," I snort. "You'll meet the town assholes soon enough."

Charlotte

I feel like I've officially entered an alternate universe. I immediately drove to the Mercer's gas station where Mr. Mercer refused to take the hundred dollars. After much pleading, he agreed to hold my necklace until I could repay him, but he said I had to have a job first before he'd take a dime from me. So Ike and I loaded up in my 4Runner and drove two miles south until we parked in front of place called *Ike and George's.*

"You own a restaurant?" I ask as I stare up at the sign.

"I did. It's all George's now."

"*Ike and George's?* Original," I try to joke and glance at him. He stares at the sign and shakes his head.

"I had two months left and I was out. I wasn't going to sign-up for another tour. I was going to come back here and run this place with him. But . . ." He lets out an audible sigh. "Plans change, right?"

"May I ask how a restaurant survives in such a small town?" I try to change the subject.

"My family owns the building so we have no rent, and we're one of only three bars in town. This is a big tourist spot, especially in the fall, like I told you. *The Plantation* is that huge place over there." He points behind us where I see some huge stone pillars leading toward what looks like a gigantic mansion. "We get a lot of business from them as well."

"I see." I nod in understanding. "And is this where you think you'll help me find employment?"

"It is. You can waitress, right?"

"Yes."

"Let's go in."

The inside of the restaurant is rustic, with barrels set up and a bar top running along them. The floors have that unfinished-but-worn look, and country music plays over the speakers. I sidle up to the bar, Ike at my side, and take a seat, glancing around, trying to spot someone who works here. There's a tin bucket of peanuts on the bar and my stomach grumbles. I didn't eat Ginger's muffins yet so I grab a handful and begin cracking the shells.

Suddenly, a blonde with way too much eyeliner appears and gives me a toothy grin. "I didn't hear you come in, hon. How are you?" she asks.

"That's because she was probably in the back snorting a line of coke or blowing the boss," Ike adds, and it takes all my strength not to go wide-eyed and look at him.

"I'm good. Thank you," I answer her after I get past my shock.

"Did you want to see a menu?"

"Tell her you're here to speak with George," Ike instructs me.

"Actually, I'm here to speak with George." Her brows furrow at my words, and she gives me a good once-over.

"Is he expecting you?" she asks, suspicion laced in her tone.

"Stupid bitch," Ike growls.

"No, he's not," I answer quickly.

"And you are?" she asks. Ike is seething beside me, but I don't understand why. Her questioning is starting to get on my nerves, but I'm not pissed like he is.

"My name is Charlotte. But people call me—"

"Misty!" a deep voice bellows from the kitchen. I turn in its direction and almost fall off my stool when he rounds the corner from the kitchen. "Misty! Where's the closeout from last night?"

My mouth drops open, and all I can do is stare. It's Ike. It's Ike in the flesh.

"Did I mention George was my identical twin?" Ike whispers from behind me as he softly chuckles.

Before I can think about it, I glance back at him, shock written across my entire face. I can't explain what it's like to see someone dead and see their mirror image in the flesh. My mind is mush right now.

"George, this little girl says she'd like to speak with you," Misty ignores his question and jerks her chin toward me, her sudden distaste for me evident in her tone.

Little girl? Did she seriously just call me that? Normally I'd be pissed, but I'm still lost in awe of Ike's brother looking just like him, so I brush off the insult and focus on the matter at hand.

"Oh yeah?" His gaze meets mine and he cocks his head to the side. "Do I know you?"

I'm still stunned frozen with my mouth hanging open.

"Okay. I should've told you, but could you please shut your mouth and stop looking like an idiot?" Ike requests from behind me. Snapping my mouth shut, I straighten up in my seat.

"Uh . . . no. We've never met," I stammer.

George looks to Misty. "Misty, can you go help Sniper unload the produce?"

"Sure." She smiles at him before cutting a quick glance at me. Once she's out of sight, George walks behind the bar and sets his clipboard down. Now that I'm able to get a better look at him, I can see some differences. Ike is buffer and broader while George is thinner. George's hair is longer, shaggier, while Ike's is buzzed, military style.

"And you are?" George prompts, and I shake my head trying to get my wits about me.

"My name is Charlotte. I'm new to town. I'm staying over at the motel." I pause, unsure of how to ask him for a job.

"Just ask!" Ike orders.

"I heard you might be looking for a waitress," I somewhat snap, irritated with Ike. It's not easy to have someone speak to you that you can't acknowledge.

"And who'd you hear that from?"

Shit! What am I supposed to say? Your dead brother? "Mr. Mercer mentioned it," I lie. Hopefully it'll never come up between them.

"You have experience?"

"Some. I waited tables in college."

"And how long ago was that?"

"I dropped out after my freshman year six years ago. Family stuff came up."

More like I started seeing dead people and thought I was losing my fucking mind, but I skip on the details with George.

"And since then?"

"Uh . . ." *Since then, I've been driving around the country helping dead people, making no money at all.* "I came in to some money, and it held me over for a while, but I need a job now." Not entirely untrue. My father basically paid me to disappear. I was given a lump-sum of money and told to travel and meet new people. In other words, I was to disappear because I was too complicated, and I freaked everyone out because I could see the dead. I took the money, hugged my parents tightly, and vanished from their lives.

George gives me a once-over and crosses his arms. "I'd like to help you, but you just drifted into town, and I have no guarantee you won't just up and leave without notice. Maybe try the grocery store down the way." He turns and bends down, sorting something in a cabinet, and I glance at Ike and shrug.

"God, he's an arrogant asshole," Ike mumbles. "Okay. He's a betting man. Tell him you bet you can pick out his favorite song on the jukebox, and if you get it, he'll give you a shot."

I glance sideways at Ike, letting him know how stupid that sounds.

"Trust me. He's a cocky son of a bitch. He'll take the bet thinking you won't win."

I shake my head no.

"Do it, Charlotte. Please." He bats his lashes at me, and I fight the urge to smile. Instead, I glare at him and take a deep breath.

George stands and faces me again, a look of surprise on his face. Maybe he was expecting me to leave after he shut me down.

"You look like a betting man to me." I stand and start digging in my backpack for spare change. "I bet I can pick out your favorite song on that jukebox. If I do, you give me a job. If I don't, I leave and never come back." I find two quarters and smirk at George flirtatiously, challenging him with a cocky shrug.

He snorts and crosses his arms again. "And who's to say I'll admit it's my favorite song? I could just lie."

"He won't," Ike adds, staring at his brother. "He's not perfect, but he's no liar."

"I'm good at reading people. You strike me as an honest man," I answer, fisting the quarters now. George's brows furrow as our gazes lock. His eyes are so dark, not like Ike's. Ike's are an earthy brown, bright and soft, while George's are like dark coffee and cold. Not a cruel cold, more like wounded, like a warning to stay away; a broken cold.

"What did you say your name was?" he asks, stepping toward me.

"I'm Charlotte, but people call me Char." *Except for your brother.*

"Okay, Charlotte." He smirks. Apparently, neither of the McDermott brothers plan to call me by my nickname. "You're on. Pick my favorite song, and I'll give you a shot."

I nod in agreement and head toward the jukebox near the entrance. Ike leans one arm against the neon machine as I put my coins in the slot. "Johnny Cash, *God's Gonna Cut You Down*," he says. I can't help it; I look up at Ike and smirk. "What? You're not a Cash fan?" He gives me a sad look.

"I am," I whisper.

"What?" he groans. "Beautiful and fantastic taste in music! Where were you when I was alive?" I smile slightly at his compliment, trying not to be too obvious to George, who is watching me like a hawk.

I flip through the selections until I find the song and enter the numbers. As I walk back toward the bar, the jukebox begins clicking, changing discs, while George and I keep our eyes locked on the other. I stop just before I reach the bar and cross my arms, matching his stance, and raise one eyebrow.

The familiar melody blares over the speakers, and I can't help but smirk when George mouths, *son of a bitch,* letting his arms fall. A triumphant smile blooms on my face as I give him a casual shrug. "When can I start?" I grab my backpack and pull it over one shoulder.

"You can start training today if you'd like, but if you suck, you'll have to move on."

"Understood. Can I go change and come back?"

"Yeah, you got a pair of black shorts and sneakers?"

Surprisingly, I do. "Yeah."

"I'll have a shirt here for you; be back in an hour."

With a curt nod, I spin around and head for the door.

"Hey, Charlotte!" George calls, and I turn back around. "How'd you know?"

I smirk. "Lucky guess." I shrug before heading out.

Ike is laughing heartily as we climb in my truck. Well, I climb in, he just teleports or does whatever dead people do. "God, I know him so well. That was too easy."

"Thanks for the warning about him being your twin, jackass," I bite out as I start the 4Runner.

"Must be hard having two insanely hot guys around you at once." I roll my eyes at him, but the truth is—it is hard. They're two identical make-my-tongue-smack-my-brains-out hot guys. But I won't tell him that.

"Yeah. Your looks have me quaking in my boots." I laugh when I make the smart-ass remark. "So George and Misty are together?"

"No, just fuck buddies, I guess. It's complicated." I can tell he doesn't like it. "I don't want to talk about her. Let's discuss how hot you think I am," Ike jests.

Shaking my head, I press my lips together to stop myself from grinning. "You're incorrigible."

"What's that? You like my body?" he says.

"Your head *is* unusually large. Must be that ego of yours," I retort.

"*If you want my body and you think I'm sexy, come on, sugar, let me know.*" Ike sings his best Rod Stewart as he thrusts his hips in his seat.

"Wow. I'm going to need you to stop that right now," I laugh.

"Why? Is it turning you on?" he asks as he continues to thrust his hips.

"More like killing my brain cells from watching it. Now, stop distracting me. I have to go and get ready for my new job."

With that, he vanishes and I do a double take. Alone. I'm alone.

One hour later, I'm standing behind the bar with Misty while she explains to me how to use a soda gun like I'm an idiot. I've waitressed before, and it's not rocket science, but I politely nod my head and smile as she babbles on. She's talking really fast and constantly stops to swallow like her throat is dry. I'm wondering if this is a side effect of the coke Ike said she does.

Ike appears and gives me a thorough once-over. The tight, black T-shirt that reads: *Ike and George's,* leaves little to the imagination.

"You're going to make awesome tips here." Ike waggles his eyebrows, and I blush as I try to refocus on Misty.

Finally, she has me sit at a table and instructs me to fill the salt and pepper shakers and sugar packet holders, keeping me busy while we're waiting for the lunch crowd to come in. Since I'm new, I can't serve today, only observe, so I'm sure she'll have me doing most of the grunt work. Ike sits across from me and watches, singing *Get Rhythm,* and I refuse to tell him it's my favorite Cash song. My parents loved Johnny and Elvis. When all the shakers and caddies are full, I set about placing them on the tables, not realizing I'm singing *Get Rhythm* out loud as I do.

I'm singing and shaking my hips when I bump into a hard body and nearly drop my tray. George stares down at me and takes the tray, placing it on the table.

Grabbing my arm, he asks, "Why are you singing that?" His eyes are dark; accusatory.

I must look as stunned as I feel because Ike says, "It's my favorite Johnny song." He runs a wide palm down his face and stares at his brother.

"I don't understand," I say to George, but I'm really speaking to Ike.

"How did you pick my favorite song earlier today?"

I stare up into his dark eyes and refuse to blink. I know what broken is. Hell, I *am* broken. He can't and won't scare me. "Anyone who likes Johnny has good taste. You look like a man with good taste." Misty just happens to approach at this moment and I take a stab for Ike. "I mean in music, at least," I say, as I glance briefly at Misty.

"Nice," Ike chuckles.

"George?" Misty asks timidly. "Everything okay?"

"I'm fine," he releases my arm, our eyes still locked in a standoff. Finally, he turns and walks off with her.

I turn back to my table and whisper, "What the hell, Ike? You did that on purpose. You knew I'd start singing it and he'd hear me," I hiss.

I glance at him and he's rubbing his buzz cut, watching George walk away with Misty. His shirt rides up, exposing his abs and that defined V that makes me want to drool. Of course, in that brief second, I realize I'm drooling over a dead guy.

Classic me.

Wanting the unattainable.

"I'm trying to help you reach him," he says as his gaze moves back to me. Luckily, he misses me checking him out.

I move to another table and slide in the booth to put the shakers in their place. "Well, don't get me hurt trying. He looked like he wanted to hit something."

"He would never hit you. I swear it."

"He'll probably fire me."

"No. But he *will* be thinking about you."

"Yeah. Like how I remind him of you and how much it hurts."

"He's a drug addict, Charlotte. Misty is his dealer. I need to get her away from him before he kills himself by overdosing."

I close my eyes. This deal we made gets more complicated by the second. Now I'm helping Ike settle his affairs by saving his *junkie* brother and somehow sending the drug dealer girlfriend away. "Look, Ike. You can give me pointers and intel, but you have to let me control this. I do have a little experience in these situations."

"Okay," he huffs in defeat. "We'll try it your way for now."

"Thank you." I smile and head toward the bar where I see Misty staring at me. She just saw me talking to Ike, except he's invisible to her so she saw me talking to myself. I decide to ignore that little fact and act like I don't notice her staring at me.

"What can I do now, Misty?"

The afternoon bleeds into the evening and the bar actually gets crowded with the happy hour folks on their way home from work and tourists from around the county. Other than *Ike and George's,* the only other places to eat in town are a restaurant named *Sam Snead's* and a tiny place called *Lindsay's Roost Bar & Grill.* There are a few other pizza and sub places around, but not in town. I follow another waitress, Anna, so she can show me the ropes. She also fills me in on all the gossip.

"So Misty and George are screwing," she whispers as we stand out back by the dumpster while she smokes a cigarette. Her curly, blond hair is in a tight ponytail and her lipstick is a deep shade of bright red. It's not a very flattering color on her, even though she's very pretty with bright blue eyes and perfect white teeth. "Misty dates Roger and she's running around behind his back, but he doesn't know," she says, in her Southern accent. "He'd be real mad if he found out."

"And no one tells him?" I mean, seriously, this town is the size of a needle point, and I imagine this is the kind of juicy gossip to get all the town hens clucking.

"You know how they say, 'don't kill the messenger'? Well, Roger would kill the messenger." Anna's eyes go wide in emphasis.

"Really? You think he'd murder George if he found out?" I ask, somewhat alarmed, wondering if, yet again, I'm faced with another dilemma in helping George.

"No," Ike shakes his head.

"Well maybe not that, but he'd definitely beat the shit out of him. And poor George." Anna shakes her head. "He's just been a mess since his brother died. His brother, Ike, was his twin, ya know? Fine piece of man, too. It really is a shame."

"I broke a lot of young ladies hearts when I died," Ike jokes, and I smile sadly. I believe he did.

"I didn't know he had a twin brother," I lie. "And how does this Roger stay oblivious?"

She takes a drag of her cigarette and answers me as smoke billows out of her mouth. "Well, between us, he's the town drug dealer, and he owns a mechanic shop on Berkley. I guess he's been too busy to notice his whore of a girlfriend is running around on him. She's not my favorite person, if I'm being honest, and she thinks because she's banging the boss she runs this place."

"Misty is a whore," Ike agrees.

"I don't think she thinks much of me," I admit.

"That's because you're pretty and new in town. Don't sweat her, girl." Anna flicks her cigarette under the dumpster. "Anyway, don't tell a soul what I just told you. I don't normally gossip, but you got me going tonight."

"She's a vault. You should totally confide all of your deepest, darkest secrets in her," Ike says, dryly, and I smile against my will.

"Your secrets are safe with me."

When we reenter the bar, George catches sight of me and narrows his gaze. He's suspicious of me, and other than the Johnny Cash song thing I'm not sure why. I give a bright smile, but he looks away.

"So you're the new girl?" A tall man with piercing blue eyes approaches me. I recognize him from the kitchen, but we weren't introduced, and I haven't been able to get a good look at him. His accent is Scottish, or Irish—something foreign. I know he works here as he's wearing the *Ike and George's* T-shirt, which is stretched across his massive, muscular chest. In fact, it's so tight, I can see his nipple rings poking out of his shirt.

"Could you close your mouth, love? You're drooling," Ike warns, and I quickly adjust my posture and close my gaping mouth.

"Um, yeah," I answer as I turn to face him.

"You didn't tell me she was bloody hot," he yells across the bar to George, who cuts him a warning look as I blush. Some of the patrons at the bar turn their heads in our direction and chuckle; the men's eyes roaming my body. My cheeks flame with heat and embarrassment. "I'm Sniper. I'm the other manager here, and if you're sensitive to sexual harassment, you should probably quit now because if I think you're sexy, I'm going to tell you." He extends his hand and I take it, noticing how little and dainty my hand seems in his.

"This is my other best friend . . . besides George," Ike explains, his arms crossed, glaring at Sniper. "We were in the military together."

"It's nice to meet you, Sniper. I'm Char. And I'm not overly sensitive, but if you touch me inappropriately, I'll bust your kneecaps out." I beam a friendly smile as Sniper's eyes flicker. I think I just excited him.

"He's a sick fuck, Charlotte. He likes pain."

"Pretty and violent. I think I just met my soul mate," he growls as he steps toward me, a look of heat and lust in his gaze. He's still holding my hand. "You're the town gossip, pretty thing. You know . . . mysterious lass rolls into town in the middle of the night."

"Not much mystery here, I'm afraid." I laugh nervously.

Sniper squeezes my hand and his gaze locks on mine. "I have a sense of these things. You're something special," he whispers as he leans in and I swallow hard. He smells really freaking good.

"And you should know you'll be walking knee-deep in bullshit every time he's around. He's a bit of a ladies' man," Ike says, as he rolls his eyes.

Taking my hand from Sniper's, I say, "Thanks. I guess."

"Sniper!" George calls, and he's almost burning a hole through us as he stares. "Get back to work!"

"Don't let George be too much of a wanker to you. He's going through some shit. You need anything, come to me, lass. I'll take good care of you." He winks and walks away. "George, you need to get laid!" he yells before disappearing into the kitchen.

"Sod off," George laughs as he grabs the remote and turns the volume on the television up. When my gaze meets the screen, I nearly keel over.

"Police have found the body of twenty-one-year-old Casey Purcell under a bridge just outside Charlottesville." My throat seizes with pain as I swallow hard and my eyes widen as I watch the screen. The reporter continues. *"Detective Andrews received an anonymous letter stating there was a body under the Ukon Bridge. Police retrieved the body and DNA testing is being done, but authorities believe it could be the body of missing UVA student Casey Purcell. At this time, detectives are asking anyone with information to call the number at the bottom of the screen. A tire track was found and police are currently studying video footage from a local gas station to see if there are any matches."*

Fucckkkkkk. . . .

"Are you okay?" Ike asks, and I nod yes way more vigorously than I should. *They're going to find me. I'm a suspect.*

"Is there a problem, Charlotte?" George calls. I quickly snap to and smile brightly.

"No. No problem," I shake off the anxiety blanketing me. *Calm down, Char. You didn't kill her, so even if they find you, you have nothing to worry about.* I take a deep breath and try to relax.

"You sure about that?" Ike asks, his brows furrowed in concern.

"Come here, please," George motions a hand and I make my way toward him. His shaggy hair sits just over his eyes and his tight, black *Ike and George's* shirt shows off his hard build. I haven't seen him smile once all day, but when the woman in front of him says something, he actually laughs.

"Oh, shit," Ike groans.

George is leaned over the bar in front of an older woman with dark, shoulder-length hair. She has a gray streak through the front and rich brown eyes. I approach George and he straightens to a full stance and motions to the woman before him. "Charlotte, this is my mother, Beverly. She helps with the books here. Just thought I'd introduce you so if you see her in here you know who she is."

"It's nice to meet you, Mrs. McDermott." I offer my hand and she takes it with a friendly smile.

"As it is you, Charlotte. What a pretty name."

"Call me Char, please."

"Of course. I hear you're new in town. How do you like Warm Springs so far?"

"It's really nice," I say, politely. *I mean, I don't have anything bad to say about it . . . yet.*

"Well, since you're new in town and working for my son, I think you need to come to my house for Sunday dinner." I can literally feel George tense up beside me. I open my mouth to protest, but she adds, "I won't take no for an answer, either. Do you like lasagna?"

"Um . . ."

"With garlic bread and tiramisu," Ike purrs. "God, I miss my mama's cooking."

I don't know what to say, so without thinking, I steal Ike's words. "With garlic bread and tiramisu."

Beverly stills, her eyes meeting mine before darting back to George. *Shit.* Why did I say that?

"Uh, I didn't think you'd repeat that. That was my favorite meal. She made it for every birthday and every time I came home on leave."

"Well," she says, softly, her eyes welling with tears. "I actually make a wonderful tiramisu."

"No. I didn't mean for you to make it. I just . . ." I shake my head, unable to finish the sentence. Oh God, I just reminded her of her dead son, and now she's crying. I am such an asshole.

"Sunday it is," she states. "George, why don't you pick her up and bring her with you?"

"I have a vehicle. I can drive," I add quickly.

"Don't be silly. George will already be on his way. There's no sense in both of you driving." Beverly gives George a little wink and he rolls his eyes. "It was nice meeting you, Charlotte. I'll see you on Sunday." As she slides off her stool, I chance a glance at George who is grimacing.

"You don't argue with my mama," Ike says, letting me know why George didn't insist we ride separately.

"Nice meeting you, too," I call as she walks away.

"I'll pick you up at five on Sunday," George grumbles before tromping away. When I turn to go, my eyes meet Misty's and she's glaring at me. I guess she heard I got an invite to dinner at the McDermott's house. *Perfect!* This night is going fabulously.

George avoids me the remainder of the night and when we close, I help Anna count out her till, and she tells me to take it to the office and give it to George and then I can leave. I do as she says, and open the office door without knocking.

My eyes bulge out as Misty snorts a line of coke off the desk while George holds his nose, apparently haven already snorted his own line. When he sees me, he jerks up and Misty follows, turning her back to me as she rubs frantically at her face.

I know my goal is to get close to him—to help him—but I can't help letting my distaste pour out of my mouth.

"Really, boss?" I question, my tone bearing every bit of my disapproval. George glances to Misty and then back to me, wiping at his nose. It's the first time since I've met him he doesn't look cold. Now he just looks embarrassed. "Here's Anna's till. Do I work tomorrow?"

"You wanna do a double? Do you think you can wait tables yet?" he asks, and I can see the humiliation in his eyes.

"I can do it," I say, jerking my gaze from his. "I'll see you tomorrow." I toss the money and receipts on his desk and shut the door loudly.

"What a bitch," I hear Misty grumble through the door. I can't help standing there a moment and listening. "She was talking to herself all night. What a fucking weirdo." Rolling my eyes, I stomp away.

"I am so glad that happened. He looked so ashamed," Ike cheers.

"Doesn't mean he'll stop," I whisper. I quickly grab my belongings and my leftover burger I didn't finish on my break and march out of the kitchen.

"Night, lass. I'd be glad to accompany you home if you'd like," Sniper purrs as he gives me a flirtatious wink and I roll my eyes.

"As tempting as that sounds, I'll pass. Night, Sniper," I call out.

As soon as I'm back in my motel room, I change into my pajamas; a pair of shorts and a tank top, and plop down on my bed. Opening the Styrofoam box my leftover lunch is in, I stuff a few cold fries in my mouth. "Wanna watch TV?" I ask Ike as I chew, whom is seated in the armchair.

"Whatever you want." He shrugs.

"So what's the deal with the sexy, foreign BFF?" I ask.

"First off, guys don't say BFF." He chuckles lightly. "We were in Afghanistan together. I promised him a job when we got back. George kept my promise for me," Ike sighs and rubs his head as I find he always does when his mind is heavy in thought.

"He seems . . . interesting," I add.

"You mean hot?" Ike snorts.

Chewing the bit of burger I just bit off, I mumble around the food in my mouth, "I mean, yeah, he is, but I mean, he's just . . . different."

"Mm-hmm. Well, let me just say, he's been with quite a few ladies, so if I were you I'd steer clear."

"Thanks for the warning, because I was totally planning on banging him," I reply dryly.

"Suit yourself."

"You can sit by me, ya know? I know you won't try anything." I pat the spot next to me.

He snorts and stands before catapulting on the bed, causing me to jerk in surprise. Just before he would land on me, he morphs and is on the bed beside me. I giggle like a little school girl and hate myself for it.

"That's a beautiful sound." Ike smiles at me, his brown eyes sparkling bright.

"Me laughing like an idiot?" I ask as I flip on the television with the remote.

He lies back and puts his hands under his head, staring at the television. "When my grandparents were alive, they had this carport attached to their house and my grandmother had, like, twenty wind chimes hanging out there. I think that's my favorite sound in the world. It's so light and whimsical. Feels like home." He looks at me, his dark eyes lit with warmth. "Your laugh makes me think of them. Of those wind chimes."

As our gazes remain locked, I have to swallow. That might be the sweetest thing anyone has ever said to me. Let alone, by a man. Of course, the first one that does is dead. And with that thought, I tear my eyes away. I cannot get attached to Ike. He will leave soon and another will take his place. Another soul needing help so they can cross over.

"With lines like that, I bet you were getting ladies left and right when you were alive," I jest to break the awkwardness of the moment. Suddenly he sits up, his tags tinkling under his shirt. "What?" I practically jump out of my skin with his jerky movement.

Ike disappears and then materializes moments later. "George is outside your door," he says, softly, as he stands by me where I sit on the bed, arms crossed.

"What?" I whisper-yell, but before he can respond, three loud knocks bang on the door.

"He's drunk." Ike's jaw tics in anger.

"Is he dangerous?"

"No. My guess is he's embarrassed." Ike huffs as more knocking sounds come from the door.

George must have gotten my temporary address from my application paperwork. I hop up and reach the door in four long strides, yanking it open. I know I'm trying to help George for Ike's sake, but for him to show up so late and drunk while pounding on my door is rude. I'm ready to give him a piece of my mind, but when I see his red eyes, filled with tears . . . I can't. His shirt is untucked, his shaggy hair sticking up everywhere as if he's been running his hands through it, and he's holding a bottle of Jack Daniel's. Instead of yelling at him, I stare at him, waiting for him to say something.

"Who were you talking to?" he asks belligerently, his eyes scanning my room.

"You must've heard the television," I answer quickly.

"No. You were laughing."

"At the television." I cross my arms, becoming increasingly annoyed with his line of questioning. "Were you standing here listening?"

His lips curve slightly. "No."

"What can I do for you, George?" He pulls himself off the doorframe and pushes past me into my room. "Sure. Come on in," I remark dryly. He ignores my comment and plops down on the pleather arm chair closest to the door.

"He's shit-faced, Charlotte."

"I know," I answer, not thinking about it.

"What?" George looks up at me in confusion.

"Nothing. To what do I owe this unexpected honor?" I plop down on my bed and cross my legs in front of me. As I do, I look up and notice Ike's eyes fixed on me. Reminding myself not to stare back, I look to George who is also staring at me, his dark eyes practically burning into me. I look down and realize the strap of my loose tank top has slid down, revealing my bra strap and the top part of my boob in the lacy cup. My face flames red. Not from embarrassment. Okay, maybe a little, but it's more the heat of their gazes upon me. I quickly clear my throat and right my top.

"You think I'm an asshole, don't you?" George slurs before swigging the Jack.

"He is," Ike nods in agreement.

"I think you're drunk," I answer, cutting Ike a quick glance.

"So, where are you from, Charlotte?"

"Is this the part where we get to know each other, boss?"

"Just trying to be friendly." George puts the bottle of Jack on the table with a thud, causing the amber fluid to slosh.

"And being friendly is showing up at my motel room at eleven o'clock at night?"

"You haven't answered my question."

"Charlotte. I know he's a drunken asshole, but please be nice. You said you'd help him," Ike pleads.

With a deep sigh, I say, "Oklahoma."

George eyes me curiously. "And what brings you to these parts?"

"Just admiring the fall beauty like everyone else," I say, snidely.

"I doubt that," George slurs.

"You know what, George? We're not doing this," I snap. "You're drunk off your ass and high on coke. Come on." Standing, I grab my keys off of my nightstand before slipping on my flip-flops. "I'm taking you home."

"Char—" Ike is interrupted when I shoot him a glare that would scare the dead. Ike is a good brother. He wants to help George, but he wants to do it with kid gloved hands. George needs tough love, and I'm going to give it to him. He can't deal with his pain and loss until he gets cleaned up.

"Get up!" I yell at George as he lulls to the side. With a lot of effort, I yank him up and drag him out the door. It takes me five minutes to get him in the passenger seat of my truck, and when I slam the door and round the back, Ike is waiting with his arms crossed.

"Don't give me that look, Ike," I warn. "You agreed to let me do it *my* way."

"Yeah, but—"

"But nothing," I cut him off. "You want my help—this is the first thing we scratch off of the list. I know what I'm doing. This isn't my first rodeo."

Ike snorts and holds his hands up in mock surrender. "Okay, let's get him home."

"How in the hell did he get here?" I ask, not seeing any other cars in the parking lot.

"Who knows," Ike grumbles. "Maybe Sniper dropped him off."

With Ike's help, I get to George's house. He has a little ranch about four miles from the bar. The grass looks like it hasn't been cut in a year, and there's a shutter hanging from one hinge on the far left window.

"This was my house. I left it to him," Ike notes from the backseat.

"He's really keeping the place up," I note, my tone drenched in sarcasm.

Ike says nothing else as I park my 4Runner and proceed to drag George inside. Luckily, I get him to walk, but his eyes are closed the entire time. When we finally get inside, the light from the range over the stove casts enough light to lead him inside and plant him on the sofa where he falls over and starts snoring.

Slowly turning, I take in the house. There are pizza boxes everywhere, empty beer bottles cover most of the surfaces, and yes, there's a white dust coating his coffee table. "This place smells like ass," I tell Ike, but he doesn't respond. When I glance at him, his expression is dismal as he stares down at George. I know he's worried about him. I know George's inability to deal with the loss of Ike is what is keeping Ike tied here, preventing him from moving on. I'm saddened with that thought. A part of me doesn't want Ike to go.

I had every intention of searching George's house, flushing his drugs and dumping out his whiskey, but I won't; he'd just get more. I know where his head is at, and he needs something big to bring him to his knees. Only then can he really begin to heal. So I put off my intervention. Tonight I need sleep. That's what I tell myself anyway. I push aside the thoughts of Ike crossing over. The truth is selfish. And it's wrong.

The truth is . . . I want more time with Ike.

Ike

One thing's for sure, Charlotte sleeps like the dead. The alarm has already sounded, twice, and she needs to wake up, but I like watching her sleep. It's only been two days since I found her on the bridge and already I feel tied to her, like she's a part of me. That's silly since we've only just met, but it's an odd bond. I'm fighting to give her, and my brother, life, while she's fighting to help me let go. Somehow we've become tethered to one another, even though we both know our time together is limited.

Staring at her, I will her sleepy, gray eyes to open. Leaning forward, my dog tags jingle under my shirt and she stirs. One eye peeks open, and she mumbles something incoherent.

"Good morning, beautiful," I whisper from my pleathered seat. I call it mine as it's where I've sat all night, watching her.

"Oh yeah. I'm sure I look really beautiful right now," she says, through a yawn, and I chuckle.

"You do," I confirm.

"The dead never sleep, huh?" She smiles at me, and I swear, if my heart still beat, it would skip once. Why couldn't I have met a girl like her when I was alive? Waking up to that smile every morning would've been the highlight of my day—every day.

"I miss sleeping," I admit as she sits up and stretches. I can't help the way I watch her, and I'm almost certain I see the faintest ghost of a smile when she notices, but it vanishes as quickly as it appears.

"I better get dressed," she mentions in a huff as she climbs out of bed. "I think I have an idea on how to get George a little closer to getting his shit together, but it's going to be ugly. I just need to know, do you trust me?"

I stare at her dumbfounded for a moment. I do trust her; it's George I don't trust. She must read my thoughts in my expression because she says, "He's tougher than you think, Ike. But he needs a wake-up call. Sometimes we have to hit rock bottom before we can make our way back up. Look at where I was two days ago when you found me. Now, I'm here."

My gut tightens with her words. She almost killed herself. The thought alone is enough to make me feel like I'm choking, and I can't speak. She gives me a nod and heads into the bathroom without another word, taking her backpack with her. I promised her I wouldn't enter the bathroom while she showers. Technically, I could and she'd never know, but I'm not a sleazeball—even though I really would like to see her naked. It seems like she's in there forever before she finally emerges, dressed for work, hair tied back in a perfect ponytail.

"You ready?" she asks, and my gaze falls to the envelope in her hands.

"What's that?"

"Just a letter." She shrugs, pulling her backpack from her shoulder and tucking the envelope inside.

"Is it a secret?"

"You said you trusted me, right?"

"Did I?" I joke, which earns me one of her death glares.

"Come on. Let's go."

Chapter 8

Charlotte

I stop by the front office to bid Ginger a good morning. When I walk in, she's sitting in her recliner in front of the flat screen. Slowly, she rises from her seat and hobbles over to me.

"Good morning, Ginger." I smile brightly.

"Good morning to you, sugar. How's your room?"

"Very cozy. Thank you so much." The kindness she and the Mercers have shown is humbling. I mentally remind myself I need to go track down Mrs. Mercer and thank her in person.

"Cinnamon rolls. You'll love them!" She shoves a brown paper bag at me and I laugh.

"Ginger, you're too good to me." I should probably at least attempt to refuse the bag, but I'm so hungry and they smell so good.

"We just gotta get some meat on those bones, dear."

"I really appreciate this, Ginger. Thank you."

"Oh, and I wanted to tell you, if you're interested, I think I found a way to help you pay for your room. I need someone to help me clean the rooms when guests checkout. Would you be interested?"

"So I would clean the rooms, and you'd let me stay for free?"

"Yes. We don't get many folks through here, but during tourist season we're busier than a one-armed paperhanger. I'm booked solid the week after next through the end of November, but my health isn't what it used to be, and it'd be nice to have someone take care of the rooms for me."

"That sounds great, Ginger. I'll do a really good job and take care of everything."

"I know, hon. You can start tomorrow if your schedule permits it."

"Okay. Deal. I'll see you later." I start to head for the door, when Ginger calls out, "I saw that foreign fella that works with you drop George off last night. George looked like he was a little . . . well, he looked a bit out of sorts. I don't want to pry, but . . . if you need help or have any trouble, just let me know."

"There was no trouble," I respond quickly. "George came by to drop off something I left at work. I took him home myself." I hate lying. Especially to someone as sweet as Ginger, but the last thing I need is for this town to start circulating a rumor George and I had a one night stand. Misty would probably stab me if she found out George was here last night. "But thank you, Ginger. For everything."

"No problem, sugar."

"Thanks for covering for him, Charlotte," Ike says quietly as we exit. "I'm sorry you had to." I give him a faint smile, letting him know it's okay. George showing up last night was definitely inappropriate, especially since he was drunk, but that's not Ike's fault. I know George is a mess right now. He's not himself. Grief can make us do funny things. Like try to jump off a bridge in the middle of the night.

As I climb into my 4Runner, I glance over at Ike. "Do you know if Sniper's working today?" I question, trying to change the subject.

"Really? Are you that attracted to him?" Ike groans.

"Uh . . . no, I'm just curious is all. Will he or Misty be working today?" I can't let Ike know what I'm up to or he'll try and stop me. I really hope this doesn't blow up in my face, but I need an in with George, and unfortunately, it won't be pretty.

"Yes. They're both working doubles."

Good. I exhale in relief. At least part of my plan will work.

"Stay straight when driving through town. I want to show you something before you go in," Ike says, as he relaxes in the seat. I nod once and do as he says and we climb mountain roads that cause my car to rev in protest. I'd love to look around at the leaves changing colors, but I'm too scared we'll end up careening over a mountain edge if I do. Ike directs me into a national forest in Hidden Valley and we park near a river. Getting out, I quietly follow him. We soon see several fishermen near a small bridge. He leads me down further so we can talk. I look ridiculous in shorts and a T-shirt out here, but I don't complain.

We stop at the bank, out of sight from the other fishermen.

"It's beautiful here," I note. The river flows smoothly, small rapids rushing over rocks, but they don't appear to be strong enough to take anyone down if they were standing in it.

"I thought you might think so," Ike says. "I'm asking a lot of you, and I just wanted to show you something pretty; something calm. That sounds dumb," he mutters as he shakes his head. Taking a few steps farther from the shore, he leans against a beautiful, gigantic tree. The branches stretch out over the water, shading us from the sun.

I follow him up the bank and stand before him. "No," I disagree. "I know what you mean. I like how quiet it is; the sound of the water." Taking a deep breath, I say, "It's calming."

Ike's stare trains on me. His brown eyes are so deep; penetrating me. I bite my lip. I don't know why him looking at me this way makes me feel so . . . nervous. After a moment, his gaze moves past me and back to the water. "I keep hoping it's like this," he says, thoughtfully.

"What?" I ask as I follow his line of sight.

"Wherever I go when I leave; I hope it's peaceful and calm. I hope there's water and color. I hope I'm somewhere that reminds me of all the happy times in my life."

A lump rises in my throat. I've helped many people move on, cross over, but when Ike leaves . . . it's going to hurt. I close my eyes as I realize how real that truth is. Ike has somehow weaved his way into my heart and when he goes, I will mourn him. As he stares at the water, I wish like hell I could take his hand and hold it. I'd give anything to do it.

"Sniper was right, Charlotte. You are a special girl," Ike says, softly.

Turning back to the water, he steps away from me, and I release the breath I didn't realize I was holding. Ike is so deep; everything seems to have meaning to him. He didn't bring me out here to impress me or anything silly like that. He brought me here to share his peace, to give me peace. My eyes tear up as I think about the last time I truly felt peace. It's been a while. Taking a seat on a large rock near the bank, I close my eyes and let the sounds of nature calm me; cleanse me. Ike is quiet until it's time for us to go or I'll be late for work.

"Are you ready?" he asks. I stand and nod, feeling a little better from my quiet time, and we climb in my truck and head back down the mountain.

"Thank you for that, Ike," I whisper.

Giving me that stellar, all-American boy smile, he says, "You're welcome."

As we near town, I realize I have something to do before I head to work. The timing is terrible, but Ike can't be with me while I do this. "Ike, I hate to ask, but could you maybe give me some privacy? I just need a little time to myself. I'll meet you at the restaurant."

His gaze meets mine, suspicion swimming in the depths of his brown eyes. It's a look I've seen on George's face a few times. "Okay," he says, simply, before he disappears. With a deep sigh of relief, I focus on the road before me and head over to Berkley.

Ike is waiting in the parking lot for me when I show up, his muscular arms crossed as he leans against a random vehicle. He doesn't ask where I've been; he simply follows me inside without a word. I head back into the kitchen to toss my backpack in the office, the skin on the back of my neck standing on end. Ike is watching me and my body is very aware of it. Sniper is in the kitchen standing over the fryer, wearing a white apron that looks way too small for him as I pass by. Sensing my presence, his head snaps up and his devilish smirk appears. His gaze begins at my eyes and moves to my chest where it seems to stay for a very obvious, long moment.

"He's staring at your tits," Ike notes gruffly. If I could talk to him right now, I'd reply, *'No fucking duh, Ike.'*

"Good morning, gorgeous." Sniper winks at me, his stare still honed in on my breasts. In his defense, he did warn me he was a perv.

Shaking my head, I reply, "Good morning, Sniper. Thanks for dropping off George last night. That was fun," I state, my tone rich with sarcasm.

Sniper cringes at my words and says, "He said you knew he was coming."

"No, I didn't." I shake my head and then realize I shouldn't be giving Sniper a hard time. "Actually, I'm glad you drove him because otherwise he might've driven himself, and if he'd made it alive without killing anyone or himself, then *I* would have fucking killed him."

When I open the office door, George is sitting at his desk, head in his hands, when he jerks up at my entrance. "Don't you ever knock?" he hisses.

"Feeling rough today, boss?" I ask snidely. What can I say? My patience for George is extremely close to being gone.

"Shut the door," George orders as he pulls out a flask and takes a large swig.

"Hair of the dog?"

"Yeah," he replies and nods. "Listen," he huffs, as he puts the flask back in his desk drawer and slams it shut. "I'm sorry about last night."

"Which part, boss? The part where I caught you snorting coke with Misty, or the part where you showed up shit-faced at my motel room and I had to drive you home?"

"Well . . . both," he admits with a slight frown. It's not hard to see he's embarrassed.

"I know you're doing things your way and all, but acting like a bitch to him isn't going to win him over. And you *are* trying to help him, right?" Ike adds, arms tightly crossed, watching the interaction between George and I. Moments like this, I wish I could zip ghosts' mouths shut. They talk nonstop, making it impossible to focus. Not to mention, this particular ghost just called me a bitch. He's definitely getting a kick in the balls for that later, figuratively speaking.

Ignoring Ike, I return my focus to George. "No worries, boss." I shrug, wishing I could give Ike the middle finger. "If you want to waste your life away on drugs, what's it to me?"

George's shameful expression twists into anger as his features "You don't know me," he snarls. "You have no idea what I'm going through."

God, if he only knew. Clearly, I know exactly what he's going through, but that's a conversation for another time and place. "I know you better than you think, George, and let me just say, when you bottom out, just remember up is the only way to go." I add, "May I have my apron, please?" I quickly change the subject. With a huff, he yanks open his desk drawer and tosses me a small, black apron.

"Thanks," I snap, and leave him to fester in his bad mood.

As I'm rounding the back line where Sniper's still manning the fryer, I make my way over to him. "Sniper. I need a favor," I say, quietly checking over my shoulder to make sure no one can hear me.

"You need a date? Someone to show you around?" He winks. "I'd be glad to, love."

"I told you he's a man whore," Ike grumbles as he crosses his arms.

I roll my eyes at Sniper. "I appreciate the offer, but that's not where I'm going with this. I have a feeling something big is going down today, and I need you to keep an eye on things."

"Are you in some kind of trouble?" he asks, turning to face me.

"No. No. Nothing like that," I assure him. "I just feel like something is going to happen, and having a tough guy like you around might keep things from getting too crazy."

"What are you up to, Charlotte?" Ike asks, and of course, I ignore him. I don't know why he bothers asking me questions when I can't answer him.

Sniper eyes me suspiciously. "Okay," he says, with uncertainty.

"Thanks." I smile brightly, leaving him to his fryer full of fries.

"Charlotte," Ike warns, but again I ignore him. He'll find out what's going on soon enough, and I'm sure he'll be pissed about it.

Misty is behind the bar, eyes dull and unfriendly as she takes me in.

"Hey, Misty," I chirp as I tie my apron on and pass by her to the hostess stand to check where my tables will be. It's no surprise I got the crappiest section as I'm the new girl, but I try to remain optimistic. I just have to show George I can do this and he'll give me better tables.

I head over to my tables to check all the salt and pepper shakers and sugar caddies when Misty approaches.

"Listen. If you want to keep your job here you'll keep your mouth shut about what you saw last night," she warns, her blue eyes scorching into mine.

"You mean how I saw you sniffing coke?" I counter and Ike groans. He thinks I'm making it worse. *He's probably right.*

"Look, bitch," she chuckles softly in disdain, as if she doesn't consider me a threat. "Keep your mouth shut and stay out of my way, and maybe I'll let George keep you on."

"Are you fucking kidding me?" Ike yells as he punches her in the face. He's the kind of man that would never hit a woman, not for real anyway, but I guess since he knows he can't hurt her, he's giving it to her. Of course, his blows don't affect her at all; his hands just go right through her. I can't help it, I laugh, which causes Misty to glare because she thinks I'm laughing at her.

"*Let* him keep me on?" I question as I cross my arms. "The sign outside says *Ike and George's*. Misty must be in fine print."

"George and I have an understanding," she says, simply.

I grin at the absurdity of her words. "Is that what they call fucking these days?" Misty's eyebrows touch her hairline.

"Jesus, Charlotte," Ike mumbles.

"I'm sorry, Misty. I'll tell you what. You stay out of *my* way and play nice, and maybe I won't tell your boyfriend you're fucking your boss," I say as I smile brightly at her.

"George will fire you if he thinks you're trying to stir up shit," Ike adds.

Ike is right, but he won't have a chance. George's world is officially about to collapse, and Misty will be out of the picture for good. Misty's eyes go wide as she stares at me blankly. She's not sure how to respond to my threat.

"You don't know who you're messing with, bitch," she bites out. She doesn't chuckle this time. I guess I've moved up on the threat meter.

"Just walk away, Charlotte. She's probably high right now, and who knows what she'll do," Ike warns, and as much as I want to lash back at her, I decide he's right. Besides, her life is about to drive head-on into a shit storm.

"Can I get to work now, or do you want to continue glaring at me?" I ask casually, as if we're not in an intense quarrel.

She backs away slowly, her eyes saying everything her mouth isn't; threatening me in all ways possible. When she finally spins around and walks away, I turn to my table and whisper to Ike, "Stop talking to me. It's distracting and hard to ignore."

"Fine. I'm trying to help."

"I know, but dial it down, please," I whisper again. "Maybe you could give me some space while I work."

"As you wish." He nods and disappears.

I check all of my tables just before George comes out from the kitchen and unlocks the doors. Through the glass pane of the door, I see Mr. Mercer with I assume is his wife, waiting to enter, and George greets them as he holds the door open for them.

"Good to see you, Mr. and Mrs. Mercer. How are ya today?"

"We're good, George," Mr. Mercer answers. "How have you been?"

"Not too bad," George replies as he makes his way to the hostess stand. "I got a table ready for you if you'll follow me."

"Actually," Mr. Mercer interrupts. "We heard you have a lovely new waitress working here. Might we sit at one of her tables?" Mr. Mercer's eyes meet mine and he winks before turning his attention back to George.

"Uh . . . sure," George agrees, grabbing two menus and two rolled-up silverwares. "You ready for a table, Charlotte?" George asks when he sees me.

"Of course." I smile brightly. "I can seat them myself." I hold my hands out to take the menus and silverware from him. When he hands them to me, his fingers skim the skin of my hand, sending tingles shooting through me. Our gazes lock for a moment until he jerks away. What the hell was that? Did he just feel that, too?

Snapping to it, I say, "Right this way, folks."

As they follow me to my section, Mr. Mercer makes introductions. "Charlotte, this is my wife, Mrs. Mercer. She's been looking forward to meeting you." Mrs. Mercer is a petite lady with blonde hair, laced with gray streaks. Her dark eyes look tiny behind her glasses, which are perched halfway down the bridge of her nose.

"I've been looking forward to it as well," I answer honestly as I indicate what booth I'd like them to sit in. As they slide in, I add, "You have no idea what your kindness means to me."

"Well, Bill here came home and told me about you, and it just broke my heart. But when he mentioned the necklace you gave him to hold and showed it to me, I knew it was a sign. Do you believe in signs, Charlotte?" She stares up at me as I place their menus in front of them.

"I guess so," I reply. "But how was my necklace a sign?"

"Our daughter, God rest her soul, left us almost ten years ago. She wore a necklace almost identical to yours every day of her life." Mrs. Mercer's eyes lower, appearing somewhat pensive, almost as if in reflection. "But she didn't have it on the day she died and we've never been able to find it. You showing up with your necklace . . . it felt right to help you. We'd like to invite you to dinner as well."

"I'd love that. And I will repay you for everything. I promise. You really have no idea how much your kindness means to me."

"How about next Wednesday?" Mr. Mercer asks. I try not to look surprised at how soon that is.

"Why not? We'll make sure you're off for it, Charlotte," George interjects as he approaches. I nearly jump out of my skin with his words. He snuck up on me.

"You should come, too, George," Mr. Mercer adds.

"Actually, I have to work, but thank you for the invite." George nods in appreciation. "Did Charlotte take your drink order yet?" he asks, and I can't help rolling my eyes. He's trying to make me look incompetent—or he's just trying to piss me off.

"We've been chatting." Mrs. Mercer pats my hand where it rests on the table.

"Wednesday sounds great, and what can I get you two to drink?"

"We'll both have iced teas, and we'd like to split the chicken Philly with fries," Mr. Mercer says.

"I'll be right back with your teas."

As I walk away, George says something I can't hear to the Mercers before trailing behind me. When I reach the kitchen, I call out my order to Sniper as I grab two glasses and fill them with ice. As I fill the first glass from the tea urn, George enters and stops, watching me.

"I'm quite capable of taking drink orders, Mr. McDermott, but thanks for coming over and trying to make me look like an idiot."

"You think I was trying to be a dick?" He snorts out a laugh.

"There was no trying there," I add as I take the second glass and begin filling it, but can't help the smile I'm fighting as I hear Sniper chuckle in the background.

"Hey, I was helping. They'd have talked your ear off if I hadn't come over there."

"So? Is it a problem if they like me and want to talk to me? Or would it interfere with your anti-Charlotte parade?"

"I'm not on an anti-Charlotte parade," he laughs, and I'm taken aback by how incredibly handsome he looks when he smiles. Both Ike and George look alike, but their smiles are different. When Ike smiles, it feels real, like his happiness is his aura. It feels like a warm, sunny beach when you've seen nothing but snow and ice for months. When George smiles, it's a gift. It's like the way the sun peeks through storm clouds. It feels like hope.

"Look at that," I say, dryly, jutting my chin to Sniper, whose elbows are resting on the top shelf that separates the front and back line, watching George and I quarrel with great amusement. "He actually laughs!"

George crosses his arms, the humor in his eyes fading fast. "I have no problems with you, Charlotte. Seriously." He gets back to the point.

"Well, your girlfriend doesn't care much for me." I roll my eyes.

"My girlfriend?"

There's no way I'm letting him off the hook. The whole town might, but I won't. "Really? You're going to play coy? Misty?"

"She's an employee. A friend. That's all," he says, matter-of-factly.

"Who you happen to fuck . . ." Sniper interrupts from behind the line, peeking over the metal shelf that separates the kitchen from the front line. I copy George's stance and cross my arms, giving him a knowing look, feeling good that Sniper backed me up.

"Fuck off," George snaps at Sniper before he shakes his head and instead of addressing Sniper or my proclamation, he pivots back toward me. "Jealous, Charlotte?" His eyes scan me from head to toe, his eyes darkening as he does. I know he's trying to unnerve me, avoiding talking about Misty, but I can't stop the heat that crawls up my neck and blankets my cheeks. It's been so long since a man looked at me like that. I quickly shake it off and get back to business.

I snort. "Wow. So desperate to avoid the topic of Misty, you'd commit sexual harassment. Nice move, boss."

"Just admit it, George. Misty hangs on your sac like a monkey on a tree," Sniper calls from behind the line. "Ooo-Ooo-Eee-Eee," Sniper heckles as he tromps around, scratching under his arms. I can't help it, I burst in to laughter.

"Put a sock in it, Sniper!" George calls, anger lacing his tone. I bite my lip to stifle my giggles and busy myself putting lemon wedges on the glasses of tea.

"No worries, boss. No judgment here," I manage as I smile and take the drinks.

As I exit the kitchen, I hear Sniper say, "She's a saucy one, isn't she?"

"She's something, all right," George mumbles.

Two hours later, the lunch rush has died down, and I busy myself sweeping under my tables and filling my sugar caddies. I'm alone on the floor as George and Sniper are in the back, and Misty went home feigning a headache. Apparently, she plans to return for the evening shift.

Awesome.

"How much did you make today?" Ike asks as he sits in one of my booths, watching me.

"Fifty," I reply and shrug. For a small town lunch shift, it's not horrible, but it's not great either.

"You work tonight, right? You'll make more," he assures me. He knows I'm worried about money. Thus far, I've had to rely solely on the kindness of strangers, and I can't stand it. It makes me feel worthless. I feel better about my motel room, but Ginger only has me staying in and cleaning one of her rooms. I'm not sure how likely it is I'll really be 'earning' my stay.

"You know, you look like a young Audrey Hepburn," Ike adds suddenly. "I always thought she was hot." I snort and shake my head at his ridiculous lie of a compliment. I look nothing like Audrey Hepburn. She was classic, timeless, and regal. I'm . . . well . . . me. "What?" he asks, as if he's offended. "I mean it. Why would I lie? It's not like I'm trying to get in your pants. I mean . . . I'd like to, but you know . . . the whole dead thing and all would make it kind of difficult. " I can't help it, I laugh out loud. Good thing I'm the only one on the floor . . . well only one alive anyway. "There it is," he sighs as a satisfied smile spreads across his lips. "You have an amazing smile, Charlotte." I can't help it. I blush. Ike McDermott is a natural charmer through and through. He can't help himself. I wish for a moment I could've seen him when he was alive, living day-to-day. I imagine the chipper demeanor I see now is only a glimmer of what he was like when he was alive. My heart pangs at the thought.

Just as I finish sweeping and head to the kitchen to put the broom and dustpan away, Anna comes in, a little, blonde girl trailing behind her. I know immediately she's Anna's daughter; they look so much alike, it's as if Anna spit her right out of her mouth.

"Hey, Char," Anna practically sings as she pulls me in for a hug. I'm a little stunned. I'm not much of a hugger as it is, and I didn't think

Anna and I were anywhere near that kind of friendly affection in our short friendship. But I pat her back awkwardly with one hand in reciprocation.

"Hey, Anna. Who is this little beauty?" I beam at the little girl as I pull away from Anna's bear hug.

"This is River," Anna replies, and nudges the little girl forward. "River, this is Mommy's good friend, Char."

"Nice to meet you, Ms. Char," River says, shyly, as she smiles.

"Nice to meet you, too." I reach a hand out to shake hers, which she takes.

"Char, could you keep an eye on her for a minute? I need to talk to George about my schedule."

"Sure. Would you mind taking the broom and dustpan back for me on your way?"

"Sure wouldn't." Anna takes them from me and scurries to the back.

"Mommy gave me two dollars in quarters before we came in so I can play the jukebox." River reaches in her pockets and pulls out the quarters. One falls to the floor, rolling away and she chases after it, hunched over as she goes.

"She's adorable," I whisper so only Ike can hear.

"I always wanted daughters," Ike notes, and I can't help the sadness that squeezes my heart for him. Not many men want daughters. They usually want sons. He would've been a great dad. I'd like to say something to him, to comfort him, but I can't. Not in front of River.

"So, what do you want to play?" I ask as she collects the quarter and tromps over to the jukebox.

"Justin Bieber," she chirps happily.

"Oh God. Please no!" Ike groans, making me giggle quietly to myself.

"I don't think there's any Justin Bieber on here, honey," I tell River.

"You pick the first one," she orders as she hands me two quarters.

"You sure? This is your money."

"Yeah. Pick one, and then I'll pick one." Running to the jukebox, her blond hair bounces as she goes.

"Please culture this child and play her some Johnny or Elvis," Ike pleads. I decide on Elvis as Johnny Cash tends to sound a little deeper and Elvis's songs are peppier.

Inserting the quarters, I select the song as Ike stares over my shoulder the entire time. When I glance at him, he smirks. "Good choice."

As the jukebox clicks, preparing to play the song, I bend down and ask River, "Do you know any Elvis Presley songs?"

"Elvis?" River scrunches her nose, obviously having never heard of him.

"Anna should be reported for child neglect," Ike snorts. "This child has obviously been starved of any type of culture."

"Are we going to dance?" I ask River, ignoring Ike and holding out my hand to her.

River shoves her quarters back in her pocket and giggles. "You first," she orders.

The first chords of *Jailhouse Rock* stream through the speakers, and I hurry to the bar and grab George's sunglasses, slipping them on.

As the words bellow out, I lip-synch and move my legs in my best imitation of Elvis' dance moves. Ike plops down in a chair at the bar. "And she can dance?" He clutches his chest. "Be still, my heart," he moans dramatically.

When it gets to the second verse, I grab River's hands and sing.

Let's rock; everybody, let's rock.

Everybody in the whole cell block

was dancin' to the Jailhouse Rock."

River laughs hysterically as I twirl her and shake my hips like crazy. I, too, am lost in a fit of giggles when someone seizes my arm and jerks me until I slam into a hard body.

"Let's show her how it's done," Sniper purrs as he twirls me around. He spins me in a series of maneuvers while River squeals with delight. I can't deny I'm impressed with his dance moves. When the song almost ends, he picks up River, twirling her while she holds her arms out and laughs. When the song finishes, we're all giggling until the sound of loud handclapping sounds throughout the room.

George stands in the doorway, one eyebrow quirked. "Maybe I should put you two on the floor to entertain the guests. Dinner and a show," he says, dryly.

"I was thoroughly entertained," Ike chirps.

"You're just jealous of my moves," Sniper jests as he twirls River around in his arms.

"Put her down, Sniper!" Anna feigns disapproval. She knows Sniper is harmless, but giving him a hard time is her way of flirting with him. I think she likes him by the way she always slaps his arm playfully in the kitchen and always gives him shy smiles. "Who knows where your hands have been."

Sniper places River on her feet and strides up to Anna. "No worries, love. I only like matured women," he adds as he waggles his brows and takes her in his arms and spins her around.

"Are you saying I'm old?" she scoffs.

"I'm saying I like MILFs, love. And you . . . are a MILF."

Anna turns bright red. "What's a MILF?" River asks innocently, her brows scrunched. We all laugh.

"A mom I'd like to be friends with, love," Sniper answers. "Very good friends, that is." He winks at Anna who turns an even darker shade of red.

Anna cuts him a look that says many things at once; *You're being naughty, but I like it, but you should stop.* "You do realize this is the only place you could ever work where the females would tolerate your behavior, don't you?" She purses her lips.

"I have been bad," Sniper answers and grins. "I need to be spanked. Think you could help me out?"

"All right," George interjects loudly. "Time for you to return to the kitchen where I can hide you from the world."

Sniper pouts his bottom lip. "It was fun dancing with you, little lady." He bows like a gentleman to River and she blushes, much like her mother.

"You, too," River giggles.

Sniper makes his way into the kitchen and Anna takes River's hand. "Time to go, bird."

"I want to dance to Elvis some more!"

"Not today."

"Next time," I promise. "I'll play you another Elvis song. Okay?"

"Okay," River huffs.

"See you tomorrow, guys," Anna calls as River drags her out the door.

George holds his hand out to me. "What?" I ask; confused. Is he asking me to dance? My heart beats rapidly at the thought. Should I say yes? No, probably not. But I kind of want to say yes. Why do I want to say yes?

"My sunglasses." He clears his throat.

Oh.

Now I feel stupid. A heat comparable to volcanic lava blankets my face. *Why would he want to dance with you, Charlotte? He hates you.* Slipping the glasses off, I hand them to him, refusing to meet his gaze.

"Sorry. I needed them for proper effect."

"I need some help stocking liquor." He turns and walks back into the kitchen.

"Okaayyy . . ." I say, cutting a glance to Ike.

"He's got a stick stuck up his ass." Ike laughs. "Always Mr. Business."

I head to the back exit where George has the door held open with a trash can. A small, black truck is backed up to the door and he's pulling boxes to the tailgate. Stepping down, I grab the first box I reach. It's opened, with eight bottles of various liquors divided by cardboard set inside.

"These boxes are heavy," George notes.

"I think I can handle it," I say, snidely. What does he think? That I'm a wuss? He takes his box and heads in and I follow behind. The box is actually pretty heavy, but I'll never admit it. When I enter the doorway to the kitchen, I forget about the last step I took when I exited, and trip. A more graceful person might have caught themselves on their knees, but this is me we're talking about. As I tumble down, I pull the box against me and twist, attempting to land on my back and save the bottles, but mid-twist I realize my effort has been in vain. I flail my arms, trying to catch my footing . . . which I don't. In the end, I'm on the floor, soaked in liquor, lying on broken glass.

"Holy shit! Are you okay?" Ike asks as he kneels down beside me. His brown eyes look panicked. I can tell it's killing him not to be able to help me.

"What the fuck?" Sniper had run from behind the line when he heard the bottles crash to the ground. "Jesus, love. Are you okay?"

Am I? I take a quick inventory. My hands seem fine. Sniper offers me a hand and pulls me up. I brush the broken shards of glass from my legs and turn my back to Sniper.

"Did I get it all?"

"What the hell happened?" George gripes as he approaches. "This is like four hundred dollars' worth of liquor." I cringe. Of course it was. Damn my clumsiness and lack of coordination.

"I tripped. I'm so sorry," I apologize sincerely.

"What a dick. He talks about money before asking if you're all right." Ike shakes his head in disappointment.

"Uh, love." Sniper taps my shoulder. "You've got a nasty cut on your arse here."

"What?" I ask, twisting my neck, trying to see my ass. Blood trickles down my leg and at the sight of it, I feel the cut. Rubbing across my butt cheek, I find the spot where the fabric of my shorts are ripped and feel the warm fluid. "Shit!" I grumble.

"Want me to take a look at it?" Sniper rubs his palms together, a mischievous grin on his face.

"I'll go to the motel and take care of it," I say.

"It's bleeding pretty badly, Charlotte. You need to seal it up. It might need stitches," Ike says, as he stares at my ass.

"I'll take you to the doctor and workmen's comp will pay for it," George bitches. He's pissed. First, I destroy eight bottles of liquor, and now his workmen's comp premium will go up.

"No. I'll take care of it." I shake my head. "Can you get me a broom, Sniper?" I ask as I survey my path of destruction.

"I'll clean it up," Sniper insists. "You're bleeding all over the bloody place."

"Either one of us is cleaning that cut and sealing it with something before you leave, or I'm taking you to the hospital. The last thing I need is for that shit to get infected," George adds.

"I'm soaked in liquor," I point out. "I don't think infection will be an issue."

"You're bleeding all over my floor. Sniper or me. Make a choice."

I look down and see the back of my leg covered in red, my white sock soaked in blood.

Shit!

Ike

George and Charlotte enter his office and he shuts the door behind them. Charlotte cuts me a look that says: *You are not watching this!*

"I wouldn't miss this for the world," I laugh. "If he gets to see your ass, then so do I."

She glares.

I laugh more.

"Okay, tell me to leave. Say it out loud. Say, *Ike, I want you to leave this room.*" She narrows her eyes in frustration. She can't say it because of George. "No? Nothing? You want me to stay, huh? Okay. You've convinced me. I'm staying."

George plops down in the office chair and pulls out the first-aid kit from the file cabinet, fumbling through it for a minute. He pivots the chair so that he's facing the desk. "You wanna lean over the desk?" he asks, avoiding eye contact with Charlotte who is bright red. It's adorable.

She quietly makes her way to the desk and turns her back to him, her ass level with his face. He stares at it a moment . . . a moment too long and Charlotte says, "It won't bite, George."

He clears his throat and rolls his eyes. As if she'll shatter at his touch, his fingers feather across the material of her shorts where it's ripped, delicately pulling back the material so he can view the cut better. "How the hell did you cut your ass, but not your hands or knees?"

"I'm talented in the arts of clumsiness. I'm a sensei, really," she retorts and he chuckles.

"I think you're going to have to pull these down, Charlotte."

"No fucking way!" she almost shrieks as she straightens to a stand. "I'm not putting my bare ass in your face, George."

"I can't see the full cut." George leans back, fighting the grin that wants to break out across his face. "You're going to have to pull them down."

"Yes! Yes! There is a God! Thank you!" I exclaim. Charlotte purses her lips, but I'm not sure if it's at George, or me, or both of us.

"Seriously?"

"We're both adults here," George assures her. "I've seen a woman's ass before."

"You better not tell anyone about this!" she grits out as she undoes the button of her shorts.

"I don't think anyone would believe me," George laughs as he runs a wide palm down his face. I know he's acting like he's just doing this to mend her cut, but he's going to enjoy this as much as me. Charlotte has an ass that makes a man want to slap it. *Even a dead man.* George's knee shakes and it dawns on me how fucked up this situation is. My brother *and* I are both getting a chub by watching a girl pull her shorts down.

Charlotte wiggles her shorts down, hissing as the waist slides over her cut, until they're just past the curve of her cheeks before bending over the desk, arching her back so her rear sticks up slightly. The room is dead silent. Even though she's facing away from us, I know she did this on purpose by the way her lips are curved. She's trying to torture us. It's working. George's lack of breathing is definitely noticeable. Her right cheek has a rather large gash on it, but even so, her ass looks amazing. And . . . she's wearing a G-string.

George scoots up in his chair, attempting to adjust his hard-on without being obvious. This situation is all kinds of fucked up. I should probably leave because Charlotte might be uncomfortable, but . . . *no.* That's not happening.

"Is it bad?" Charlotte places her forehead to the desk; embarrassed.

George takes out some antiseptic wipes and says, "This is going to sting a little." With that, he begins to rub around the area before dabbing the cut itself. As soon as the wipe makes contact with her wound, she hisses and lurches forward; her body tensing. George just stares at her ass. Jesus Christ, we're some sick fucks. Why was that so fucking hot? I know he's thinking it, too. He's my twin. I can read him like an open book.

"It fucking stings!" Charlotte bites out as she pushes her ass back out, almost daring the pain to return.

"Sorry," George finally manages, swallowing hard, his Adam's apple bobbing.

In hopes of easing her discomfort, at least mentally, I decide to torture her back by joking with her. "I'm really enjoying this, by the way, Charlotte," I note and she tenses, clenching her fist. I love seeing her become all fire and feisty.

"Okay. Let me try something," George says. When he applies the wipe again, he blows gently on her flesh. Her skin immediately pebbles with goose bumps.

"Will it leave a scar?" Charlotte murmurs with her eyes clenched closed.

"Why? You got a lot of people looking at your bare ass?" I ask.

"I think I can use some butterfly bandages to close it, and just place gauze over it. We'll need to check it and clean it once a day," George mumbles. "Maybe with some Neosporin the scar will be minimal."

"We?" Charlotte snorts. "I don't think so." Just then, George pokes her cut, making her yelp.

"Sorry," he says, lacking sincerity. He did it on purpose. George makes quick work of cleaning the wound, applying ointment to it, and then he butterflies it and tapes the gauze on top. "There you go. I'd remove the gauze when you shower." He slides his chair back and fumbles in the first-aid box, but I see him watching her as she slides her shorts back up. *Dirty, rotten bastard.* I shake my head and chuckle silently to myself. He's just like me.

"Well, despite how incredibly awkward that was, I appreciate your help." Charlotte turns and smiles faintly.

"You're welcome." George nods and stands, tossing the first-aid kit on the desk.

"Guess I need to go and change. Do you mind if I wear a jean skirt? These were my only black shorts."

"No, that's fine. You can take the rest of the day off, if you want," George offers.

"No. I need the money," Charlotte quickly adds. "I'll be back in twenty."

Chapter 10

Charlotte

"Thanks for staying to add to that completely mortifying moment, Ike," I moan as we drive to the motel.

"Charlotte," Ike says, simply. "I'm dead. I have so little true happiness. Don't feel embarrassed. Feel good you've given a dead man a small glimpse of heaven."

I narrow my eyes and glance sideways at him. "You're ridiculous."

After I get to the motel, I wash off quickly, slipping on my jean skirt, and making it back to the restaurant in twenty minutes. The afternoon is slow and George seems to be hiding away in his office. I'm not sure if he's hiding from me, or maybe he's back there snorting drugs or getting drunk.

The uneventful afternoon tapers into the evening and Misty appears looking refreshed.

"She's high," Ike notes when he sees her.

She doesn't speak to me as she busies herself preparing the bar for the night shift. *Fine by me. Like I care.* Sniper introduces me to two of the other cooks, Greg and Winston. Greg is a tall, black man with a stellar white smile and Winston is a thin, pasty-faced man with cornrows. They both greet me and we share the typical pleasantries of introduction. Two other servers show up around five, Peyton and Libby—the charming pair are brother and sister.

"So you're the new girl?" Peyton grins as his eyes run up and down my body.

"That's me," I reply awkwardly as my face heats from his very obvious perusal.

"Please ignore my brother," Libby says, as she rolls her eyes at Peyton. "He's twenty-one and still hasn't finished puberty." When I laugh out loud, I immediately turn away from them and try to stop when I see Peyton glare at his sister.

"Apparently every man in town is going to have the hots for you," Ike notes gruffly as he stares at Peyton.

When my gaze darts to him briefly, he's standing with his signature McDermott stance—arms crossed—and his mouth is in a tight line. *Is he jealous?*

Ignoring Ike's statement, I make small talk with the siblings until the dinner crowd begins to trickle in. The night is pretty busy, and I keep making a point to check on George, wondering if my plan was a bad idea. I've been expecting some sort of event tonight, but so far there's been nothing. After we close down, George tells me I'm scheduled for the lunch shift tomorrow and sends me on my way. As I head out to my car, Misty is leaning against my hood, one leg crossed over the other, smoking a cigarette as if she hasn't a care in the world.

"Did you need something, Misty?" I ask with an *I-don't-give-a-shit* tone.

"This is your truck?" she asks, glancing back at it.

"It is," I admit as I cross my arms and cock my head. What the hell does she want? Momentarily, I wish Ike were here, but I wonder if maybe she knows what I've done, and I don't want Ike to know about that just yet.

Exhaling her last drag, she flicks her cigarette onto the parking lot and stands to her full height. She's an attractive woman, but you can tell life's had its way with her. She looks way older than she is, and just plain mean. There's no softness to her, not from what I can see, and I wonder why George would even give her the time of day. Maybe he thinks he doesn't deserve better. That thought makes me incredibly sad. For the most part, George has been a major dick to me, but I know there's good in him. I've seen it.

"I think we got off on the wrong foot," she begins, and it takes all of my strength not to roll my eyes at her.

"Is that so?" I ask.

"Maybe we won't be friends, but I'd like us to be amicable to one another." I want to exhale a huge breath of relief, realizing she apparently doesn't know about the letter. I'm not sure what to say to her. I know she hates me every bit as much as I hate her, but I decide to just roll with it. Maybe it'll make working together somewhat tolerable.

"Sounds good to me." I nod and head to the driver's side door of my 4Runner, but I stop, noticing Misty standing in front of my vehicle, eyeing my license plate.

"Oklahoma, eh?"

"Yep," I answer, quickly becoming increasingly suspicious of her. *She's memorizing my license plate.* Does she know someone that could look it up? It doesn't matter, I'm no criminal. She can look all she wants. "Would you like a pen to write it down, Misty?" I ask sweetly, and her eyes jerk to mine as she glares, but she quickly composes herself and smiles.

"Your tags are expired," she notes.

"Yeah, thanks for that," I say, sardonically. "I hadn't noticed."

Just then, a huge truck pulls up and my eyes just about pop out of their sockets. It's Roger's truck. When I left my letter on his windshield under a wiper, I had no doubt it was his. After all, the license plate did say 'ROGERZ' on it. "That your boyfriend?" Did he get the letter I left him? *Shit.* Is he here for George?

"Roger's out of town, bowhunting. Won't be back for a few days," she answers as she walks toward the truck. "That's his brother. His truck broke down so he's using Roger's, and my car has a flat."

Without another word to me, she climbs in the truck and they pull out of the parking lot. Shit! Did the brother get the letter? Will he tell Roger or Misty about it? As I climb into my truck, Ike appears in the passenger seat.

"You okay?" he asks, taking in the sight of me. The truth: *Hell no.* I had a plan and now it's all gone to shit and I have no idea what to expect. *Dear God,* I silently pray, *please don't let George get hurt. I was only trying to help. Amen.*

"Yeah." I swallow hard and start the truck. "I'm fine." For now, anyway.

Ginger tells me not to worry about starting on cleaning the rooms until my first day off, stating she doesn't want to overwhelm me and I'm already paid up, thanks to the Mercers, through the end of the week.

After I work my lunch shift, I head back to the motel and almost orgasm at the thought of taking a shower and crawling in bed. And I do just that. The restaurant closes early on Sundays so everyone is off tonight.

"Lie down with me, Ike," I order him.

"Careful, baby girl. You might get so used to it you won't be able to sleep without me," he jokes as he morphs to lie beside me. He's on his back, his hands behind his head as I turn toward him. He has a perfect profile, strong jaw, and straight nose.

"Can I ask you something?" I inquire.

He smiles and turns his head toward me. "Do you want me to take a look at that cut on your ass? Make sure it's not infected?"

I roll my eyes, fighting the urge to smile. "Never mind," I reply in a huff as I flop back, feigning annoyance.

"No. Ask away," Ike insists, and I roll back toward him.

"Were you with . . . ?" God, why in the hell am I asking him this?

"Was I with . . . ?"

"I mean . . . were you with a lot of women when you were alive?"

His eyes dart back to the ceiling and he sighs. "I wouldn't say a lot, but there were girls. Why do you ask?"

"Were you ever in love?"

Ike snorts. "Define love."

"Like, love," I say, simply. "You know what I mean."

"If by love you mean I dated a girl all through high school and planned to marry her, then yes, I was in love . . . or at least I thought I was."

"What happened?"

Ike smirks and runs a wide palm down his face. "Eh, you know. We graduated and she went to college, I joined the army, and we went our separate ways. We just kind of grew apart. She did come to my funeral and she cried. Just because we grew apart doesn't mean we didn't love each other, we just didn't have that forever love, I guess."

I roll to my back and stare at the ceiling just like Ike. "You miss her?"

"No," he answers quickly. "What about you? Ever been in love?"

Now it's my turn to snort. "Hardly. My brother made sure no guy came near me in high school, and in college I—" My moment of sharing is interrupted by a knock at the door. "Who is it?" I ask Ike.

He morphs and returns within seconds. "It's George."

"What the—" He knocks again, interrupting me.

Climbing out of bed, I tromp to the door and whip it open. George steps back, his gaze running up and down my form, causing heat to blanket my entire body. I'm wearing nothing but a large T-shirt that cuts just below my ass. It was Axel's—one of his favorites.

"That your boyfriend's shirt?"

Pinching my lips together, I look down and fight the urge to punch him in the jugular. "Hello to you, too, George. What an unexpected surprise. Should I just start expecting you to show up at my room unannounced every day?"

He rolls his eyes. George looks a little more groomed this evening; his hair is combed back and he's wearing jeans and a black dress shirt. He actually looks . . . hot. "It's Sunday," he says, sarcastically.

"And?" I ask pointedly.

"You were invited to dinner at my parents.' But if you're busy, I'll just let them know you can't make it." I can tell by the lilt in his voice that it's exactly what he hopes I'll do.

"Fuck. I forgot."

"You're going," Ike states.

"Clearly," George mumbles. "As much as I'm sure my parents and little brother would love to see your ass hanging out of that T-shirt, maybe you should put something a little more modest on."

Did he just say 'little brother'? I decide to ask Ike about it later. "Give me ten minutes. Come in." I open the door wider and stand to the side so he can enter. Slipping by me, he enters, his eyes scanning my room. Of course my bra is hanging over the pleather chair he heads straight for. Picking it up, he hands it to me.

"I think you might need this."

Snatching it out of his hand, I say, "Thanks."

After I lock myself in the bathroom, I hear him say, "Lord, give me strength."

Twenty minutes later, I'm ready to go and George leads me out to the parking lot. I lock my door and turn to find him straddling a motorcycle, causing my heart to drop to my feet.

"I brought a helmet for you, don't worry," he says, as he holds out a small, black helmet for me.

My eyes are wide as I stare at him. The sounds of screeching tires and bright lights flicker through my mind, making my throat constrict.

"What is it?" George asks, his mouth curving slightly. "Don't tell me you're scared of a little bike ride?"

Shaking my head, I step back, my hand searching blindly for the doorknob to my room. Nausea overtakes my stomach as I fumble to open the door, accomplishing it just in time before I make it to the bathroom to vomit. My breathing is labored as I begin to dry heave, and I know I need to calm down or I'll hyperventilate.

"Shit, Charlotte. You're having a panic attack. What is it?" Ike asks as he stands beside me, but I can't answer him. My arms are clutching the toilet as my body continues to rack itself painfully, trying to purge the contents of my stomach.

After a minute, I feel my hair being slid to the side, followed by something cold and wet on my neck. "Calm down, Charlotte," George says, quietly, as he kneels beside me. "Everything is okay. You have to slow your breathing. Look at me," he orders, and as I continue to suck in air, I raise my gaze to his. I expect to see fear or pity, but I see neither. George stares pointedly at me, trying to find me where I'm lost inside my head. "Inhale with me, nice and slow." Together we breathe in and exhale slowly, and after a few minutes, George has calmed me down almost completely.

"Do you want to talk about it?" he asks.

"No. I'd rather not." I sniffle, feeling like a total lunatic for freaking out that way. He must think I'm insane. "God. I'm so sorry," I manage as I wipe frantically at my face, positive it's covered in mascara.

"So am I. I didn't mean to make fun of you. I should've brought my truck." He pushes himself up then offers me a hand, helping me to my feet.

"Thank you for that," I whisper.

"I know a thing or two about panic attacks," he says, softly. "Had a few of them when . . ." He pauses, a pained expression seizing his features. "A while ago," he finishes. I know he means when Ike died, but as far as he knows, I don't know much—or maybe, anything at all—about that part of his life. And I'm sure discussing it is painful for him, so I don't press. "I'll let you get cleaned up. Would you mind driving your truck to my parents'?"

A huge part of me doesn't want to go after the meltdown I just had, but I know Ike wants me there. "Okay, thanks." I nod and George slips out of the bathroom, shutting the door behind him. I set about cleaning my face and reapplying a light coat of makeup.

"Are you okay?" Ike asks from behind me. In the reflection of the mirror, I can see his brows furrowed in concern. I know George is just outside, in my room, so I nod yes in answer even though the truth is—I'm not.

We make it to the McDermotts' place by four. Thankfully, we drove my truck and I haven't suffered any more panic attacks. As we stand in front of the gigantic house, my eyes widen—I'm in awe. The McDermotts own a bed and breakfast. The enormous house has a plantation porch with large, round pillars. It's beautiful, especially with the mountains as a backdrop.

"This is where you grew up?" I ask, somewhat raging jealous.

"Trust me, it's not all it's cracked up to be. We had to share our home with strangers for a large portion of each year."

"Still," I add. "This is just . . . beautiful."

"I guess," he agrees. "My mother is very excited about you joining us for dinner," George says, as he rests a hand to my back to lead me up the stairs. My body stiffens at the contact. I'm still not used to that feeling; the feeling of a man touching me, leading me, using his body to guide me. I think it's one of those little things people take for granted. "I think she has some twisted idea in her mind that we might date," he snorts as if the thought was ridiculous. I scowl where he can't see. Am I that unattractive to him? I can't help remarking on his comment.

"Gasp," I say. "Has she not heard about your *Charlotte is the Antichrist* parade? I figured you'd have the entire town in on it by now."

He chuckles as he opens the front door and shoves me gently, but forcefully enough to cause me to stumble. After I catch my footing, I glare at him. "Oops," he feigns. "I don't know my own strength sometimes. And no, I've only managed to get half the town in on it." He rolls his eyes.

"Dick," I say, under my breath, but apparently he heard it because he winks at me.

"You two are ridiculous," Ike mumbles as he morphs beside me.

"Ma!" George yells. "We're here!"

The house is just as beautiful inside as it is outside, with worn wood floors and a grand staircase. I follow George to the back of the house as my eyes scan the place. Everything is antique and feels so authentic to the house. The smell of food wafts in the air, causing my stomach to grumble. It's been so long since I've had a home cooked meal and my stomach is eager for it.

"George!" A tall, black boy calls as he comes barreling down the stairs. He's younger than George. If I had to guess, he's maybe seventeen, and extremely handsome.

"Cameron." George grins as they slam into each other, giving one another a hard pat on the back. "Good to see you, little brother."

So this is the little brother.

Cameron pulls away and his gaze finds mine. "And who do we have here?" he asks as he swaggers toward me.

George rolls his eyes again. "Charlotte, this is my little brother, Cameron. Cam, this is Charlotte."

"Nice to meet you," Cameron says, as he eyes me.

"You, too," I add. "I didn't realize George had a little brother."

"Well, he doesn't tell many people. It's obvious I'm much better looking so he tries to hide me from the world."

"Yeah. I'm jealous of your good looks," George retorts.

"How could you not be?" Cameron asks. "I mean, look at all this," he motions his hands down his body, "this beautiful mocha skin, these mahogany eyes, and this stellar smile."

"There's no denying it," George agrees mockingly. "You're much better looking."

"And let's not even get started on the size of my—"

"Cameron!" Beverly scolds as she approaches.

Cameron smiles and pulls her in for a hug. "I was going to say heart, Mom. I have the biggest heart in the county." When she pulls away, she gives him a knowing look. "What'd you think I was going to say?" Cameron asks coyly. "You didn't think . . . oh no . . . come on, Mom," he feigns disbelief. "Get your mind out of the gutter, woman."

George and I are fighting hard not to laugh as Beverly turns bright red. Ike, on the other hand, is laughing loudly. "Cameron McDermott, I'm going to beat you senseless."

"Gutter mind and abusive," Cameron tsks. "Charlotte, save me," he whispers. "I have such a young, impressionable mind, and I'm being raised by a really twisted woman, here."

Beverly smacks Cameron's arm. "George," she says. "I may need you to dig a hole out back. One big enough for a body."

We all laugh as Cameron picks her up and twirls her around. "I love you, Mom. You know you're the best."

"Yeah, yeah," she replies as he places her back on her feet and she touches at her hair to make sure it's still in place. "I'm still going to beat you." Turning to me, she takes my hands. "It's so good to see you again, Charlotte."

"You, too, Mrs. McDermott. Thank you for having me." I smile.

"Dinner won't be ready for a while, but I know George can keep you entertained. George, your father is down at the river, fishing. Why don't you take Charlotte down and introduce them."

"Sure," George agrees. "You coming, Cam?" George asks.

"No, he's not," Beverly adds. "Cam is going to set the table."

"Did I mention she's an advocate for child labor?" Cameron says to me.

"Is that so?" I laugh.

"Cameron," Beverly mumbles. "You better get in there and set that table." At this point, Beverly is fighting hard not to laugh herself.

Cameron leans toward me. "That's code for she's going to beat me," he whispers.

"I'm glad I'm not you," I whisper back. "She looks tough."

"You have no idea," he replies.

George leads me out the back door and onto the porch. There he slips off his boots and puts on a long pair of rain boots. Picking up some poles and other belongings, we head down toward the water. As we near it, an older man comes into view, flinging his pole back and forth over the water.

"Hey, Pop," George shouts, and the older man waves in response.

"The trout are biting, today, son. You better get in here and get your line wet," his father yells back.

Once we've reached the water, George drops everything and points to some overalls-looking thing with rubber boots attached to it. "Put that on."

I look down at my outfit. I'm wearing my best jeans and a fitted, black, long sleeve T-shirt. Not the nicest outfit, but I don't look like a schlub and I don't want to ruin my jeans.

"It'll protect your clothes," George adds as he picks up his pole and starts playing with the string attached to it. It doesn't look like your classic fishing pole.

"Protect them from what?"

"The water." He points.

"Oh. I'm not doing . . . that," I state adamantly. "I've never fished before."

George's mouth curves into a smile, but he doesn't look at me. "Then you're about to learn." I look to Ike but he just smiles as he stares at his father.

"You'll like this, Charlotte. Fly-fishing is a religion in these parts."

I fight the urge to roll my eyes. Whatever that's supposed to mean.

George and I bicker back and forth for a few minutes until he threatens to tackle me and put the, what he calls, *hip-waders* on me. I concede and put them on. Of course, they're about seven times too big for me and waddling to the water is a feat; I can only imagine how hard it'll be to wade through the water.

"Hold my hand," George offers as he steps into the river. Taking his hand, I can't deny the warmth I feel as his fingers intertwine with mine. It takes a few minutes before we reach his father because I keep losing my footing over the slick rocks.

"So you're the beautiful girl my wife came home raving about?" Mr. McDermott asks and my brows rise in surprise. Was Beverly really raving about me?

"It's nice to meet you, Mr. McDermott," I say.

"Please, call me Henry. How's my son treating you at the restaurant?" he asks as he gently whips his rod.

"Horrible," I reply certainly. "He's pretty much the worst boss I've ever had." Cutting my gaze to George, I stick my tongue out at him as his father laughs.

"Yeah, well, she did destroy a four-hundred dollar box of liquor, so I wager I deserve to be a little tough on her," George argues as he plays with his rod.

"And I paid for that mistake," I point out, "in blood." As embarrassing as it was to have my ass in George's face while he tended to my cut, I'm trying to laugh about it now. Of course, George can't just laugh with me. *Noooo.* He has to embarrass me even more.

Henry's brows furrow and George snorts. "It's a long story, Dad," George says, noting his father's perplexed expression. "Maybe one I'll save for dinner tonight." My eyes widen as I whip my gaze to George. He wouldn't dare tell them all the details . . . *would he?* George stares back at me with a face-splitting grin. "Or would you rather tell it, Charlotte?"

Glaring at him, I push some of my hair behind my ear, and say, "Of course not. While we're at it, I'm sure I have a few stories I could tell them about you as well."

George doesn't respond as he pulls at the line of his pole. *That shut him up,* I laugh to myself.

Glancing back at Mr. McDermott, I find him smirking at me. "George needs a good girl to keep him on his toes," he chuckles. "Looks like you found her." He turns and winks at George.

"Yeah. I need a girlfriend like I need a hole in the head," George replies gruffly, earning a deep scowl from me. Mr. McDermott, sensing our . . . what is it? Animosity? Whatever it is, he senses it and changes the subject.

"Have you ever fly-fished before?" he asks.

"No, sir. I've never done any kind of fishing."

"Well that's a travesty," he states. "Show her how it's done, son," he instructs George.

For the next hour, George describes the parts of a fly rod and how it works. He shows me how to cast the line. At one point, he and his father cast almost in sync and it's oddly beautiful. The casting seems almost like a dance, the wrist and the elbow guiding the line that bends and wafts through the air. And almost as soon as the line hits the water, they pull it back. It's elegant and serene and for the first time since I've met George McDermott, he seems peaceful.

"I'm heading back up. Don't be too long, you two." Henry winks at me.

"Now it's your turn," George states as his father wades back to the shore.

"I don't mind just watching," I say. As simple as it looks, it still seems to involve coordination, which I lack.

"Come on. You have to at least try it," George insists.

My first few attempts, I fail miserably, and at one point I drop the f-bomb, then frantically look around to make sure his father is actually gone and didn't hear me. George laughs loudly, taking the rod from me. "Let me show you," he says, as he moves behind me. With his front pressed to my back, my body heat rises and my heart pounds. Taking my hand, he places the rod in it and helps me arrange the line.

"Now," he breathes in my ear. "Imagine the rod is an extension of you; like you're one. It has to be smooth and quick. The bait, or the fly, has to land lightly on the water. When it lands, it has to float. If it drags, the trout will know by the way the water moves around it, and they won't bite at it." After he arranges my hands where they need to be, his left arm weaves around my midsection, his hand resting on my belly. His other hand holds mine softly, guiding it back. My body begs to press back against him, to feel all of him, but I fight it. Together we cast the line and pull it back, and I forget for a moment how awkward this should be because honestly, it feels amazing. His mouth remains close to my ear as he speaks, sending delicious vibrations down my body. George smells incredible and while he keeps babbling on about the art of fly-fishing, my mind is honed in solely on every point where our bodies are contacted.

Eventually, after I've casted successfully a few times, we head back to the shore and George holds my hand as he tries to help me through the water. Once we're on dry land, he laughs as I step out of the hip-waders and my heart beats a little faster. His laugh is deep and rich, achingly beautiful. "So, what did you think?"

"It was nice," I admit, sheepishly. I can't look into his eyes; I'm afraid he'll see all my thoughts. I think I'm starting to like George. Am

I crazy? But out there, in the water, with his body pressed to mine, I reacted to his touch. I wanted him against me. What the hell is wrong with me? After a beat, I manage, "Thank you." I look around for Ike, but he's nowhere to be seen. I frown, wondering where he went.

"You did good," he lies with a smirk.

"If by good, you mean sucked ass, then yes, I did good," I grumble and am blessed with another knee weakening George McDermott laugh.

"I'm glad you liked it," George says, as he takes my hand and leads us toward the house. "Now it's time to eat."

The evening is amazing. I'd been nervous about this dinner, but I've loved every minute of it. The McDermott family is warm and inviting and after being cold and alone for so long, it brings a kind of contentment I haven't felt in a long time; a feeling of home.

After I tell them where I'm from and some very vague details about my family, avoiding discussing Axel at all costs, we have dessert. Beverly made tiramisu, just as she promised. Afterwards, Beverly assigns the men to dish duty and she leads me into the family room. The walls are filled with family photos of Ike and George in football and baseball uniforms. The boys at a young age, fly-fishing with their father. There are even pictures of Cameron as a baby. I'm staring at a photo of him with a pair of sunglasses on at the piano; my guess is he's impersonating Ray Charles.

"We didn't get Cameron until he was twelve. We managed to get the baby photos of him from a relative of his." She smiles as she looks at the very photo I'm holding. "That boy has so much personality. I thank God every day for bringing him into my life."

"He seems like an amazing guy," I agree.

"His mother worked for Henry and passed away in a car accident. Cameron had always been around the office after school, and Henry insisted we take him in if Cameron agreed. Luckily he did, because in the last year laughter has run short, and Cameron seems to always find a way to keep it here." She pauses for a moment before stepping toward the wall.

"And this," she pulls a frame from the wall, "is my Ike. I'm sure you've heard, but we lost him in Afghanistan." Her features soften and her eyes glaze over with emotion.

"I have heard, and I'm so sorry for your loss." She hands me the frame and I smile at Ike dressed in a tux for what I would guess was his senior prom. The girl beside him is wearing a long, red dress and smiling brightly. They look like they were the cool kids, prom king and queen. This must be the high school girlfriend he spoke of.

"I want to be angry he's gone . . . blame God or everything, but I can't. That beautiful boy came into my life, and it was my honor to love him every day he was here."

Something causes me to look back, and I see Ike has returned. He's watching us, his expression soft as he listens to his mother speak about him.

"If you could say anything to him right now, and know for sure he could hear you, what would you say?"

Her brows furrow as she stares at his photo. "I'd tell him he made me proud. Every day of his life I was so proud to be his mama. I'd tell him that I love him more than words could ever convey, and he'll always be in my thoughts, every day for the rest of my life."

Tears threaten to spill from my eyes with her words. "I bet he'd tell you what an amazing mother you are," I speak for Ike. Anyone can see this woman is mother of a lifetime material.

She smiles and hangs his photo back on the wall. "I'm glad you came tonight, Charlotte. I hope you and George become good . . . friends."

I chuckle. "Our friendship thus far has been very futile."

"George is a bit of a mess right now, but I think he just needs to find a nice—"

"You ready?" George interrupts from the doorway leading in to the family room. His jaw is set and his mouth is in a hard, flat line. It's not hard to tell he's unhappy about something.

"We can stay longer if you'd like." I actually want to stay. I've really enjoyed this evening.

"No. I need to go. Meeting up with someone in a bit," he says, irritably. I glare at him. Probably meeting up with Misty. I fight the urge to say something shitty to him as his mother is standing right beside me.

"Why don't you go say good-bye to my father and Cameron. I need to speak with my mother for a moment," he states curtly.

The tension is thick in the air as I turn to Beverly and hug her. "Thank you so much for an amazing dinner. I truly enjoyed it."

"Anytime, dear. You'll come back soon, won't you?"

"I'd like that."

As I slip past George, he doesn't look at me. I make my way into the kitchen where Mr. McDermott and Cameron are arguing about football. They both hug me good-bye, and I head back to the family room to let George know I'm ready, but as I near the room, I overhear George speaking loudly.

"I'm fine, Mom," he says.

"No. You're sad and that's okay, George. Ike was your twin, your best friend. But at some point you have to give yourself permission to be happy again," Beverly says.

"I am happy, and I don't need you trying to set me up with some drifter. I'm okay. I don't need a woman to fix me."

"She seems like a lovely girl," Beverly argues. "I just want to see you happy, George. Really happy."

"Mom . . . I'm okay. Trust me. The last thing I need right now is a girlfriend, let alone one with issues like her."

Issues? Is he fucking kidding me? If that's not the pot calling the kettle black . . . Having heard enough, I stomp obnoxiously the remainder of the way to the family room, alerting them to my approach. When I peek in, they're both silent, and Beverly looks embarrassed and apologetic.

"I'm ready," I chirp with a bit of bite. "Thank you again, Beverly."

"Anytime, honey."

With that, I tromp out to my truck, and George follows shortly after. He directs me back to my motel and when I park the truck, I get out and slam the door. "Thanks, George. See you at work," I call over my shoulder as I pull out the key to my room. Just as I'm about to insert it in the lock, I'm pulled back, my gaze meeting George's.

"What's with the mood swing?"

I laugh, haughtily. "Mood swing?"

"Yeah. Why are you acting so bitchy?"

"I'm not," I say, as I unlock my door. "I just have some *issues* I'm dealing with." With that, I slip inside and slam the door in his face. After a few minutes the sound of his motorcycle firing to a start blares and he takes off.

"That went well," Ike snorts from where he sits in his chair.

Glaring at him, I warn, "Not another fucking word, Ike."

After changing in to my pajamas, I crawl in bed and Ike lies beside me. And to his credit, he doesn't breathe another word.

Chapter 11

Charlotte

Due to my work schedule, I have to swing by the Mercers' gas station and postpone dinner. Mr. Mercer understood how badly I needed the money, and we agreed I'd join them for dinner early next week. As I'm leaving, a dark-haired girl is standing in the back of the store, watching me. I give a faint smile and exit, wondering if her wide-eyed expression is a sign. Did I just recognize another soul?

I've just made it to my truck and Ike has already morphed inside when she appears beside me. "You can see me?"

I close my eyes and sigh loudly. "Let me guess," I say, defeated. "You're the Mercers' daughter?"

"Maggie," she replies simply, pushing some of her dark hair behind her ear.

"Do you know why you're here?"

"No."

"I only see souls with unfinished business. Is there something you feel you left unresolved in your life?"

Her brows narrow. "My mom has been looking for something she couldn't find when I passed. I want her to have it."

"Who are you talking to, Charlotte?" Ike asks as he appears out of nowhere.

My gaze jerks between them. "You can't see her?" I ask.

"See who?" they both reply in unison.

My brows rise to my hairline. I never knew these souls couldn't see others. "I'm talking to the Mercers' daughter," I answer Ike. Then looking to Maggie, I tell her, "I'm talking to Ike McDermott. I can see him, too."

"Oh, yeah. I heard my parents say he died in Afghanistan."

"She's here right now?" Ike asks, unable to hear what Maggie is saying.

"Yes," I answer. "Let's get in the truck before someone sees me standing here talking to myself. They both morph inside and their souls are intertwined, making it hard to tell who is who. "Ike, can you get in the back for a minute? You guys are all intermingled. I'm getting you two confused."

Ike morphs into the backseat and Maggie's gaze, filled with eagerness, meets mine. "Listen, Maggie. Do you want to cross over?"

"Something is pulling at me. Like it wants to lead me away, but I don't know where. Is it heaven?"

I let out an exasperated breath. I wish I knew. The truth is, I don't know. Many souls have described that pull to me, but no one knows what lies ahead. "I wish I could tell you," I answer her as I start my truck. "Do you want me to help you with your mom? Help you tell her where the necklace is?"

"Charlotte, I hate to sound like a dick, but you can't tell the Mercers what you can do before helping George," Ike says. "If it gets out, it could make things complicated."

He's right; it could. George is a mess right now, and we have no idea how he'd take it. "Maggie, I need some time before I can help you. I'm in the middle of helping Ike and his situation is complicated. If you'll be patient, I promise I'll help you." I have no idea how the Mercers will take me telling them I can communicate with their long-deceased daughter, but if I can bring them peace, I must. They've been so kind to me.

"I've been gone ten years. What's a little more time?" She shrugs.

"I'm Charlotte, by the way."

"I know. My parents think a lot of you." My heart swells with that. I showed up to this town looking like a homeless addict, and her parents have shown me such warmth and kindness.

"They're great people," I tell her. "Some of the best I've ever known."

"I'll see you at dinner at their house next week," she tells me.

"Hey, just a heads-up. Try not to talk to me too much . . . it gets distracting, and since I'm the only one that can see you, it wouldn't look good to seem like I'm talking to myself."

"I hear ya," she replies and smiles faintly. "I'll try to keep quiet. Bye." Then she vanishes. I frown slightly. She is by far the easiest soul I've ever had to deal with.

"Is she still here?" Ike asks from the backseat as I turn out of the parking lot of the Mercers' gas station.

"No, she's gone."

He morphs into the front seat and stares out the window. "It really isn't easy being you, is it, Charlotte?" he asks.

"Just another day for me," I answer somberly.

Misty has been off the last two days, which has been wonderful, but George has been here, of course, and hasn't spoken a word to me unless he's grunting an order. After dinner with his folks and his attitude toward me, I need some space. Otherwise, I'm likely to snap at him and blow this whole plan to help him. Luckily, he decided to close early this evening since it's slow and we're not making any money.

As I'm sweeping under my tables, Anna saunters up to me. "I'm heading out, but I'll pick you up at your motel in an hour."

"I'm sorry?" I ask, confused.

"It's Friday, and my mom is keeping River overnight. They have a decent band at the dance hall tonight. I'll pick you up in an hour."

"I don't have anything to wear, Anna. I think I'll just head home and sleep."

Putting her hand on her hip, she purses her lips and says,

"Charlotte, you're going. I have a bunch of dresses, and I'll be there in an hour."

"Dresses?" I ask, baffled. The closest I've gotten to wearing a dress in the last five years is a jean skirt. "Is it a dressy dance?"

"No," she sighs. "But it's nice to dress up a little when you can. I'm not bringing you prom dresses to try on. Chill. I have one I know will look great on you. Do you have any boots?"

"Some black ones . . . knee-length."

"Okay . . . see you in an hour."

After I finish up my tables, I head to the back where Sniper is almost done closing down the kitchen. "Are you going to this dance, tonight?" I ask, hoping to God he is so I know more than one person there.

"Yeah, Anna's making me."

I laugh. "You really like her, huh?"

Glancing sideways at me, he smirks and winks. Guess that was my answer.

An hour later, my makeup and hair are done, and Ike and I sit as I wait for Anna.

"Is this too much?" I ask him as I motion at my face.

"No, you look hot," he assures me with that fabulous knee-knocking smile of his. "You'll be the hottest girl there."

"I doubt that," I say, as I blush.

"I don't." When my gaze meets his, heat blankets my cheeks. The look he's giving me is so intense.

I don't know why, but I ask, "Would you dance with me tonight if you could?"

His brows rise, surprised by my question. Standing, he looks down at me, his expression serious. "Every fucking song. You wouldn't have a chance to dance with anyone else the entire night." When he swallows, his Adam's apple bobs. My heart tightens. There's no denying there's an attraction between us and I've wondered if it was just me, but now I know. Ike is feeling it, too. "But since I can't, will you dance with me now?"

This time, *my* brows rise. "How . . . ?"

"It might be weird since we can't touch, but we can move together."

"What about the music?"

Smiling, he says, "I'll sing."

"You sing?" I grin.

"Uh, I try to, but I know I can pull this song off."

"Jack-of-all-trades, huh?" I tease.

"Master of none," he quips back.

"Okay. How do we do this?"

"Stand here and put your hand on the back of the chair."

"Why?"

"To keep balance." I do as he says and he gets as close as he can. My body urges me to lean toward him, but I resist. There's nothing to lean in to. "Now close your eyes. Imagine my hands on your hips, your arms draped over my shoulders, and sway slightly to your right and back again."

I move as he's instructed and when he speaks again, his mouth is close to my ear and his voice vibrates through me, causing me to tremble. I want so badly to feel him, to touch him. He begins singing an old Travis Tritt song, *Drift Off to Dream.* It's a song a man is singing to the woman he hasn't yet found, but he's telling her how much he wants her and what they'll do when he finds her. Ike's voice is amazing; rich and deep. With my eyes closed, his voice gently sounds in my ear, and my body sways as I imagine us on a dance floor, surrounded by other couples, smiling at one another as the band plays in the background and he lip-synchs the words to me. That's what it should be like. Ike shouldn't be dead; he should be here right now, holding me close and dancing with me. I want to get angry, but the words of the song cut me so deep, it brings me back, forcing me to recognize this moment before it passes.

Then we'll dance to the radio, right up 'til dawn.

'Til you drift off to dream in my arms.

My heart aches as I take in the meaning behind the lyrics. Ike is telling me what we *would* do if we could; if he were alive and able to touch me. My eyes water as tears threaten to spill, my throat tight with emotion.

"Open your eyes, Charlotte," Ike whispers, and I realize the song is over. I squeeze my eyes closed tighter, wishing I could hang on to this beautiful moment. I don't want to let it go; the vision that's all so clear in my mind of dancing in the arms of Ike McDermott. When I open them, we're still swaying side-to-side in perfect unison. "Thank you for dancing with me," he says, quietly, and smiles softly, his brown eyes shining. God, he's a beautiful man. Before I can respond, there's a knock at the door and he quickly morphs outside, and then back in. "It's Anna."

I'm still holding the chair, frozen in place, trying to figure out how to move again. That was the best dance I've ever had and we didn't even touch. Anna knocks on the door again, bringing me back to reality. Shaking off the completely romantic moment Ike and I just shared, I saunter to the door and open it.

"Damn, you look good, girl," Anna cheers. She looks pretty good, too. She's wearing a black dress with a tight cardigan and her hair is down; straight and sleek. "Here." She shoves a green, cotton dress toward me.

"This is it?" I hold the dress up and try not to grimace at how small it looks. "I thought you were bringing a couple dresses for me to try on?"

"This is the one. I know it will look hot on you. I have a knack for these things."

"If it will even fit," I mumble as I hurry into the bathroom and change.

When I come out, Anna grins. "I knew you'd look hot."

My gaze moves to Ike briefly and he's staring at me, his jaw set tightly. "Beautiful," he whispers, and I can't help the smile that breaks out on my face. "I'm going to go check on my folks," he says to me, even though I've torn my eyes from his and am busy collecting my purse. Then, he disappears. I frown, wondering if he's upset about something.

"It hugs you in all the right places," Anna says, speaking of the dress.

"Little bit low in the front, don't ya think?" I ask as I attempt to tug the low-cut dress up to cover my cleavage, which is spilling out. I slip on my leather jacket and check myself out in the mirror one more time.

"Yep, and that's why George is going to have a stroke when he sees you in it."

"Excuse me?" I almost choke as I spin around to face her. "George?"

"Yeah, he and Sniper are outside waiting for us."

Don't roll your eyes and groan, Charlotte. Why does George have to be going? I'm surprised he didn't back out the moment he found out I was going.

"And why would I want to impress George?" I ask with a little edge to my voice.

She gives me a knowing look. "Because you have a crush on him."

Anna and I sit in the back of Sniper's car while he and George sit up front. I insisted she was wrong about the crush on George, but she just smiled and patted my shoulder, saying, "If you say so, honey," then hightailed it out to the car.

They all make small talk while I stare out the window, wondering where Ike is. That dance was truly one of the most romantic things I've ever experienced. It isn't until we reach the dance hall that everyone is able to see what I am wearing. George gives me a once-over, his lips flattening, before making a beeline for the bar. Guess he isn't too impressed, after all. Once Sniper sees my outfit, he—of course—tells me I look *sexy as hell.* I feel a little awkward as Anna is right beside me, but she doesn't seem to care. I guess it helps he has his arm around her waist.

Sniper, Anna, and I take a seat at a table near the dance floor. Anna was right, this isn't a dressy dance, and I wish I would have fought her on making me wear this. I'd feel so much better in my jeans. "I'm going to go get us all a drink." She stands and scurries off toward the bar.

"You two don't seem to be getting along too well, lately," Sniper mentions.

"Have we ever gotten along?" I counter, knowing he's speaking about George. My gaze moves to find him, and I spot him at the bar, laughing with a guy he's speaking with.

Sniper's lips form in to a sad sort of smile before he opens his mouth to respond but Anna appears with our drinks, stopping him. "Sniper, I love this song," she tells him, obviously hinting she wants to dance. He takes his beer from her and draws a long swig before setting it down, taking her hand, and leading her to the dance floor. "I'd love to dance with the most beautiful woman here," he tells her.

The song is pretty upbeat, and the two dance together amazingly. They laugh as he twirls her, and while I smile, my heart aches a little. Sometimes I don't realize how badly I need something until I see someone else with it. I want to be happy and basking in the glow of early love; that prelude to the delicious things to come. I haven't thought much about it over the past six years; I mean, not really. I've been lonely, but it never occurred to me I craved that kind of relationship; mostly because I truly believe no one could deal with me and my gift. My own parents sent me away, so why would any man want to burden himself with me? So I settled into a life where love didn't exist. At least not until the McDermott brothers came in to my life. Ike has certainly made an impression, which makes me even more pathetic. I can't have a relationship with him, so why am I allowing myself to even imagine it? Then there's George. Our relationship to date has been so hot and cold, I'm not sure what to make of it. No matter what, George has some changes to make, and they're deal breaker changes. I chance a glance at him and see he's still standing at the bar, facing the back. Misty approaches and rests a hand on his shoulder. I make a gagging motion, not thinking anyone might be watching.

"What's a pretty girl like you doing sitting over here by yourself?" a voice asks, and when I look up, I see a very tall man with wide, broad shoulders and a beard. He looks like he's maybe thirty or so, attractive in a rugged and country kind of way. Before I can respond, he takes the seat next to me and scoots closer.

"You must be the new girl in town everyone keeps talking about," he says, before sipping the bottled beer in his hand.

"I didn't realize I was gossip worthy," I reply.

"A beautiful woman shows up and you can be sure the women are talking smack, and the men around here are eager to check you out."

"Is that so?" I chuckle, slightly humored by his bluntness. A smile sneaks across his face, and I can't help smiling, too. Although I find him attractive, I wouldn't say I'm attracted to him. I can admit, however—sad and pathetic as I am for feeling it—I like that he's flirting with me. Sometimes it's the little things. Sometimes a woman just needs a man to give her attention so she knows she's attention worthy.

"You're serving over at Ike and George's, right?"

"Wow. I guess everyone does have the 4–1-1 on me, huh?"

"Small town, small minds. What else is there to do around here?" he asks.

"Apparently, dancing is an option." That feeling of warmth spreads across my back, and I get the sense someone is watching me. Darting my eyes to the bar, I see George watching my interaction with the man before me. His mouth is set in a hard, flat line and he's almost glaring. Misty follows his line of sight and her brows touch her hairline when she realizes he's looking at me.

"Well then," the stranger stands, chugging the last few sips of his beer and setting the bottle down. "May I have this dance?"

My gaze moves from George to the handsome man before me. Chugging a few sips of my own beer—liquid courage in a bottle—I take his hand and let him lead me onto the dance floor. We pass by Sniper and Anna on the way and they stop to watch us before glancing at one another. Another upbeat song starts playing and without discussion, my dance partner and I fall into a two-step and we're nailing it. He's a great dancer, and I'm laughing the entire time, not remembering the last time I danced like this; so carefree.

When the song ends, a slow one comes on and he pulls me to him, taking my arms and draping them over his shoulders, putting his hands at my waist, his fingers applying gentle pressure. This is a little more intimate than I'd like, but I don't want to offend him so I try to make conversation, but he starts to speak first.

"You got something going on with George McDermott?" My expression must indicate I'm floored by his question because he quickly adds, "He's been watching you since you arrived." *Has he?* That's news to me and obviously this guy is mistaking glaring at me for watching me in appreciation.

"We work together, that's all," I respond, unsure of why George is even bothering to stare at me at all. "You're a pretty good dancer," I tell him, trying desperately to change the subject.

"You're not so bad yourself, Char," he replies, and I'm stunned he knows my name until I remember that apparently I'm the town gossip.

"You know my name. Do I get to know yours?"

"Roger," a voice interrupts, and I nearly choke. It's Misty, and she's attempting the daunting task of trying to shoot fire from her eyes at me and obliterate me to nothing but ashes. This bitch has some nerve acting like she's jealous when she's cheating on Roger with George. And then the thought hits me; this is Roger; her drug-dealing boyfriend she's cheating on with George. I've been dancing with a drug dealer.

"May I cut in?" George asks from behind me. And as Misty glares at me, Roger eyes George with a look that says, *I know;* at least, that's what it looks like to me.

"Um . . . sure," I say, completely thrown by the last few seconds. "Do you mind, Roger?"

"No. Not at all." Taking my hand, he kisses it and Misty's eyes are as big as saucers. "Lovely to meet you, Char. I'll see you around." With that, he saunters off the dance floor, Misty scurrying behind him in a huff.

Looking back to George, he steps toward me, but waits for me to meet him halfway. His gaze is almost blank, as if he's just going through the motions and he doesn't really want to dance with me. "I'll spare you the grief, boss. I know you two were just trying to break it up. I didn't know that was Roger, okay? I wouldn't have said anything about you two even if I had known. And now they're gone so you don't have to torture yourself and dance with me." As I step around him, he takes my wrist and pulls me back, slamming my body against his. God, he smells really fucking good.

"I asked you to dance because like every other guy here, I want to dance with the most beautiful woman in the room." My mouth falls open with shock.

"Was that a compliment?" I ask sarcastically. "I'm waiting for the punch line."

"Do you always have to be such a pain in the ass?" he questions, earning a lethal glare from me.

"Forgive me, but you're the one giving me whiplash with your hot and cold mood swings," I pipe back. "The other day I was a girl you wouldn't waste a minute on because of my issues. Now I'm the most beautiful girl in the room." The band starts playing *I Believe in Love* by Don Williams when George snakes one arm around me, resting a firm hand on the small of my back. His other hand finds mine and holds it to his chest. My traitorous body simply, and stupidly, falls into rhythm with him as he begins to sway.

As he pulls me closer, his mouth is next to my ear. "Let's put our crazy away for three minutes and just dance, Charlotte. Okay?"

Swallowing hard, I nod twice, and allow myself to get lost in the moment, drowning in the feel of him against me, the beautiful song playing, and his enticing scent. The song plays on and for a moment, I think George is whispering the words, but so quietly I can barely hear them. I know he's only singing just for the purpose of singing, not singing to me, but I find myself trying to catch every word. When the song ends, George pulls away; his dark eyes meeting mine and he smiles faintly. "Thanks for the dance." Then he's gone. What the fuck?

"Ladies' room. Now." Anna appears out of nowhere and drags me away. I'm relieved she did because otherwise I'd still be standing in the middle of the dance floor looking like an idiot. When we enter the ladies' room, she quickly checks the stalls to make sure we're alone before taking me by the shoulders.

"Dude," she says, simply. "You have just somehow created a love square."

"What?" I ask, confused.

"It was a triangle with Misty, Roger, and George. You just changed it to a square."

"What? No." I shake my head adamantly in disagreement. "I just danced with them. That hardly qualifies as me infiltrating their fucked up love triangle, or whatever." In fact, that thought makes me ill. I can't quite figure out why I detest the thought of George with Misty. I mean, we're not together, hell . . . he thinks I have *issues,* and he definitely doesn't like me. But when I see her smile at him or him smile back, it makes me queasy.

"Roger approached you to fuck with them, ya know?"

"Who? George and Misty?"

"I would bet my life he did it to piss both of them off."

"So you think he knows . . . ?"

"I bet he's had suspicions." Anna pulls out a tube of her infamous red lipstick and begins applying it.

"I'm not interested," I tell her. "In either of them." Not entirely true, but I'd rather not think about George in that way at all. "I didn't even know that was Roger. A guy asked me to dance, so I danced."

Anna rubs her lips together and tosses the tube back in her purse. "You keep telling yourself that, sugar," she chuckles and leads me out of the bathroom.

Chapter 12

Charlotte

The rest of the night at the dance was calm and enjoyable. George's parents showed up and hugged and fussed over me, which I loved. They're amazing people. His dad and I did a line dance, and he begged me to marry George, and if I couldn't, would I wait until Cameron was of age. George ignored me and chose not to ride back with Anna, Sniper, and I when we left. I assume his parents took him home. My consolation after the dramatic evening was that Ike was waiting for me when I got back to my room, and I found great comfort in that.

The next day, the first half of my double shift is rather drama free. George and Misty are both off. I imagine sniffing coke and boinking like rabbits. I hate how ill the thought makes me. I shouldn't care; this is business, after all. I'm only helping George so Ike can cross over. At least without George and Misty at the restaurant, I had a day of peace; no nasty looks from her and no attitude from him. Ike wanted me to go to George's house and make up some excuse for being there, but I couldn't do that. Not after what happened the other night. I know I'll see him and Misty tomorrow at work.

Today has been slow and awkward. Misty is pretending to be nice to me, and I *despise* her for it. I don't want her fakeness, mostly because she's so much better at it than me. Very rarely can I smile at a person I dislike and speak to them without my every thought being obvious, and I have no doubt my distaste for the white trash princess is evident every time we speak. George is working the back line with Sniper and Greg, avoiding me for the most part.

But *I've* noticed him.

Unfortunately.

He's wearing a tight, black T-shirt, showcasing his amazing body and muscular arms. Since I met him, he's always been slightly thinner than Ike, but still ripped. I wonder if it's only the drugs that have made him smaller, because other than the slight difference in their size, haircuts, and shades of eye color, they are identical. I find myself ogling him, forgetting what an ass he is for a mere second until he speaks.

"How's your ass?" he chuckles, snapping me out of my state of admiration. Sniper bites his lip to keep from laughing as he winks at me. *Damn him.* I blush with embarrassment. I can't believe I had my ass in George's face. It's no secret he likes to get a rise out of me and he's succeeded. Score one for George. Two can play at this game.

"I don't know." I bite my lip seductively. "Might need you to check it out for me again. Would you mind?"

All three men on the line stop what they're doing and stare at me. I chance a glance at Ike and he rolls his eyes as if he's annoyed. I resist the urge to toss a lemon at him. What's his problem? It's only a joke.

"Uh, sure. I could—"

"It was a joke, George," I interrupt him as I laugh. He glares at me as his perfect lips flatten into a hard line. "You will not have the pleasure of having this ass," I turn slightly and point to my butt, "in your face again," I tease. I know I shouldn't. George hates me, but I can't deny I'm attracted to him and his brother. The McDermott twins are good-looking men. And as much as I know George dislikes me, I can feel his dark eyes on me every so often. The attraction is mutual.

Before he responds, I take the two hot plates from the line and head out to drop them at Peyton's table. As I exit the kitchen, I hear Sniper say, "You're a lucky wanker, you got to see that ass." They all laugh in response, and I smile to myself because I'm an idiot.

After that, Ike leaves me alone most of the night, which I'm grateful for. The fact he's dead and tries to talk to me—constantly—is distracting enough, but add in his good looks, and I can't focus on anything. Even though the lack of his presence helps in some ways, I find myself looking for him, scanning the restaurant and the kitchen just to make sure he's still with me. Sounds stupid when I've asked him to give me space, but some part of me needs to know he's near. I've mentally scolded myself for that feeling. Becoming dependent on his presence is bad news; it is an infinite fact Ike will leave this world for good soon. Then what will I do? But for now, as long as I know his soul still lingers in this world, I need to have him close as much as I need to breathe. He's the one and only thing I can count on right now, and I know how absurd that is since he's dead and can do absolutely nothing for me other than hang out, basically.

Peyton and Libby are standing at the bar watching the television when I join them, my gaze moving to the screen to see what they're so entranced by. It only takes a glance at the news segment playing to send my heart catapulting into my throat.

Police are looking for the driver of this vehicle in connection with the murder of Casey Purcell. Purcell's body was found under a bridge in Charlottesville, Virginia and authorities would like to speak with the driver of this 1996 Toyota 4Runnner. Due to poor video footage, authorities were unable to make out the license plate, but they do know the vehicle was gray and believe a female operated the vehicle. Investigators have also retrieved evidence they're using to aid in locating the owner of the vehicle. If you have any information, please contact . . .

The words are drowned out by the beating of my own heart. *Evidence retrieved? What evidence?* I didn't murder Casey, but that doesn't mean I want to go in for questioning. How would I explain how I found her? It's highly unlikely they would believe Casey's soul directed me there. *Shit.* I thought I had been careful.

"You okay, Char?" Libby asks, laying a hand on my shoulder, making me jolt.

"Uh, yeah," I shake my head and swallow. "Think I just need a break." My fourth table is just getting up, and I know now is the perfect time for that break after I check my other two tables, making sure they have everything they need and their drinks are full. I don't smoke, but I head to the back, planning on getting some fresh air where Anna and I chatted the other night.

"Where are you sneaking off to, love?" Sniper calls.

"Just taking a quick break," I answer.

"Be careful out back by yourself, Char," Greg warns. "Make sure you leave the door open so if you need us, we can hear you."

That's a strange warning. Is this town dangerous for women? My expression must indicate my thoughts because Sniper explains, "Greg used to be a police officer in Chicago. I can't seem to make him understand that Warm Springs is nothing like Chicago."

"Always better to be safe than sorry," Greg adds as he tosses the vegetables in the frying pan he's holding.

"I appreciate your concern, Greg." I smile. "Thank you."

When I take my first step to head out back, Ike morphs in front of me and my heart nearly bursts from my chest as I stumble back. Goddamn it, *I'm going to kill him if he doesn't stop doing this shit to me.* But my plans for his demise are quickly obliterated when his wide panicked eyes meet mine.

"What is it?" I ask instinctively.

"I didn't say anything," Sniper says, as he eyes me suspiciously.

"It's George," Ike practically pants.

"Where is he?" I ask, the hair on my arms and the back of my neck standing on end.

"Where's who?" Sniper asks.

"Where's George?" I add, still focusing on Ike.

"Out back. Misty's boyfriend and his brother just showed up and beat the fuck out of him." Ike turns his head to the back door.

"Shit," I hiss.

"Are you okay, love?" Sniper asks as he takes a hesitant step toward me.

"Sniper. I need you. Follow me," I call as I bolt to the back.

"Watch the line, Greg," Sniper orders as he hurries behind me. Greg steps in and takes over.

"What the hell is going on?" Sniper asks as he trails behind me.

I don't answer. Instead, I burst through the back door, my heart pounding in my chest. I didn't even think about the fact Roger was back in town after seeing him at the dance. Shit! I didn't look out for George like I was supposed to. Now he's hurt, and it's all my fault.

When we hit the pavement, we find George motionless on the ground, blood covering his shirt and face. "Shit," I breathe.

"What the fuck?" Sniper bellows as he pushes past me and runs to George. I follow behind him and kneel beside George. His face is already swollen, his cheek bubbled up, his lip busted open and bleeding.

"That mother fuck . . ." Sniper growls aloud, but doesn't finish. He lays George on his back, stretching him out.

"We're trained for this. Sniper knows what to do," Ike assures me as he stands over us, arms crossed, concern painted across his face.

The night air is slightly humid from all the rain, enough to make anyone sweat, but I'm perspiring profusely; my shirt is clinging to my back and strands of my loose hair are stuck to my neck and forehead. I didn't mean for this to happen. I just wanted to out George so maybe it would separate him and Misty. I thought Sniper and I, together—albeit Sniper had no idea this was happening—could stop George from getting hurt.

"Is he okay?" I ask, reaching my hands out, wanting to touch George but unsure if I should or even where I should touch him.

Sniper smacks George's face on the side that isn't pulverized. "Wake up, ya wanker." George flutters open the eye that's not swollen and groans. "That's a lovely shiner you have there, mate," Sniper notes as he attempts to sit George up. "Go get a bottle of bourbon," Sniper orders me as he reaches in his pocket and tosses me his set of keys. I hurry inside, groaning as I try each key on the lock to the cabinet. Of course, the last one works. I grab the bourbon, and as I slam the cabinet closed, Misty appears.

"What the fuck are you doing?" she squawks as she glares at me with her arms crossed. She thinks I'm stealing bourbon.

"It's for George," I answer nervously. Not because of her, but because my nerves are a fucking wreck.

"He asked you for this?" she questions and quirks a bitchy brow.

"Now's not the time for your shit, Misty. Your boyfriend—ya know, the one you've been cheating on—just beat George's ass," I counter before spinning around and sprinting to the back door.

"What?" she calls, shock laced in her tone.

By the time I get outside, Sniper has George sitting up. Peeling the plastic off, I twist the top open before handing the bottle to Sniper. "Chug this." Sniper holds the bottle to George's lips and George gulps it. I cringe. I can hold my own, but I could never chug Wild Turkey.

"George," Misty gasps as she kneels beside him, placing one hand on his leg. I can't help the gigantic eye roll I make.

"Misty, lass." Sniper shakes his head as if trying to reel in his anger. All I've ever seen of the burly line cook is flirtatious winks and perverted smiles. This look on him is quite terrifying. "We both know who did this. You need to go. Take a few days, and let's see how things play out."

Misty shakes her head vigorously. "Roger wouldn't—"

"Misty!" Sniper snaps. "Get the fuck out of here, and tell that asshole boyfriend of yours Sniper's coming for him." Misty is stunned silent. So am I. I wonder how he would react if he knew I was also responsible for George getting hurt. Sniper is incredibly scary when he's pissed off. "Go!" Misty stands stiffly and rushes back inside. "You have to take him home, Char. I have to stay and close this place down for the night. The only other people to call would be his mom and dad, and he'd kill us both if we did that."

"Shouldn't we take him to a hospital?" I ask.

"No," Ike and Sniper say, almost in unison.

"I have tables," I add.

"I'll have Peyton take over your tables."

I help Sniper drag George to my truck where he straps him in, leaving the bottle of bourbon in his lap. George's head lulls as he struggles to keep conscious. Sniper shuts the door and his head drops for a moment. Slowly, he turns back toward me and his expression makes me freeze. Is he pissed? At me? When he grabs my arm, jerking me away from the truck a few feet, I know he definitely is.

"What the fuck, Sniper?" I hiss. "You're hurting me!"

"I might hurt you worse if you don't tell me how the hell you knew George was going to get the shit kicked out of him tonight."

"I didn't," I lie.

"Bullshit! What was that the other day, that little *I just feel like something is going to happen and having a tough guy like you around might keep things from getting too crazy* bit? You knew this was going to happen. You ratted George and Misty out to Roger, didn't you?"

"Is that true?" Ike gasps, but I don't look at him. I'm too busy staring at the vein swelling off of Sniper's throat because he's so angry. I was naïve to think the truth would never get out.

"Yes," I answer, which coincidentally answers them both.

"What the fuck?" Ike groans.

Sniper takes me by both arms, holding me firmly in place. "Do you know what he's going through? What's your game here? Trying to break him and Misty up so you can move in on him?" he snarls.

"No!" I shriek as I panic. Sniper's understandably irate. He thinks I've just gotten his friend badly hurt, and I'm trying to take advantage of him, which technically, I did, but I had good intentions. I'd be pissed, too, if I were him.

"Tell him you see me, Charlotte," Ike insists. "Tell him *friends share the joy and divide the sorrow*." I repeat Ike's words and Sniper freezes. "He said that at my grave, months after they buried me. He didn't make it in time for the funeral."

"You missed Ike's funeral," I wheeze, still panicking. He turns slightly, fixing his lethal, narrowed gaze on me.

"Anyone could know that," he hisses, releasing me. "What are you doing here?"

"Tell him the truth," Ike says.

Closing my eyes, I take a deep breath. I have to tell Sniper the truth, or he's liable to break my neck. I hate this part. They never believe me at first. Then they ask you fifty questions trying to prove I'm lying. "Listen, Sniper," I begin, "what I'm about to tell you is going to sound crazy, but I just need you to hear me out, okay?" He crosses his arms and glares at me, but doesn't argue. The muscles in his jaw tic, and I have to swallow my nervousness and fear before I continue. "Ike brought me here. I'm a medium . . . of sorts."

Sniper doesn't speak. He just continues to stare at me so I continue to babble to fill the awkward silence. It's a bad habit of mine. "Ike and I met a few days ago, and he asked me to come here to help George. You see . . . Ike is in limbo. He can't cross to the other side because he has unfinished business." Again, Sniper stares, his jaw still twitching angrily.

"He doesn't believe you," Ike mumbles, shaking his head.

"No shit, Ike," I snap as I glare at him.

Sniper takes a step back, shaking his head. "You expect me to believe you're talking to him right now?"

"Yes," I answer simply. "Ask me something only Ike would know the answer to. Maybe an inside joke or a secret between the two of you."

"I'm not doing this, you crazy bitch." His words make me wince. He's never spoken to me like that before. Sniper suddenly takes one large step toward me, muscles, bulging, fists clinching and I cower slightly, but refuse to step back just yet. I'm not lying and I refuse to be scared away. "Again, I don't know what your game here is, but you better get out of my face and out of this town before you get hurt." I swallow hard as I back away.

"Charlotte, repeat after me," Ike orders. As he speaks, I shout after Sniper who is now walking back to my truck to retrieve George.

"Number one on the bucket list was to piss in Sgt. McForbe's canteen and watch him drink it." I give Ike a narrowed glance. "That's disgusting," I say.

"We hated him." Ike shrugs before speaking again, to which I repeat to Sniper, who has stopped dead in his tracks.

"Number two was to go to the Super Bowl together if the Steelers and Seahawks were playing. And you have a pink unicorn shitting a rainbow on your ass!"

My gaze immediately jerks to Ike's, and I give him a *What the fuck?* look. Ike laughs. "He lost a bet and he was wasted."

"Really?" I turn back to Sniper, who's steadily approaching. "You have a pink unicorn shitting a rainbow on your ass?"

"Bloody hell, Ike," he grumbles. When his gaze meets mine, his eyes are brimming with tears. Watching a man like Sniper become emotional is a beautiful thing. It's like witnessing a baby take its first breath. You know it's rare and because of that, it's beautiful. "He's really here? He can hear me right now?"

"Yes," I answer and smile faintly as my gaze flicks to Ike. His eyes are brimming with tears, too.

Sniper crosses his massive arms again. "This is fucking crazy," he sighs.

"I know," I answer honestly.

"Ike, man, I . . . I'm sorry," he apologizes.

Ike tells me what words to say and I repeat them to Sniper. The conversation is emotional on both sides, and even I begin to feel a bit weepy after a while, but the two say very wonderful and loving things to one another, things only brothers of war would understand. When men walk into hell together, they believe they will walk out the same way and when that doesn't happen, when one brother comes home and the other doesn't, there's a guilt so choking, you can't breathe. Sniper lives with this pain and through me, Ike tells him, "It wasn't your time, brother. God has plans for you still. Live for us both. And it would mean the world to me if you'd help us help George so I can rest in peace." As Sniper cries, the emotions rolling off of him are like strong waves crashing over me. I can feel the weight of guilt and sadness he's carried since Ike's death. They say a few more things, promises from Ike that he'll always be looking over Sniper, and promises from Sniper he'll always take care of the McDermott family. And when they are through, Sniper drags me into his large arms and hugs me tightly.

"I'm so sorry I manhandled you, Char. You have no idea what this has meant to me. Thank you," he whispers in my ear as his breath hitches. When he releases me, he steps back and rubs his face roughly with both hands. I've heard that a million times when I've communicated the words of the dead to a loved one, but this time, it feels good to hear. Ike is quiet when I glance at him, tears still streaming down his face, and I realize Sniper's gratitude means more than I imagined; in helping Sniper, I helped Ike. And more than anything, I want to help Ike.

"I take it George doesn't know about you seeing Ike and all, since he acts like a wanker to you."

"He's not in the right frame of mind to really accept the truth," I say.

"So Ike told you to tip Roger off about George and Misty?"

"Uh . . ." I pause and give Ike a sheepish glance. "Not exactly. I kind of took that initiative all on my own. Ike wants George to stop seeing Misty because she's supplying him with drugs."

"That lass is a bit of a crack whore, isn't she?" Sniper snorts.

"I thought with you being here, and me staying on alert, we could prevent George from being hurt. I just wanted Roger to . . . I don't know . . . scare him, I guess."

"Well, a good ass-kicking is probably what he needed most. You get him home, and we'll talk more tomorrow. I'll help in any way I can." Sniper pats my shoulder as he glances around as if trying to catch a glimpse of Ike. "I love you, man," he says, before walking toward the back door.

"You okay?" I ask Ike, who watches him with me. When his eyes meet mine, anger flashes in them.

"You could've gotten him killed," he growls.

"You said Roger wouldn't kill him," I argue.

"You should've asked me, and I could've kept an eye on things before my brother got hurt!"

"Look!" I snap. "I'm sorry, but something drastic had to happen. The people in this town see George falling and keep handing him a fucking crutch because they feel sorry for him because he's grieving you. If I'm going to help *him,* so that I can help *you,* he needs to be clean, which means he needed some sense knocked into him."

"This wasn't your call to make."

I laugh bitterly at him. "Oh. I see. So I'm just a fucking puppet for you? You call the shots, and I simply obey, is that it?"

"He's my brother!"

"I'm well fucking aware of who he is, Ike!" I shout. "And who am I?"

He stares at me blankly a moment. "Who are you?" he asks, confused, as if he doesn't understand my meaning.

"I'm the only fucking person here that's able, and willing, to help you, so get off my ass!" I stomp away and head toward my truck, leaving Ike to fume.

Chapter 13

Ike

After Charlotte cleans George and removes his bloodied shirt, she leaves him on the sofa, placing a blanket over him. I'm mad as hell at her and decide it's better not to speak or I may say something I'll regret. How could she be so reckless with his life? What if Roger had pulled a gun on him?

After she scrubs his house top to bottom, ignoring me as she works, she dozes off in the recliner near the couch around one in the morning and I simply stare at her. Maybe this was a huge mistake. Maybe I was wrong to make her help me. I need her to help me save George, not get him killed. Another hour passes and George begins to stir. Sitting up slowly, he places a hand to his swollen eye, wincing when he does. "Fuck," he grunts.

Scooting forward, he reaches for the coffee table, his hand fumbling across the surface, freezing when he finds it cleaned. Charlotte got rid of all the trash, and even polished the table with Windex. His head jerks to the recliner where Charlotte sits and he jumps up, groaning as if his bruised ribs are screaming painfully in torture. Of course, Charlotte doesn't wake at the sound of his agony; she could sleep through a hurricane. George stumbles into the kitchen, ripping open the drawer closest to the fridge, looking for his stash, only to find it empty. Charlotte looked in every drawer and cabinet, flushing anything she found. She even looked in the toilet tanks.

"Charlotte," I say, loudly, as I watch George morph into anger and panic. He wants his drugs badly, and he knows exactly who to blame for not being able to have them. She doesn't flinch. George slams the drawer shut and opens the cabinet above the stove where he keeps his liquor. It's all poured out. Gone.

"Charlotte!" I boom, and her eyes barely crack open as she shifts her position in the recliner. "Wake the fuck up! He's pissed!" George slams the cabinet door shut and beelines straight for her. Charlotte snaps up like someone's electrocuted her, shooting her gaze to George. I expected to see fear in her eyes—after all, he does look like he's going to murder her—but instead, she welcomes it. She wants his wrath.

"Are you fucking crazy?" I ask as she fights the smile dancing on her lips.

"What the fuck have you done?" he shouts as he stomps right to her, rage pooling in the one eye not swollen shut, fists clenched at his sides.

"Whatever do you mean, George?" she asks calmly, as if he isn't practically breathing fire in her face.

"Where the fuck is it?"

"Where is what?" She plays dumb.

He steps back and tugs at his hair as if he's trying to keep control. "My whiskey, my . . ." He pauses. He knows she knows about the drugs, yet he can't even say it.

"Your coke?" she questions.

His head snaps up, his one eye glaring at her. "This is my house. You have no right to be here messing with my shit!"

Charlotte shrugs nonchalantly. "I drew the short straw. Had to bring you home after you got your ass kicked by Misty's boyfriend."

"It was a misunderstanding," he grumbles.

"Was it?" she asks sardonically. "I mean, the entire town knows you've been sleeping with her even though she dates the town drug dealer."

"Well it's none of their business, and it sure as hell isn't any of yours! You owe me three hundred dollars!"

"I don't owe you shit!" Charlotte yells back, her own fists clenched at her sides. "I'm trying to help you."

George steps back, shaking his head. "I didn't ask for your help," he says calmly, but the bite is still there.

"Well, you're getting it anyway. You need it."

"What are you? Some kind of fucking martyr? Gee, thanks, Mother Teresa, but I'm good. You can go." George stomps into his bedroom, and Charlotte stares after him.

"Maybe you should go," I urge, not wanting her to push it. He'll have nothing to do with her if she pisses him off anymore. Then what will I do?

"No," she grumbles and stomps off after him.

"Shit," I moan as I slide a wide palm down my face. This is going to get ugly.

I morph to George's bedroom. Charlotte is already standing in his doorway watching him dig through his bottom dresser drawer before pulling out a small bottle of pills.

"You're fucking kidding me, right?" Charlotte groans.

George stands and shakes the bottle in her face, the pills rattling, as he pushes past her. "You can either stay and watch or you can get your ass out of my house. Your choice." He leers at her and she rolls her eyes. George crouches down, slowly paying mind to his injuries, in front of the coffee table and dumps a pill on the glass. He takes the picture of me in the frame from the day I graduated basic and begins crushing the pill with it.

Charlotte's eyes nearly bulge out of her head. "What the fuck is that?"

George snorts. "Oxy."

"You're going to snort oxycodone? Are you fucking kidding me?" she shrieks.

George doesn't answer her. Patting his pockets, he finds his wallet and pulls out his license and continues to break up the pill with the card. Charlotte stands, arms crossed, staring down at him in disbelief.

"You want some?" George asks snidely, knowing she doesn't, as he pulls out a dollar bill and begins rolling it up. She may not realize what he's doing, but I do. He's trying to scare her away; let her see the worst of him.

"Don't do it, George," Charlotte warns, and even I'm surprised by her tone.

"Or what, Mother Teresa?"

"I'll tell your mom," she threatens.

George laughs haughtily. "She'd never believe you."

Charlotte bites her lip as George bends down to snort his first line. In a rush, she throws herself on the table and the pill dust flies everywhere as the glass crushes and combusts into a thousand tiny pieces.

"What the fuck?" George yells as she hops up, white residue and glass covering her black *Ike and George's* shirt, her expression hard with anger. "Get the fuck out of my house!" George growls.

Picking up the photo of me George used to crush the pill off the ground, she yells, "What would Ike say if he could see you now?" as she shoves the photo in his face.

George freezes. "Really, Charlotte?" I mumble. "This has gone too far. You should go," I encourage. George's expression is unreadable, and as his twin that knows everything about him, that worries me. I'm not sure what he's capable of right now.

George slowly looks up at her and drops the dollar bill, yanking the picture frame from her hand and tossing it on the sofa behind him. With his injuries, it takes him a minute to fully stand and Charlotte waits, her jaw set.

"Leave!" he roars. "Leave right this fucking minute!"

The room falls silent as they both breathe heavily. Charlotte's eyes move to the pill bottle that lays sideways amidst the table she just destroyed, and I can practically read her mind.

"Don't," I warn, but it's too late. She's darted to the table, seized the bottle and bolts to the bathroom. George, even in his pain, manages to catch up to her rather quickly, cursing at her as he moves, but by the time he makes it to the hall bathroom, the toilet is already flushing. Her eyes are fixed on the toilet bowl as the water spins around and the pills swirl with it. George is in the doorway, shirtless, every muscle in his body coiled. His rage rolls off him like pulsing heat as he stares at her in disbelief. I'm a little thrown, too. She's a very drastic woman. Not even I could have predicted she'd do something like that.

When she raises her head, she twists the lid back on the pill bottle and approaches him in the doorway. She's not smiling, but there's definitely no apology in her eyes. Pressing the bottle to his chest, she looks him directly in the eye and without one ounce of fear, says, "Here. I'll be leaving now. Thanks for having me over." She releases the pill bottle, which George doesn't attempt to catch, letting it fall to the floor. Pushing past him, she walks calmly to the living room, but before she reaches the entrance, George seizes her arm and jerks her around. Her eyes widen slightly before returning to their usual calmness. I've never seen George so angry, and I know he'd never hit a woman, but even I'm worried I could be wrong about that, judging by the look on his face.

With his fists tightened at his sides, he steps toward her. "You roll into town and I give you a job. You come to my home and flush my booze and drugs. As pissed as I am, I might be able to forgive you for that shit, even though I'll probably fire your ass tomorrow. But don't you *dare* act like you know shit about my brother, and what I'm going through." After everything she's said and done tonight, I'm surprised that seems to be what he's most pissed about; her use of my memory to influence him.

"And why is that?" Charlotte shouts angrily as she pushes his chest, rage brimming in her eyes. *Holy shit!* Why is she so pissed all of a sudden? She was the definition of calm a few moments ago. "Because you're the only one that's ever lost someone?" She shoves his chest with more force and he winces. "Because you're the only one that's ever wished it would all end?" Again, she shoves him, this time making contact with his arm, hard, and George stumbles back, surprised by her aggression. "The drugs. The booze. You're fucking hiding, George, and Ike would be destroyed if he could see you right now!"

She swings her arm to slap him, but in a flash, George grabs her by the arms and corners her against the wall. "You don't know me, and you don't know shit about Ike, so fuck you, Charlotte! Where the fuck do you get off saying this shit to me?"

"Because I know you!" she yells as she struggles to get free from his grip as tears stream down her face. "I know you wish it had been you that died and he had stayed. You think he was the better one, the one that always knew what to do, or say, and now that he's gone, you feel like no one will ever know you like he did!" She takes a deep breath as her body stills for a moment, leaning heavily to the wall he's pressed her against, her lips trembling.

George's grip stays firm on her arms, but his expression softens slightly as his chest heaves with each ragged breath he takes. He's hurt from the beating Roger and his brother gave him and his exhaustion is evident. Swallowing hard, he asks, "And how do you know this, Charlotte?"

"Because . . ." She shakes her head and jerks, trying to free herself from his grip.

"Stop!" he orders, pressing her back against the wall.

"Fuck you," she sobs and knees him in the groin. When he lurches forward in pain, Charlotte moves to escape, but George grabs her and they tumble to the ground together, both of them grunting. She claws and twists, but George crawls up her body and straddles her, pinning her arms to her sides. "Tell me how you know this," he pants. Charlotte stops fighting him, realizing he's much stronger than her. Her chest heaves up and down as she tries to catch her breath.

"Tell me," George repeats.

"Because I see myself in you," she growls through clenched teeth as if she hates him for making her admit it. "Every time I look into your sad, brown eyes, I see my own despair staring back at me. You think because I didn't grow up in this tiny-ass town that I can't know you? Well, you're wrong. I know you better than anyone here does. Maybe better than your brother did."

"Charlotte," I whisper. "Where is this coming from? What are you doing?" She ignores me as her gaze locks with George's. It's like they're seeing something I don't, or can't, and I'm not sure if it's because I'm dead or because I'm not privy to it.

George sighs. "Who was it?"

"My brother, Axel," she says, quietly. "Six years ago."

How have I not heard about her brother? I should've asked. I should've asked about her life, but I was too caught up in saving George's. How could I be so stupid to think a job and a place to sleep were all the answers to her problems? They're both in leaking boats, and I've asked Charlotte to get in George's and help him bucket out the water while her boat steadily sinks.

"How'd it happen?"

Charlotte swallows hard, the thought causing tears to trickle down her face. "Motorcycle accident. We were both riding. He died. I didn't," she answers mechanically.

George's eyes clench closed as realization dawns on him. "The panic attack the other day . . ." he whispers. It all makes sense now. "Shit," he says, under his breath. "I'm so sorry." George releases her arms and rolls off of her. They lie back side by side staring up at the ceiling, both of them still breathing heavily. "Ike was in Afghanistan. IED."

"Anna told me," Charlotte replies as she wipes at her face. "I'm so sorry," she adds as her gaze moves to me briefly. And I believe her. She is genuinely upset over my passing. As our eyes lock for that brief moment, I finally see what she described to George. I see her despair, her hurt, and I hate myself for not seeing it before. I found her at a pivotal moment, a time when she was choosing the unknown to escape this world. I knew there was pain, but not like this. How could I have been so senseless?

After a few moments, George stands up, reaching a hand down to help Charlotte up. When she's on her feet, she wipes at her face once more, running her fingers under her eyes to clear any smeared mascara. "After a brawl like that I could use a drink," he laughs. "Too bad some Billy Badass came in here and dumped it all out." He's trying to joke with her; lighten the mood.

Charlotte smiles faintly. "I won't interfere again, George." With that, she grabs her keys off the table by the sofa and opens the front door.

"Wait!" George practically shouts. "Where are you going?"

"I'm going back to my motel room to sleep. I'm leaving

tomorrow."

"What?" George and I ask in unison.

"I hope you get it figured out, George." With that, she shuts the door, leaving me and George feeling lost.

Turning, George runs a hand through his hair, his eyes clenched closed. He has to know he's really FUBARRED big time when it comes to Charlotte. After a moment, he opens his eyes and picks up my picture from the couch. "What do I do, Ike?"

"Go after her, you ass!" I yell, but of course, he can't hear me.

Chapter 14

Charlotte

As I drive back to the motel, the tears fall freely. Revealing my pain to George and Ike was like peeling back my skin and exposing my insides. It's been so long since I let the memory of my brother, and his untimely death, wreck me like that. I never intended to tell George or Ike about Axel, at least not how destroyed his passing left me.

Pulling into the motel's parking lot, I put the truck in park and rush inside, hoping Ginger won't see me in this state. It's dark out, so it's unlikely, plus it's two in the morning, but I hurry anyway, just in case. Once inside, I flip the light on and nearly jump out of my skin when the first thing I see is Ike. I know he's disappointed in me. I left his brother. I'm leaving tomorrow without helping him resolve his unfinished business.

"I'm sorry, Ike," I say, hoarsely. His brown eyes soften and he runs a hand over his hair, like he does a lot, and sighs.

"Why didn't you tell me?"

"Because it's hard to tell," I answer honestly.

"I'd like you to tell me now. Please." His gaze meets mine and he reaches a hand up as if he wants to wipe the tears from my cheek, but his hand stops midair and he pulls it back slowly, realizing he can't. I quickly wipe at my face and let my gaze fall to the floor. I hate he can't touch me right now. A hug, a touch from him, would be amazing. It's been so long since someone, anyone, held me, gave me some kind of physical comforting. Maybe I'm partly to blame for that; I haven't exactly been making myself available. But right now, I'd give anything to feel Ike's touch. And as fucked up as it sounds, I'd love to feel George's, too. The brothers are so different, polar opposites in fact, that I find myself drawn to each one for different reasons. One is so strong and responsible; so much so, not even death can keep him from taking care of those he loves. The other, broken and lost, wishing time could rewind on one hand, but using any method necessary to forget time on the other. In George, I recognize myself and my desire to save him has a lot to do with wanting to save myself; as if by yanking him out of the black hole he's sinking in, maybe I'd have a chance of surviving this hell I've lived in for six years. In Ike, I see hope. I see that maybe with enough love, being saved is possible.

Before I can respond to Ike, there's a knock at the door and I have a feeling I know who it is. I open it and see George, his swollen eye and busted lip painfully on display, his forearm leaned against the doorframe. He doesn't wait for me to invite him in; he just pushes past me, forcing me back and shuts the door behind him. We stand facing each other, our gazes locked. I loathe the weak and pathetic girl I am right now. All I want to do is breakdown and sob. There's a saying that misery loves company, and it's true. At least for me it is. George is a reflection of every horrible feeling I have, and even though the moments we've shared together have, for the most part, been anything but pleasant, being with him feels like being with someone who understands.

He stares at me with his good eye and his mouth curves at the corner. Before I know it, he's wiping my tears away. And when I press my cheek into his hand, his other arm snakes around me and pulls me to him. My thin arms wrap around his torso, causing him to hiss slightly, so I immediately loosen my arms, realizing his ribs hurt, but he presses me to him.

"Don't stop," he orders, so I strengthen my hold and press my forehead to his chest. Minutes, hours, I don't know—time passes and we hold each other. It isn't intimate or sexual; it's the comfort in finding someone who finally understands. When we finally pull away from each other, I scan the room and don't see Ike anywhere. My heart breaks a little. He wanted to comfort me this way and couldn't.

"Don't go, Charlotte." George breaks the silence. "I know I've been an asshole. I'm just really fucked up, but I think you should stay." He runs a hand through his shaggy hair and sighs. "I think if you do, we could be good friends, and to tell you the truth, I really need one."

I lick my dry lips. "I'll stay, if you promise me something."

He snorts. "What's that?"

"No more drugs. I mean it, George. None."

He swallows hard and nods once. "Okay."

I was given the day off, perks of being friends with your boss, I guess, so I sleep in. Shortly after I awake, I dress and head over to the main office to seek instructions from Ginger. No one other than me was checked into the motel last night, but I volunteer to do a thorough cleaning of the rooms, agreeing to get three done today. Hopefully by next week when things get busy, all of the rooms will be in tip-top shape. Ginger seems tickled pink, and after she shows me where to find the cart with the cleaning supplies, she sends me on my way. Truthfully, I'm grateful for anything to keep me busy and my mind off the events of last night.

George left shortly after our agreement. We're both venturing into unchartered waters. Neither of us really knows how this friendship is supposed to work, but we've both agreed to try. Ike never returned last night and I'm worried. I imagine he's still pissed at me for leaving the letter for Roger. I understand why he feels that way; his brother got the shit beat out of him. Of course, he's angry with me.

After I finish cleaning, I return to my room and prepare to shower. Just as I've undressed, a knock sounds at my door. Wrapping a towel around myself and opening the door, I find George, swollen eye and smile on his face. He's holding a brown paper bag with grease stains.

His one good eye goes wide at the sight of me in my towel. "Hi," he finally manages after swallowing hard.

"Hello," I say, as heat crawls up my neck and blankets my face. Pulling my towel a little tighter around me, I clear my throat.

"Do you always answer the door without asking who it is in nothing but a towel?" he scolds me.

"Nice to see you, too, George," I grumble. "What can I do for you?"

"I brought lunch for milady," George finally manages. "Thought I owed my new friend a thank you."

My heart feels heavy in my chest. I would've never expected such a sweet gesture from him. "That's awesome. I'm starving." I open the door to let him in, but he steps back. "I'll wait out here while you get dressed. Maybe we could make it a picnic. I know an awesome place."

"Okay. I'll be just a few minutes," I tell him as I close the door. Slipping on my last pair of clean underwear, I quickly dress in dirty jeans and a T-shirt before grabbing my jacket off the chair near the door. Taking in his jeans and tight, gray sweater, I realize I haven't bathed today. I don't bother checking myself in the mirror. I know I look like hell. "I haven't taken a shower today so I apologize if I'm stinky."

"I was wondering what that foul odor was," he teases as I shut the door and we head toward his Bronco. It's jacked up, worn, and painted bright red.

"You're hilarious," I retort. "Nice ride. What does this thing get, like negative five miles per gallon?"

He laughs and my tummy clenches. What an amazing laugh he has. His laugh is like the pop of a fired gun; it's surprising and leaves me stunned and a little wired. He opens the passenger side door and helps me climb in, his hands grasping my hips gently and lifting me. I can't ignore the zing that travels through me when he touches me. I wish I could control the reaction my body has whenever he touches me, but I can't. I can only hope it's not obvious to him. "It was me and Ike's first car. Took our joint life savings, but we were sixteen with the baddest ride in school."

Grinning at the thought, I glance around for Ike, but he's still nowhere to be seen. I frown slightly at that realization. I hate not feeling him near. George drives us up the mountain and pulls into a wooded area about ten minutes away. The entire time he points out houses and tells me who lives there and how he knows them. Apparently, he knows every freaking person in this town because we don't pass one house or farm where he doesn't identify the family living there. The roads are steep, and if I look to my right, it's almost a direct drop down the mountain. One bad turn or swerve and we crash to our deaths. As his Bronco lurches over the rough terrain, I question, "You bringing me out here to kill me?"

"I think I thought about it once last night when I realized you dumped out everything," he answers with a half-quirked smile.

"How are you feeling? Any withdrawals?"

"Not yet, but it will probably hit me harder tonight or tomorrow. But I have to work so maybe that'll work as a distraction. Unless you'd like to come in tonight and distract me." He winks. "I'm sure you could find a few ways to piss me off."

"True," I admit before sticking my tongue out at him. It's not very hard for me to make George mad. "As tempting as that sounds, I have plans."

"You do?" he questions, his brow furrowed.

"Dinner with the Mercers, actually," I clarify as I dig through my bag and grab my Chap Stick.

As we climb out of his truck, I pray he's right about being able to distract himself from the symptoms of his withdrawals, but I have a feeling it's going to be worse than he thinks. Pulling a blanket from behind his seat, he lays it on the ground and we sit in the center of an opening in the woods. The leaves have started to change and a beautiful array of yellow, orange, and red kiss the leaves slightly. "Where are we?" I ask as we sit and George pulls out burgers wrapped in wax paper.

"This is my father's land. We come camping here sometimes."

"It's beautiful," I note as I tear open my burger. "Very peaceful. I love the color of the leaves."

"Just wait until the next week or two. It'll put Crayola to shame. Things will get really busy around here starting around the end of next week."

Taking a huge bite of his burger, he looks up and chews, a thoughtful expression on his face. "Ike and I used to come here a lot." I glance around for Ike, but he's still nowhere to be seen. Where is he? "We used to bring girls here, too," George says, with a slight smirk.

"We were real classy guys."

"Oh," I feign insult. "And here I thought I was special," I tease. "I'm just one of many."

"It was in high school and where else is a teenage boy supposed to bring a girl for some privacy around here? It was either this or a barn. This was where we hid."

"Is that what you're doing?" I can't help questioning. "Hiding me or hiding us together from the town?"

"Why would I hide our friendship?"

"Maybe Misty would get pissed if she knew?"

He takes another bite of his burger and chews slowly, and I wonder if he's buying some time before he responds. Finally, after he swallows and sucks some ketchup from his thumb, he says, "I know I must look pretty pathetic to you."

My head rears slightly. That's not at all what I think. "No. Not at all," I tell him.

"I mean, hanging out with a girl that's taken and the drugs. They're not things I'm proud of." His gaze lingers off somewhere, notmeeting mine. He's ashamed.

"We all cope differently," I admit. I'm the last person in the world that could judge George. Sure, he is doing some things I think poorly on, but I was about to kill myself a few days ago, so who am I to say anything? At least he was trying to survive his pain, I was ready to end it; period. Maybe I'm not the stronger one like I thought.

"The thing between Misty and I just kind of happened and seems to have snowballed from there. But we're not together . . . we're only friends."

"But you still wouldn't want her to see us together, right?" He cocks his head to the side, giving me a look that says he's baffled by my question.

"Do you want to be seen with me, Charlotte?" he asks seriously and my brow furrows in confusion with his question.

"What do you mean?" I ask before biting into my food.

"I just thought *you* might not want others to see you with me. Apparently, it's no secret I've been seeing Misty, and with you knowing about the drugs and all . . . Plus, I look like I've been beaten with a bat."

Licking my lips, I shake my head. "You think I'd be ashamed to be seen with you?"

"Well, aren't you?"

Leaning forward, I lay my hand on his leg. He stills as his gaze moves to my hand. "You're my friend now, George. I'm not ashamed of that."

When his coffee eyes meet mine again, his mouth quirks up on one side. "Yeah. You're pretty lucky to have me as a friend," he laughs.

Rolling my eyes, I take another bite of my burger. When I'm done chewing, I ask, "So, what the hell do people do around here for fun?"

"You mean other than attending epic dances at the dance hall?" he jests.

"Yeah," I chuckle. "Other than that."

"Hunt, fish, hike, and drink," he answers simply.

"Sounds riveting," I snort, but on some level, it sounds wonderful. It sounds peaceful and isn't that what I've wanted more than anything the last few years?

"Well, it's not for everyone," George notes. "But it's home. Why don't I take you on a tour one day?"

"Oh my," I say, in my best Southern drawl, placing a hand to my chest. "I get the grand tour of Bath county with George McDermott. It's my lucky day."

"Yeah, well, you're growing on me. Kind of like a fungus."

"You really know how to make a girl feel special, George," I reply, tossing my crumpled up wrapper at him. "That burger was awesome, but I probably just gained a thousand pounds eating it."

"You could stand to gain a few pounds," he notes before shoving the rest of his burger in his mouth.

"Well, I think I just gained a third butt cheek."

"God, I hope not, because that ass of yours is perfect," he notes with a devilish smirk on his face. Heat crawls up my neck and onto my face, causing my cheeks to redden.

"I'm so suing you for sexual harassment," I joke as I lie back and stare up at the sky. He laughs a genuine laugh and my chest tightens. *Damn.* I *really* like his laugh.

Looking down at me, he leans forward. "You have something right . . ." His thumb grazes the corner of mouth, wiping away a spot of ketchup. Sucking it off of his thumb, he smiles. "Lucky ketchup."

Warmth, once again, inflames my cheeks as I dart my eyes away from him. *Why was that so hot?* George lies down beside me and when his arm rests against mine, tingles surge through me again. I shouldn't be reacting this way to him. I'm only meant to help him so Ike can cross over, not to mention the feelings I've developed for Ike. I'm seriously messed up in the head. I mean, what kind of person develops a crush on a set of brothers, let alone with a dead one in the mix? But I can't deny I'm drawn to the McDermott twins. In Ike, I crave his warmth and good heart. In George, I crave his likeness, the understanding we share. Glancing around for Ike once more and not seeing him, I try to relax even though I'm worried sick that he's disappeared.

George and I fall into an easy conversation. We share stories about our childhoods, our brothers, and George fills me in on the town gossip, which is sad. His seeing Misty and getting beaten up by Roger is the most dramatic thing to happen in Warm Springs in years.

When he drops me off back at the motel, we stand awkwardly at my door. "Thanks for joining me today, and I'm sorry I was such a dick last night or . . . well, every day since we've met."

I laugh. "I'm glad we're friends now, George." And it's true. He's a good guy once he lets his guard down, but the thought of us being true friends simmers in my mind. I'm lying to him about everything; about who I am, and how I came to be here. When the truth comes out, it won't be pretty. Another awkward second slips by before he leans toward me, making my breath hitch. Is he going to kiss me? Oh God, no . . . but yes. Do I want him to? I think I do. Licking my lips, I prepare myself for his mouth to meet mine, closing my eyes. But when his warm mouth brushes gently across my cheek, my eyes fly open, embarrassment flooding me. Did it look obvious I wanted to kiss him? *I am mortified.*

The corners of his mouth are turned up as he pulls back, and I know he's laughing at me on the inside. I *did* look obvious. *Son of a bitch.*

"Not yet, Charlotte, but soon," he says, shoving his hands in his pockets. Is he implying he plans to kiss me soon? That has to be what he means. Before I can play dumb and ask him what he meant he turns to leave, calling over his shoulder, "See you tomorrow, Charlotte." Then he climbs in his Bronco and drives away.

There's still no sign of Ike when I enter my room and guilt slithers through me. He really is mad at me. *Shit.* My heart twists at the thought. I just want to help him by helping George. I should've told him my plan. He's right. George could have been really hurt. *Shit.* He was hurt. With a few hours to kill and no one to talk to, I decide to take a nap before heading over to the Mercers' house for dinner. But my sleep is unsatisfying. It's the kind of sleep where you dream so vividly it feels like you've never slept a wink.

I don't remember the entire dream, but what I do remember is George walking up to me, his dark eyes hungry with desire. My body instantly reacted; my breath coming out in quick pants, my sensitive nipples hardening, wetness pooling between my legs, and heat blanketing me everywhere his gaze lingered on me.

When he whispered, "Charlotte," and pulled me close, I whimpered. Yes, whimpered. And when his lips met mine, something in me ignited. His body pressed to mine, his arms holding me close as I threaded my fingers in his hair and ran my hands down his back. But when he pulled away, everything came to a halt. It was Ike staring back at me, smiling in that way he does that makes my insides liquefy.

And then, I woke up.

Even though it was only a dream, my mouth feels swollen as if the kiss was real. Touching my fingers to my lips, I brush them softly.

"Hi," Ike says, and I gasp, jolting upright on the bed. "Dude, you have got to stop sneaking up on me like that. You scared the bejesus out of me."

"Sorry," he replies and smiles slightly. He's sitting in the pleather chair, elbows resting on his knees, fingers laced before him.

"Where have you been?" I pull my legs up and sit cross-legged.

"Why? You miss me?" He waggles his brows and I snort.

"I was worried you were still pissed at me. Ya know. Over me leaving that letter for Roger. I'm sorry, Ike. I should've told you before I did it."

Ike sighs and rubs his hand over his head, his dog tags jingling as he moves, slouching back in his seat. "I'm not mad. It looks like it worked. I'm madder at myself."

"For what?" I question.

"Because I never asked about your story. I never asked what you've been through. I'm an asshole for asking you to help George when you're going through so much yourself."

I fidget with the edge of a pillowcase, flicking the material back and forth between my fingers. My story is so . . . depressing, I'm not sure I want to tell him.

"I'd like to know, Charlotte. Tell me. Please." When I look up, I meet his gaze and nod.

"Well . . ." I start and sort of snort. "Where the hell do I begin?"

"I want to know everything," he answers, and I take a deep breath.

"Well . . . I grew up in Jackson County in Oklahoma. My mother's a school teacher, she works in special education," I add, "and my father is a pharmaceutical rep for a company called Lincoln. And I had an older brother, Axel," I nearly choke as I say his name. I've rarely said it out loud in years, and I forgot the emotion speaking his name evokes from me. "He was three years older than me," I finally manage. "We weren't twins, but we were close. I don't think anyone cried harder than me when he left for college," I laugh and meet Ike's gaze. "I suppose I was more enamored with my big brother than he was with me. I saw him as my confidant, my best friend, and he saw me as his baby sister he had to protect from everything. But he wasn't overbearing or anything. I think he knew if he tried to tell me what to do, I would stop confiding in him. He was smart that way." I stand and stretch before moving to the dresser where I have a half-filled bottle of water, taking a large swig before I continue.

"So of course, when I graduated, there was no other college I wanted to go to other than the one he was at. I'm not sure how he felt about it, but he never said anything to deter me, so off I went. Six years ago I was a freshman at Oklahoma State University. At the beginning of the second semester, I had joined a sorority and made some friends. I hung out with Axel every chance I could, but his fraternity kept him busy. One night, I was at this mixer, a paint mixer," I laugh sadly. "Drunk off my ass and covered from head to toe in fluorescent paint several college boys had graciously rubbed all over me."

"Lucky bastards," Ike chimes in with a smirk.

"There was this girl, Melissa, I was friends with that had a huge crush on Axel. Somewhere along the evening she managed to grab my phone and take a picture of me dancing, sandwiched between two guys and texted it to Axel."

Ike snorts a little laugh. "Let me guess. Axel showed up?"

"Yeah. But he didn't try to drag me out or anything. I found out later any guy he saw talking to me got a very stern threat to remain two feet away from me at all times," I laugh. "I couldn't understand why guys started avoiding me." I sip my water again, my hand trembling as I bring the bottle to my mouth. "So eventually I got bored and asked him to take me home. He rode this badass Harley, spent his life's savings to get it. He'd only had it a year, and the purchase had definitely caused a rift between him and my parents. But Axel was . . ." My gaze moves to the ceiling as I search for the best way to describe him. "He was loyal to a fault. A good son, always had good grades, played football, yada yada. He rarely went against the grain, and when my parents threatened to stop paying his tuition, I was surprised he wouldn't budge. He loved that bike."

I move back to the bed and sit with my legs crisscrossed again, grabbing my hair tie off the nightstand and twisting my hair into a messy bun. "He gave me his helmet to wear that night. Less than a mile from my dorm, a drunk senior turned left in front of us and we hit him going forty miles per hour. When I woke up, I was in an ambulance, the paramedics messing with me, and Axel was beside me, unscathed, staring down at me. I could tell I was in bad shape by the look on his face."

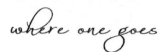

I pause, willing myself not to breakdown. "'Hold tight, Char. Everything is going to be okay,' he'd said." Tears brim my eyes as I remember him, the way his voice trembled as he spoke to me. "I went unconscious. I had broken my back and my right leg. I had some swelling on my brain, even though I had been wearing a helmet, and they put me in an induced coma until the swelling went down. When I finally came to, my parents were so relieved and crying. I was really groggy and tired, but when I saw Axel smiling at me, I thought everything would be okay. He nodded once at me and said, 'I love you. Always remember that.'" I swallow hard around the lump in my throat.

"I was in and out of consciousness for a day or two, but when I finally came to fully, the doctors began telling me about the road ahead and my recovery. When they left, I looked at my mother and asked, 'Where's Axel?'"

I let out slow, deep breaths. "She wouldn't answer me at first, but left to fetch my father. When they both returned, they were sobbing uncontrollably, my father to my left and my mother to my right."

I shake my head back and forth as more tears cascade down my face. "'Axel didn't make it, Char. He's gone,' my father had whispered as his voice shook. I had never seen him so distraught. He has always been so strong. I just stared at him; perplexed. 'He was here when I woke up,' I'd replied adamantly to my parents. 'I saw him.' But my mother just wept and told me, 'I'm sorry, sweetie, he's gone.'"

I meet Ike's eyes and try to smile through the tears. "As you know, with grief comes denial. I refused to believe it. I thought maybe I was dreaming, that I would wake up any moment and realize it had only been a horrific nightmare. But as time went on, I realized he really was gone." I wipe my nose with my forearm.

"He didn't cross over until he knew I was going to be okay. I was his unfinished business. I missed my chance to say good-bye to him because I didn't know what was happening."

"I'm sorry, Charlotte," Ike says, grasping for something more to say.

"Shortly after, I started seeing people and talking to them, and my mother would always ask me who I was talking to. It took me a while, since I was on a lot of medication then, to understand what I was seeing. When I figured out the dead were talking to me, I tried to tell my parents, and they, of course, thought I was nuts and sent me to a psychiatrist and a neurologist. They put me on antipsychotic meds, which completely fucked me up, and I still saw dead people," I grunt. "Eventually, I stopped talking about it, for the most part. I became severely depressed; my friends had all abandoned me when they thought I went nuts," I say, sadly. "My parents were dealing with the grief of losing Axel on top of my issues. A year later, I was back to normal, mostly physically, and my father had some business associates over for dinner. Of course, his boss's father had died recently, and he came to the party too. I tried to get him alone, to tell him what his father needed him to know, but my father caught me. His boss was sobbing and hugging me, but that didn't matter," I recall. "My father was done. The next day he gave me a check for thirty thousand dollars and told me I should travel. It was part of the money the insurance company had paid for the accident. I knew he just meant I should disappear. So I did."

Ike's expression is grim, his mouth in a hard, flat line. He shakes his head, I assume in disbelief, before lowering it. When he raises it again, he smiles sadly. "So you've been wandering around for the last five years helping the dead? All alone." It's not a question, more of a confirmation. I swallow hard and nod, resuming flicking the material from my pillowcase to occupy my gaze. I can't look at him or I'll cry again. Standing, he walks over to me and sits beside me and places his hand on the bed next to mine. "I think this is the worst part, ya know. I can see you, hear you, but I can't touch you."

"I know," I answer quietly. I would give anything if he could. I've only known him a few days, but he's the first person I've had a real connection with in years. As I stare up at him, I can't help but wonder what Axel would think of him. It's a silly thought, and I don't know where it came from, but I believe Axel would have liked Ike very much. Maybe George, too, despite his issues.

Taking a deep breath, I stand and pull my hair from the knot I tied it in. "I have to get ready. I have dinner plans with the Mercers, ya know."

"Yeah," he replies and nods. "Do you want to go alone or do you want me there?"

I'm surprised he's asked. Every other time I've wanted to be alone I've had to demand it from him. But last night, worrying about where he was and what was going through his mind, I hated it. I need him to stay with me. "Would you mind coming with me?"

"Not at all," he answers and grins, his pleasure with my asking him evident.

Chapter 15

Ike

"So, tell us about your family, Char. Do you see them often?" Mr. Mercer asks as he sets a glass of iced tea on the table where she's seated. Mrs. Mercer went all out and prepared a meal that could feed twenty people. The food is spread out over a clean, white tablecloth and she's using her best china. My mouth waters as I stare at the fried chicken and mashed potatoes.

"I'm sure not as often as they'd like," Charlotte answers before taking a sip from her tea. She's wearing a loose, blue top with her jeans, her black hair half pulled up. She looks . . . beautiful.

"Do you have any siblings?" Mrs. Mercer asks as she takes her seat and picks up the dish of mashed potatoes. Charlotte's eyes dart to mine very briefly before returning to the Mercer's.

Smiling somewhat stiffly, she says, "I had a brother. He passed away about six years ago."

Mr. Mercer's brows furrow as if pained by this news. "I'm sorry to hear that. As you know, we know what it is to lose someone you love dearly."

Charlotte sits up and takes the dish of potatoes from Mrs. Mercer. "This all looks amazing, Mrs. Mercer."

"Best fried chicken in Bath County," Mr. Mercer adds, causing his wife to grin as she gives Charlotte a bashful look.

"Like you'd say otherwise, Bill," Mrs. Mercer quips and Charlotte smiles. “Maggie loved fried chicken. We had it every Sunday.”

“It was her favorite,” Mr. Mercer adds sadly.

Mrs. Mercer smiles softly. “She’s been gone ten years, and it still feels as though it was yesterday she was here.”

“She fought. Lived a hell of a lot longer than they said she would when she was diagnosed.”

“May I ask what it is she passed away from?” Charlotte asks delicately.

“Dyskeratosis Congenita . It’s a rare disease that can lead to bone marrow failure. Eventually . . . her body gave out,” Mr. Mercer answers as he spoons a helping of green beans onto his plate.

They chitchat back and forth, mostly speaking of Maggie, and Charlotte listens intently as they describe Maggie from the way she smiled to what an ornery toddler she was. When they’re done eating, Mrs. Mercer shoos her husband and Charlotte into the living room while she clears the table. Their house is modest; not huge, but not exactly small either. Antiques and numerous clocks hang on the wall, ticking mercifully.

“Say, could you tell me the time?” I jest, and she rolls her eyes. “Do you think they like clocks?”

But she doesn’t seem to hear the last part of what I said; when Charlotte enters the living room, her entire focus is on the mahogany grand piano against the back wall. Like a moth to a flame, she goes to it, running her fingers along the wooden lid that covers the keys.

“Do you play?” Mr. Mercer asks as he watches her.

“I did,” Charlotte answers, staring at her hand where it rests on the lid.

“Will you play for us?”

Charlotte turns and smiles sadly. “Would you mind?”

“Not at all. It hasn’t been played in years.”

Lifting the lid, she pulls the small bench from under it, taking a seat.

“A woman of many talents, I see,” I say, and she smiles but doesn’t look at me.

"Any requests?" she asks Mr. Mercer.

"Play me your favorite," he answers, taking a seat in his worn-out recliner.

Charlotte turns back and tests a few keys tentatively; I assume checking the tuning. "It's been a while so I might be a little rusty," she warns, and Mr. Mercer chuckles.

"No worries, my dear. Go ahead."

As her fingers dance across the keys, a beautiful melody fills the room and I'm stunned. She's playing some kind of classical music; maybe it's a piece by Mozart. I don't know shit about pianos, but this is my best guess. The melody is deep and raw, like all her emotion is lingering in it. Her body is erect, her eyes fixed on her hands, and it almost seems like she's connected to the piano. As if it's an extension of her, a place where emotion and feeling can run free. Music can be angry and deep and people call it beautiful. But for people in the real world, those emotions are considered weakness.

She plays for a while and when she finishes, she nods to her hands as if to tell herself she still has it.

"That was . . . amazing," I manage.

Mr. and Mrs. Mercer break out in applause and Charlotte stands, smiling sheepishly. "Where did you learn to play like that?"

"My mother. She's a teacher. Besides her special education classes, she teaches piano, too."

The remainder of the evening they sit outside on the porch and sip tea. And when it's time to go, the Mercers hug her tightly. Charlotte pulls some money from her back pocket and hands it to Mr. Mercer. "I owe you sixty more and I should have it by the end of the week."

"No. You owe us nothing."

"Please, Mr. Mercer," Charlotte pleads. "A deal's a deal. I get my necklace back when you get the rest of your money."

His thick, gray brows furrow and his lips form a smooth line as if he's fighting the urge to argue, but instead, he nods his head once in compliance.

"Would you like to come for dinner next week?" Mrs. Mercer asks with a hopeful tone.

"Yes. Sure. I have to see what days I'll be off, but yes. I would like that very much."

"And you'll play for us again," Mr. Mercer says, not really asking.

"If you'd like me to," Charlotte laughs. They watch her as she climbs in her truck and pulls out of their driveway.

"They're very lonely. People like them should be covered in grandchildren," Charlotte notes as she turns down Emerson Ave.

I shrug and say, "I think you're right."

"Are employees allowed to sit at the bar and drink, or no?"

"Yeah. If it's your day off you can go in and drink," I reply.

"Good, because I think I'd like to have one or two," she answers. She looks pensive for a moment before she puckers her lips in a thoughtful way and says, "Hmm."

"Everything all right?" I ask.

She smiles faintly. "Just been one of those days where I've been reminiscing."

"Was Maggie there the entire time?"

"Yes, but she didn't say a word to me until we left."

"I guess that was helpful," I chuckle. "What did she say?"

Charlotte frowns and answers, "She told me not to forget about her." We ride for a few minutes in silence when Charlotte asks, "Can I ask you something?"

"Of course," I reply.

Licking her lips, she inhales deeply and releases. "Are you scared?" Her question surprises me. "Of crossing over," she clarifies.

Now it's my turn to inhale deeply and release slowly. I can't deny I'm concerned, but I wouldn't say scared. "Not scared so much, maybe just sad."

"Sad?"

"It's hard to leave the people you love. My family and friends. And

I know we haven't known each other long, Charlotte, but it'll be really hard to leave you, too."

Her lip trembles and I close my eyes wishing to God I could touch her. "I'm going to miss you, Ike," she whispers.

I smile sadly and face forward. I don't like seeing her cry. It fucking shreds me. "And when I go, remembering that will make me smile," I tell her, and she wipes a tear from her cheek.

"If you were alive, Ike McDermott . . ."

"You'd strip me naked and ravish my body?" I tease, and she laughs even though she's still wiping at her face.

"You know, I think I would." I'm getting excited, and I can't help but join her in this game of what-if. How could I not?

"If I were alive, I'd ask you out on a date. What would you say?" This is a terrible road for us to go down, but we're finally admitting there's an attraction between us, and even though nothing could ever happen for obvious reasons, I want to know. I need to know, as sick as it is. My blood is pumping and I flatten my palms to my thighs as I await her answer.

"Depends," she answers. "Tell me how you'd ask."

I scratch the back of my neck. "I think I'd do date by ambush. That way you couldn't really say no. I'd just show up at your job and bring flowers and say, 'Would you join me for dinner?'"

Grinning, she asks, "And we'd have dinner right there where I work?"

"Why not?" I scoff. "It's the best restaurant in town, is it not?"

"Sure it is. So you'd put me on the spot, eh?" she chuckles.

"Oh, yeah," I agree. "So, what would you do?"

"I would join you for dinner." She smiles sadly.

"I'd tell you about my time in the army and my family."

"I'd hide from you that I see dead people," she adds.

"Would you?" I ask, surprised. Hearing that makes me sad. There is absolutely nothing about her I wouldn't want to know. Does she think if I were alive I wouldn't believe her?

"At first, until I knew you were in love with me and wouldn't freak out." Her gray eyes dart to mine quickly before returning to the road.

"That wouldn't have taken long," I tell her. The first time I heard her laugh, I was done. If I were alive, I'd be making a fool of myself to make her mine. Her gaze lowers for a moment and she breathes deeply. We should stop, I know we should, but I can't. Not yet. "I'd take you home and kiss you good night."

"I'd let you," she says, sadly.

"After we'd been dating a while, I'd take you back to that spot by the river I took you to the other day, and to show my love for you, I'd carve our initials in that big tree. *I & C* inside a big heart." I can see it all; her gray eyes bright with love as she watches me mark the tree, the way she smiles at me when I finish. God, I wish I could give that to her.

"And then you'd get laid," she jokes and chuckles through her tears.

"Right there by the water?" I ask and laugh. "Aren't you the exhibitionist," I tease.

"Why not? I'd be caught up in the awe of your romantic gesture. I wouldn't have cared if anyone saw. We'd be all that mattered."

A long moment of silence plays out as we both bask in the intensity of her last words. *We'd be all that mattered.* I'm choking on my emotion: it's knotted in my throat. A living man or woman could relate to wanting something you can't have, but this is different. I literally can never have her. It's soul crushing. I need to say something—anything—but Charlotte saves the day and says, "You would've brought a picnic and there'd be a blanket."

Clearing my throat, unable to stop myself from playing out this fantasy with her, I add, "I'd lay you down."

"And you'd kiss me," she breathes, urging me on.

I grin. "And the water would be rushing and the branches of the tree would cover us with leaves of fall colors."

"The air would be chilly, and we'd be covered in goose bumps, but we wouldn't care."

"Because we'd be one," I say, before swallowing hard. The vision of her beneath me, naked, and staring into my eyes is something beautiful and torturous all at once. I can almost feel her breath on my neck as she whimpers. I can imagine the way her lips part as she moans. And I'd treasure every fucking minute of it. I would've loved her like she was my last breath. How the hell did we get here? We're building a fantasy that could never come to fruition. I know deep down this is wrong. We're connecting ourselves further, and it will only make it that much more difficult to let go.

"It would be . . ."

"Amazing," I finish her sentence. The image of it all is so clear it tears at my heart. I stare straight ahead, anger bursting inside me, with no one or no way to take it out on. I'm raging on the inside, clenching my teeth; hoping she can't sense the wave of emotion that's come over me.

"I'm sorry, Ike," she says, and her voice trembles. "It's so unfair."

My chest tightens with her words. I'm trying to be strong and not resent my situation. It is what it is. I died. People do it every day. But I can't fight the bitterness surging through me. I'd make her mine if I could. I want her more than I've ever wanted anything. But I can't have her and it occurs to me that if I continue to let our friendship or attraction grow, I'll only hurt her more when I go. I've asked her to take on the gigantic task of saving my addict brother on top of the problems she's struggling with. I can't add to it. I can't do that to her. I need to start distancing myself. And as much as I enjoy our teasing, what I really want is to see her happy. I don't want to leave her the same way I found her—sad and alone. I don't know where I'd be without her. She's become my best friend. And I'll always be grateful for what she's doing for my brother. He was a better man than me before the drugs got to him. And what he's become is not who he is. He has so much potential. I know he'll get back on track. He's a fighter.

Thankfully, the weight I've been carrying has lightened some. George is getting better, little by little. Maybe the two of them could make a go of it. My heart twists at the thought. It's selfish to be jealous, but I am. But if I can't have her, he definitely should. And I know he really likes her. She'd be good for him, and he'd always protect her. I've noticed the playful way she is with him. And even when she doesn't know I'm looking, I see the longing she has for him. Maybe if I back away a little, they can grow closer.

"You okay?" she asks after a long moment of silence.

"Yeah," I say, even though I'm the furthest thing from it. "Thank you for everything you're doing, Charlotte."

She nods once. "You're welcome, Ike.

Charlotte

It's almost nine by the time we reach the bar. Just as I'm walking in, I see Anna approaching the door from the inside.

"Hey, girl," she chimes merrily as she opens the door for me, her lipstick bright red just like the first night when I met her.

"Hey." I smile. "This place is dead tonight," I remark as I pass by her and enter.

"Yeah, we're closing early."

"Damn," I mumble. "I came up here to get a drink."

"Well then," she loops her arm through mine and leads me toward the bar. "You came to the right place. We're having a staff party."

"Staff party?" I ask as we reach the bar where Peyton is wiping it down. Ike walks beside me.

"Yeah. We stay and play cards sometimes. Dance, get wasted. So you got here just in time." She pats my back before untying her apron.

I want to ask if George is here, but I don't want to be too obvious. "So, who all's here?" I ask as nonchalantly as I can.

"Sniper and Greg are closing down the kitchen, and George is in his office with Misty."

"What?" I say, a little too . . . well, too eagerly.

Anna leans toward me and whispers, "I think she came here to beg for her job back. Probably trying to get George to take her back, too." Anna shakes her head. My gaze flickers to Ike and he disappears to go check on George. "I gotta finish cleaning my tables," Anna says, as she moseys away.

Why do my insides feel like they're on fire? George promised no more drugs. And why is he behind closed doors with her, anyway? Okay, calm down, Charlotte. Just because she's back there doesn't mean anything, right? *Then why are you stomping to the back like a jealous girlfriend?*

When I round the cook line on my way to George's office, Sniper's head snaps up and his eyes go wide. "Wait, Char," he calls as he darts for me. Just before I reach the office, he snakes one strong arm around my waist and pulls me back, turning us away from the office.

"Put me down," I growl as I struggle to release myself from his hold.

"It's not what you think," he whispers as he sits me down. "No need to be jealous."

Jealous? Is that what I am? No, he's wrong. "I'm not jealous!" I state adamantly. "George is trying to get clean, and she is a weight set to drag him down with her."

"And she's been his lover," he points out, his mouth turning upwards.

The look I give him is fit to annihilate. *That was a low blow.* My fists clench with his words. Scowling at him, I ask, "And what does that have to do with anything?"

"You know exactly what I'm saying."

He's reiterating he thinks I'm jealous. I ignore his statement as I'm not ready to admit that just yet. After all, I barely know George and our relationship, as of yet, has been volatile. "What does she want?"

"Her job." He shakes his head and rolls his eyes.

"Is he going to let her continue to work here?" My eyes are practically bulging out of my head as I think the unfathomable. If he lets her continue to work here, he's fucking nuts.

"What's it to you?" A voice comes from behind Sniper and we turn to acknowledge it. Misty is standing with her hip cocked and arms crossed over her chest.

Sniper runs a wide palm down his face. "She was just curious, Misty," he says, but his tone is drenched with annoyance. He doesn't like her either.

"If it pleases you," Misty sneers, "I will no longer work here. I guess that leaves you plenty of opportunity to move in on him." Leaning toward me, she whispers, "We just had our . . . well . . . we said good-bye." The taunting smirk on her face validates what her wording was meant to imply. "He's all yours, baby. But I doubt you could ever be as good as I've been to him."

My mouth drops open. What a fucking skank. I hate being bitchy or catty, but I can't help myself. Smiling pitifully at her, I say, "If I wanted him your presence wouldn't be an issue. And if you are so good, as you say you are, why's he letting you go? Because in the end, men don't want skanky coke heads."

She laughs in disbelief. I've one-upped her in the insult game. "You better watch your back, Char," she warns as she steps toward me again. Sniper stands tall and watches her, wondering if she's going to attack me.

I grin at her and as she passes by me, I say, "You look a little tense, Misty. Why don't you go home and snort a line. Might make you feel better."

"Charlotte!" George's voice booms, jerking Misty's, Sniper's, and my gaze to his seething glare. I glare back at him. Is he mad at me? Is he defending her? His eye is still swollen, but at least it's open now, and a deep purple surrounds it.

"Yes?" I snap back, placing my hands on my hips.

Misty smiles and continues on her way. "Bye, Charlotte," she calls, her voice almost in a singsong tone. "George, if you need me for *anything*, you have my number," she says, as she walks out.

"I believe I'd like to see you take her down, Char," Sniper notes with a nod.

"Shut it, Sniper. Charlotte, in my office. Now!" George shouts, and I straighten my back in protest. Is this anger for me, or a symptom of withdrawals?

"I'm off the clock, boss. You can't tell me what to do!" I stomp past him and head for the back exit, but he grabs me and yanks me in to his office. I look around, but don't see Ike anywhere. Did he leave me?

"What the fuck was all that out there?"

"What the fuck was all this in here?" I counter. "She said you two had a good-bye fuck." *Those weren't her exact words, but it's definitely what she implied.* "Was it good for you? To bang the woman whose boyfriend beat the shit out of you?"

"I didn't fuck her!" he shouts. "We ended things, okay? She's not going to work here anymore."

"Then why'd she say it?" I ask, calmly, in an effort to rein in my anger.

George's head rears back slightly, his anger draining from his face. Tilting his head to the side, his mouth quirks up slightly. "Are you . . . jealous?" Disbelief is rich in his voice.

My mouth clamps shut as anger and embarrassment swirl inside of me. Why am I acting like a fucking lunatic? I have no right to. I shouldn't feel this jealousy. But, God, I *am* jealous. I despise Misty and hate the fact she's ever touched him. As the realization dawns on me—that I do, in fact, want George McDermott—like want, want him—my knees go weak. Placing a hand on the desk behind me, I attempt to hold myself up without looking that way. I can't tell George I have feelings for him. How could I? How could I admit that to him, or anyone, when I have the same feelings for Ike? I'm a fucking mess right now. I need to change the subject. "No. You asked me to stay, and you made a promise to stay clean. She's your dealer. I'm concerned, not jealous."

George steps toward me, closing the distance between us. My heart beats wildly as my stare remains trained on him as I refuse to look away. "Listen, Charlotte," he whispers. "I realize you're concerned, but you can't make outbursts like that. All of my employees will think it's okay to behave the same way." My lips fall into a hard line and I stare at my feet. Damn it, he's right. "Charlotte, please look at me," he says, softly. When I continue to stare down, he brings his hand under my chin and cups it, tilting my head up. "With that said, I know I'm a hypocrite because I want to kiss you so bad right now. More than I've probably ever wanted to kiss a woman before. But I want to be clean, and I don't want my face to look pulverized when I do it." His confession weakens my defenses. My shoulders slouch as I succumb. I have no idea what to say so I nod once in understanding.

He removes his hand from my face and asks, "Would you let me take you somewhere?"

"What? Now?" I ask; my brows furrowed.

"Yeah. It's a really cool place."

"Okay." I shrug.

George lets Sniper know we're leaving and pulls me out the back door. Once again, he helps me into his jacked up truck and we drive. During the day Warm Springs is a bountiful abyss of color with sloping fields and round hay bales everywhere, but at night it's the darkest place I've ever seen. You can't see any of the day's beauty here at night.

We drive just past the gazebo with the *Welcome to Warm Springs* sign on it, and turn down a gravel road. "Where are we?" I ask as I squint my eyes, trying to make out the building in front of us with the limited light from the truck's headlights.

"The Jefferson Pools," George answers as he parks in front of a round, rundown-looking building.

"There's a pool in there?" I ask.

"Well, it's a warm spring, hence the town name. It stays ninety-eight degrees all year round. It's kind of what put our town on the map." He grabs a flashlight from the glovebox then climbs out of the truck and rounds it, opening my door and helping me out. As my body slides down his, it seems as if it happens in slow motion, but every single nerve inside me is aware of it, and I love every second of it.

"So this is where Thomas Jefferson used to come to soak and rejuvenate?" I ask, remembering Ike telling me something to that effect.

"It is. You're going to swim in water our third president swam in."

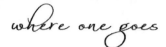

I stop in my tracks. "We're swimming? I didn't bring anything to swim in, George."

I can't see his face, but I can hear the smile in his voice. "Looks like we'll have to skinny-dip."

Shaking my head, I follow him and say, "So it's too soon to kiss me, but not too soon to see me naked?"

"I've already seen your ass," he points out.

"You're never going to let me forget that, are you?" I grumble.

"I don't think *I'll* ever forget it," he says, as if the thought gives him great satisfaction. I'm thankful it's dark out so he can't see my cheeks blush.

"You really expect me to skinny-dip?"

He laughs. "I won't look, Charlotte." He pauses. "Much," he corrects himself. "I won't look much." I want to protest, but I can't. I love this side of him; the carefree and fun George. His laugh is my drug; I need more, and I'd do almost anything to have it.

When we get to the door George pulls out his wallet, removing a credit card. "What is that for?"

"To pick the lock," he says, casually, as he inserts the card between the door and doorjamb.

"We're breaking in?" I hiss as my eyes dart around frantically.

"No. My debit card is the key to this place," he jests, earning an eye roll from me he doesn't see. "Relax," he urges me. "I know the guy that manages this place. If we get busted, we won't get in trouble. I promise," he assures me. "There it is," he cheers quietly as he pops the lock and opens the door. "Give me your hand." In the darkness, I find his hand and he leads me inside. The smell of sulfur assaults my nostrils and I cringe, but it soon fades as I quickly become accustomed to the odor. "Stay close to the wall or you'll fall in."

"It's so dark, I can't see a damn thing," I complain as I plaster myself to the wall.

"Well get undressed and hop in. I can't see a thing anyway. That's what I'm doing."

"You're undressing?" In the darkness, I sense him bend and hear the ruffling of clothing. He must've taken his shirt, underwear, and pants off.

"Done," he answers. Then there's the sound of a splash. "Come on, Charlotte. It feels awesome. Don't dive in though. It's only about four feet deep."

Good thing he can't see me roll my eyes. Removing all of my clothing, even my bra and panties, I prepare to hop in. "What about my cut?"

"You'll be fine. Come on," he encourages. I bend down and slide off the wooden floor surrounding the pool. The pool feels like bath water and I have to admit, it feels fantastic.

"Where are you?" I wade through the water, careful to step softly as there seem to be several large rocks, when suddenly a light comes on.

"Right here," he answers and tosses the flashlight twenty feet away from us in the water. My arms wrap around my chest as I attempt to cover myself. The water is clear, which means with the flashlight illuminating it, it's easy to make out our very naked bodies in the water.

"George!" I shriek.

His brows rise to his hairline as he takes in the sight of me. "I didn't think you'd get *completely* naked." He's laughing loudly, and mentally, I recant my previous sentiments about how addicted I am to his laughter.

"I wouldn't have if I had thought you'd throw a flashlight in the water!" I snap. "Turn it off!"

He only laughs harder.

"It's in the water. Shouldn't it have died already?" I squawk.

"Nope." His laughter ebbs as his dark eyes focus intently on me. "Waterproof." The word drifts through the air, deep and throaty.

Why did the word 'waterproof' just sound so erotic coming out of his mouth?

In an attempt to remain focused, I ask, "Did I mention that one of the first things my brother ever taught me was how to kick a guy in the balls?"

He's laughing again.

One of those open mouth, I can see his amazingly-white-straight-teeth laughs. Okay, I really am addicted. *Damn, him.*

"I hate you right now," I say, as I fight the laughter that's attempting to bubble up my throat and out my mouth.

"Okay, okay," he sighs and steps toward the flashlight before sinking in the water and crying out in mock anguish. "My ankle! I can't move! I'm sorry, Charlotte, I can't turn off the light."

Glaring at him, I say, "I should blacken your other eye."

As he continues to laugh, he swims toward me, causing me to back into the deck surrounding the pool. When I can't back away any further, I'm forced to wait until he's just a foot before me. My arms are so tight around me, my boobs are smushed up, the tops completely on display.

George's brown eyes are trained on me as he stands to his full height, the water's surface meeting his hips. Keeping my gaze on his, I refuse to let myself look down and see what's below the water's surface. "I don't mind if you see me naked, Charlotte."

"Shocking," I say, dryly. "I'm sure you don't. You're a guy."

"Maybe that's part of it," he concedes. "But you've seen more of me than anyone has in a long time. All the ugly parts. Things I'm not proud of." When he runs a hand through his hair, my eyes disobey me and move to his abs and the delicious, deep V-shape on his hips. God, they're beautiful. My fingers itch to reach out and slide down them. Then he says, "I want to know all of you, too. The good, the bad, and the ugly."

My heart beats wildly with his words. I know deep down this is the moment I should tell him about me, about what I can do, but I'm not ready to come clean for a multitude of reasons. One being, what if he thinks I'm a liar? Or worse, what if he hates me for keeping this secret all this time? Or even worse, what if it speeds up Ike's cross over? God, that's such a selfish thing to even think. Ike wants to cross over. He's been living in limbo for months, but that selfish part of me still isn't ready for him to go yet. Ike is the only friend I have. I can't tell George the truth. Not yet. So I stand to my full height and let my arms drop. Standing naked in front of someone makes you vulnerable, exposed. Maybe I can't tell him everything, but I can show him this, something I've never shown anyone before. I can't breathe as George's gaze moves down my body and back up again. His mouth is in an even line, his chest rising and falling with each breath he takes. The lighting from the flashlight in the pool illuminates his skin and hair, flickering in his eyes. Even battered and bruised, he's beautiful.

I've never been completely naked in front of a man before. I was a virgin before the accident and probably would have lost my virginity to Will, the guy I had kind of been dating at the time. But the accident took that from me and being a freak that can speak to the dead for the last six years hasn't helped my love life at all. But feeling George's eyes on my body excites me, preventing me from being embarrassed.

"I lied to you," George says, quietly stepping toward me again. I tilt my head. That's not what I was expecting to hear. "I said I wouldn't kiss you until I knew I was clean and didn't look like a punching bag, but I can't wait that long."

Swallowing hard, I tilt my chin up, inviting him to give me the kiss I want so badly even though I shouldn't. George is still recovering and this may all be symptomatic. I may only be a method to cope, and maybe later he'll regret it. But I can't fight it. If he wants to kiss me, I'll let him.

One hand finds the back of my neck and he pulls me toward him. When our mouths collide, his other hand wraps around my back just above my waist and he slams me to him. As his tongue dips in to my mouth, I moan, letting my hands rest on his biceps. In the warm water I can feel his length, hard, pressing against my belly, causing a delicious ache to blossom between my legs. The kiss is fierce and bold, the two of us clinging to each other for dear life. After all, George and I are floating, desperately seeking footing so we can stay planted to the ground. Perhaps we'll ground each other.

When George pulls away, I tremble, my body missing his warmth against it. The corner of his mouth curves slightly as his soft gaze lingers on my lips. "Thank you," he says, quietly.

George just gave me the best first kiss I've ever had. Will never kissed me like this—with such intensity. I'm pretty sure it's the best first kiss *any* girl has ever had. *I* should be thanking him. So I do. I slam my body to his and kiss him again, my want for him conveyed by the desire on my lips. My kisses tell him there's more, so much more to me, but I'm not ready to tell him everything just yet. He groans with arousal and I kiss him harder one last time. When I pull away, I say, "Thank you for bringing me here. It's . . . amazing."

Chapter 17

Ike

I stood outside the Jefferson Pools while George and Charlotte were inside. When they exited, they were holding hands, and I could feel my brother's happiness radiating from him. He's falling for her. My brother and I are in love with the same girl. I half laugh at the ridiculousness of this situation.

Flashing back to the motel, I wait in my chair for Charlotte to return. I won't tell her I followed her. I don't want her to feel like she can't be herself around George or for her to get the creeps because I was following her.

An hour later, the door opens and she flips on the light. She jumps when she sees me, but laughs as she grabs her chest. "You're trying to give me a heart attack, aren't you?"

I smile and stand. "Just keeping you on your toes."

"Where have you been?"

"You told me to give you space to work so I've been trying to do that."

"Oh," she mumbles as she tosses her bag on the floor by the bed. She climbs on the bed and yawns, her hair still damp from the water. "George took me to the Jefferson Pools. It was pretty nice."

Shoving my hands in my pockets, I say, "I'm glad you're getting the full Bath County experience." When her gaze meets mine, I see the sadness and the guilt in her eyes. I know she feels bad about wanting us both, but she feels worse because she knows I can do nothing about it, no matter what.

"Will you lie down with me?" She pats the bed beside her and I want to say no, to resist, but I can't. If this is all I can have of her for this short time, I'm going to take it, no matter how wrong it is. I lunge and jump as if I'll land on top of her. She shrieks and laughs when I morph and end up lying beside her.

"Why does that always freak me out?"

"I don't know," I chuckle. Turning to face her, her gray eyes meet mine and she smiles softly. "How'd it go tonight?" I ask, even though I already know.

Her eyes dart away for a brief moment before meeting mine again. "He likes me . . . like, really likes me," she says, quietly.

"Do you like him?" I ask, even though, again, I already know the answer.

Her eyes brim with tears and she turns her face into her pillow. "This is such a fucked up situation, Ike," she says. I close my eyes, pained by all the things I am incapable of. I want to hold her and kiss her, and press my body to hers, but I can't. None of what I feel for her matters because I can never give her what she needs. And I have to remind myself of that. I have to let her go eventually. She cares for me . . . I know it. I feel it every time she looks at me. But I'm dead. She shouldn't feel guilty about caring for my brother, too. I have to let her know it's okay; that I understand.

"It's okay to like him, Charlotte," I tell her softly. "Don't feel bad because you . . ." Like me, too? Should I say that?

"It's not just about you being dead, Ike. Who lets themselves fall for twin brothers? What kind of person am I to say that I love you both?"

And there it is. She loves us both. My heart twists. "If you are going to share your heart with another man other than me, I'd want it to be George."

"If you were both alive, I'd never choose, Ike. I'd leave. I could never choose one of you over the other. I'd never want to hurt either of you."

Smiling, I say, "I guess it's a good thing it worked out this way. You weren't given a choice, Charlotte. The choice is already made."

"How do I save him, and let you go at the same time? How do I do that?" Her crying has morphed into sobs at this point, and I can't stand watching it.

"Because you know I will be at peace. Because I can rest easy knowing the woman I love and my brother—my best friend—are happy. I'll know you'll both be okay." I smile softly and add, "Charlotte, you're my best friend, too. I'm okay with you being with George. I think you two are good for each other." And that's the truth, even though it hurts. She gives me a small smile but still has a worried look on her face.

"We have to tell George soon," she says, as she wipes at her face.

"We will, but you need rest now, baby girl."

"Will you stay? Please don't go," she begs, and I move closer to her.

"I'm here." *And even when I go, a part of me will always be here, with her.*

We lie back, side by side, and eventually she drifts off to sleep. I stare at her, her fair skin and dark hair on display, and I know I love her because letting her go will be one of the hardest things I'll ever have to do, but I'll do it gladly knowing she's safe and happy. I hope she stays and makes a home here. This town is good for her. I pray George can convince her.

The night lingers into the morning, the sun peeking through the curtains. Charlotte is in a sleep coma but is startled awake when someone beats on her door.

"Who the—?"

I morph out of the room and morph back. "It's Sniper," I tell her as she walks toward the door rubbing her eyes. "He looks like something is wrong."

"George," she gasps as her eyes go wide with panic. Ripping the door open, she says, "What's wrong? Is it George?"

"No, lass. Your truck was broken into last night at the bar. George is there with the police right now."

"He called the police?" she shrieks as her body tenses.

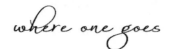

"Yeah. Someone broke into it," Sniper says to her, as if she's dense.

"Shit!" she mumbles. Closing her eyes, she clenches her fists.

"What's wrong, Charlotte?" I ask. Why is she freaking out?

"I'm thinking!" she snaps.

"Is Ike here?" Sniper asks as his eyes dart around the room.

"Yes," she answers as she moves toward the bed, grabbing her bag. "I've got problems, Sniper."

"Okay," he says, stepping inside the room and shutting the door behind him. "What's going on?"

"Have you seen those clips on the news about the Purcell girl? That missing UVA student and how they found her body?"

His brows rise in thought. "I think I heard about it." He shrugs.

"Well . . . I'm the one that sent in the anonymous letter telling the detective where to find her body." We're all silent for a moment until she adds, "Casey showed me where her body was."

"You didn't kill her, so what's the problem?" Sniper asks.

"How am I supposed to explain I found a corpse under a bridge? They'll never believe I can talk to the dead."

He bites his lip and nods. "No, most likely they won't. What does Ike say?"

Charlotte looks to me, and I use both hands to scratch the back of my head roughly as I think. "Tell the truth, Charlotte," I tell her, and she rolls her eyes.

Looking back to Sniper, she asks, "Who messed up my truck?"

"I have a pretty good guess," I remark.

"Probably that twat, Misty," Sniper answers and Charlotte's shoulders slouch.

"I guess we better go get this over with," she sighs and pulls her backpack on her shoulders.

"It'll be okay, Charlotte," I promise her. "Don't worry."

On the drive to the bar, Sniper tries to take her mind off things, mostly telling embarrassing stories about me. "You know, when we were in basic training, all the guys had to share a bathroom. There weren't any stalls or doors or anything, so we were all out in the open in front of everyone."

"Is that so?" she asks dismally, her mind obviously remaining fixed on what's ahead.

"Yeah, so we're men, right? Men need . . . to release, if you know what I mean," Sniper continues and Charlotte turns her head toward him.

"Oh, he is such an asshole," I say, as I clench my eyes closed, knowing exactly what he's going to tell her.

"Ike just called you an asshole. My curiosity is officially piqued." Charlotte grins and Sniper's body shakes as he works to keep his laughter in control. The bastard hasn't even finished the story, and he's already in stitches.

"Well, sharing a room and bathroom with sixty dudes doesn't exactly give you the privacy to jerk it," Sniper explains.

"So you went six weeks without whacking off?" Charlotte asks.

"Kill me now," I say.

"You're already dead, Ike," Charlotte points out.

Sniper laughs, beating the side of his fist against the steering wheel. He's enjoying this way too much. "It'll cheer her up, Ike. Don't be such a wanker."

"Keep going. I'm on the edge of my seat over here," Charlotte encourages Sniper.

"Well, Ike decides to get up in the middle of the night to use the bathroom." Sniper uses his fingers to make quotations when he says, *use the bathroom*. "There was this guy in our unit, Williams . . . total sod. He was really good at ragging on people about shit. Of course, when Ike made his little bathroom break, Williams went in after him and caught him spanking it. He woke us all up laughing so hard."

Charlotte turns to me, grinning from ear to ear. "You got caught whacking off in the middle of the night?"

"Yes," I admit grumpily. Not exactly a story you want a girl you're crazy about to hear.

"Thanks for that, Sniper," I say, even though he can't hear me.

"He says thanks," Charlotte tells him as she chuckles at my expense.

"No problem, Spanky," Sniper replies. "That was his nickname for the remainder of basic training."

"Spanky?" Charlotte asks as she smiles brightly and shakes her head. Sniper just embarrassed the fuck out of me, but it worked. He relaxed her a little bit, but now we're pulling into *Ike and George's* parking lot, and her smile fades rapidly.

"It'll be okay," I assure her again.

She nods a few times as she stares at her truck. A police officer is standing near the passenger side looking inside, but not touching anything. When George sees Sniper's truck pull in and park, he comes straight to the passenger door where Charlotte is and opens it.

"Hey," he says, simply. The swelling of his lip and eye is much better, but there's still a nasty pink and purple hue surrounding it. Reaching out his hand for Charlotte, he helps her out of the truck, and she smiles faintly in gratitude.

"When I got here this morning the windshield and driver's side window was busted out. I didn't touch it, but when I looked inside, it looked like maybe they went through your glove box." George's hand finds the small of her back and he leads her gently toward the police officer. Shoving my hands in my pockets, I remain standing near Sniper's truck. Sniper stands about four feet from me, unbeknownst to him.

"Don't worry, Ike," he says, quietly. "I'll help her." Then he heads toward Charlotte's 4Runner.

Chapter 18

Charlotte

"Are you the owner of this vehicle?" the officer asks as I stare at the shattered glass on the hood of my truck.

"It's in my father's name," I clarify, meeting his gaze.

"Are you aware the tags are expired?" he asks, and I want to roll my eyes. I have no idea if my father paid to renew the tags and license plate after I left. I've been pulled over countless times for those damn tags and the expired inspection, and I've collected a great deal of tickets for it as well. But as I've been drifting state to state for the last five years, I've never felt the need to pay those tickets or even mind their existence.

"I am," I answer.

"Randy," George says, annoyed. "Shouldn't we be focusing on who broke into her truck?"

At that moment, Officer Randy's partner approaches and pulls him aside, leaning toward him to tell him something. George steps in front of me and shakes his head at them. "Bath County doesn't see a lot of excitement in the way of crime around here. He's just trying to show off," George assures me. I nod as I suck in a deep breath. I wonder if I tell the officers to leave, if they would. The longer they're here, the more my stomach knots up. George places his hands on my arms and squeezes gently as he leans in and kisses my forehead. "It'll be okay," he whispers. When I look up at him, my brows furrow. He looks pale and a light sheen of sweat covers his face. He doesn't look well at all.

"Are you okay?" I whisper. "Do you feel sick?"

He swallows hard, and his mouth curves to the side. "A little," he admits. "I threw up a few times this morning."

"George, you should go home and rest," I insist as I touch the back of my hand to his forehead, which he quickly swipes away.

"I'm fine. I'm not leaving you here to deal with this alone."

"Ms. Acres," Randy calls me and I turn toward him, surprised to be addressed by my last name. Did George tell him my last name? He tugs the brim of his hat down before placing his hands on his belt. His partner stands just behind him.

"Yes?" I answer.

"We're going to need you to come with us," Randy says, and I tense as George steps farther in front of me.

"What the fuck for, Randy?" George snaps, and I realize how horrible the timing is. George is going through withdrawals and is already on edge. The last thing he needs is to be put in a situation that upsets him.

"That's not your concern, George," Randy's partner says, as he steps forward.

"The hell it's not, Willard. Someone broke into her truck last night, and you're taking *her* in?"

"That's Officer Lloyd to you, George, and if we say she needs to come with us, she needs to come with us," Willard snaps back.

I have to step in and calm down George. Rounding him, I face him and place my hands on his chest. "It's okay, George. This is probably about some outstanding tickets I have." Cutting my eyes to Sniper, I try to tell him to help me out. He gets my message loud and clear. Stepping forward, he takes George by the shoulders and pulls him back a bit.

"It's all right, mate. We'll follow her to the station and get this all cleared up."

"This is fucking bullshit, and you know it, Randy," George growls as he pushes Sniper off of him and steps back to me. Placing his hands on my shoulders, he bends slightly to meet my gaze. "We'll be right behind you. My mom can come and open the restaurant, and Greg is working the kitchen today so he can handle it." My heart drops to the pit of my stomach. Here he is being so sweet and wonderful while going through drug withdrawals, and I'm keeping things from him. It feels amazing to have someone care for me this way, but dread blooms inside of me. *He's going to hate me when he finds out the truth.*

"You really don't have to come, George. I'm sure it's the tickets. I'd feel bad with you coming down there. Besides, you should be resting."

"I'm coming with you, Charlotte," he says, sternly, before leaning in and kissing me softly on the lips, shocking the hell out of me. When I glance to Ike, he's staring at the ground, and when I look to Sniper, his eyebrows are touching his hairline. "Don't worry. My dad is a lawyer, and if we need him he can help," George assures me.

"Let's go," Randy orders from behind, and I roll my eyes.

"Can I grab my bag out of Sniper's truck?"

He nods in answer, and after I get my bag, I climb into the back of the brown cop car and we head toward the Bath County Sheriff's department. Ike morphs beside me and gives me a reassuring smile. "It's not about the tickets," he says. I nod, letting him know I know that.

"So what's this about? Why are you bringing me in?" I ask Randy and Willard.

"An APB was put out on your vehicle and you last night. You're wanted for questioning in the Casey Purcell investigation."

I lean my head back against the seat and exhale loudly. This is going to be a long day.

Once we reach the sheriff's department, I'm placed in a small room with a table and two chairs on each side. It even has one of those mirrors like in the movies, and I know I'm being watched from the other side. Ike stays with me, even though I can't speak with him. It's still nice to know he's here.

It's been three hours, and I've had four cups of strong, stale coffee when the door opens and a tall, dark-haired man enters wearing a light blue button-down shirt and khakis. He's holding a folder in one hand and a bottle of water in the other.

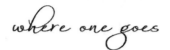

"Ms. Acres." He nods in greeting. "I'm Detective Andrews with the Charlottesville Police Department." I don't respond as he pulls out the steel chair across from me and sits. "Bottled water?" he asks, holding it out toward me. I shake my head no.

Leaning his forearms on the table, he asks, "Do you know why you've been brought in?"

"The officers that brought me in said there was an APB out on me that had to do with the Casey Purcell investigation."

Leaning back, he eyes me. "Did you know Casey Purcell?"

"Don't answer anything yet," Ike warns.

"Am I under arrest?" I ask.

"No. But you're a person of interest. Your vehicle was seen at the nearest gas station to where Casey's body was found."

"And that makes me a person of interest? You think I had something to do with her murder?"

"Did you?" he asks simply, and I smile with disdain.

"Are you serious?"

"We know, at the very least, you're the one that reported the whereabouts of her body," Andrews replies as he flips open the folder. "Does this look familiar?" He slides a piece of paper in a plastic sheet protector forward. I recognize it immediately. It's the anonymous letter I wrote.

Swallowing hard, I take a deep breath. "It's a letter," I state because I have no idea what to say. In an attempt to calm myself, or at least appear calm, I place my hands on the table and lace my fingers together.

He smiles sadly at me as if to say, *You're only prolonging the inevitable.* "And what about this?" he asks as he takes the sheet before me back and places a photo in front of me. My heart stops. It's a picture of the flashlight I dropped in the water that night. I could deny recognizing it if not for the **ACRES** written across it in bold letters. My father always had a thing about labeling our belongings. I'm an idiot. How could I forget about the flashlight?

"I'm working on a warrant, and I'm sure we can match the paper the anonymous letter was written on to maybe . . . a notebook in your possession."

Pulling my hands back in to my lap, I shake my head. This is what I get for trying to help. "I think I'd like an attorney."

Chapter 19

Ike

Detective Andrews steps out and Charlotte immediately stands and starts pacing.

"Just tell the truth," I tell her, but she shakes her head no. "There's no one on the other side of the mirror right now and there aren't any cameras in here. You can speak to me."

"Who would believe me?"

"Charlotte, relax. I know you're freaking out, but they have no proof you were there the night she disappeared. Just tell them everything you know, and maybe they can find the real killer."

"And how do I tell them I know all of those details, Ike? Maybe they can't charge me for murder, but it would certainly look suspicious."

"George will get my father and he'll help."

"I'm not using your dad for this, Ike. I can't. Not when I've lied to your family about us and . . . you," she finishes.

"Then it's time for you to tell my father," I state. Stepping in front of her, she stops pacing and meets my gaze. "He'll believe you. I'll make sure he does."

She hangs her head and sighs. "I'm not sure I'm ready to do this."

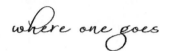

An hour later, my father strolls in the room and immediately takes Charlotte in his arms. "Are you all right, dear? George is fit to be tied out there worrying about you," my father says.

When Charlotte pulls away, her eyes are filled with tears. "Thank you for coming, Mr. McDermott."

"I told you to call me Henry. Now sit. Let's get this mess sorted out." He leads Charlotte to her seat before rounding the table and taking his own seat across from her, pulling out a large, yellow paper tablet from his briefcase.

"Did you tell George what this is about?" Charlotte winces with the question.

"You asked me not to, and everything we discuss will be confidential. I've spoken to Detective Andrews briefly. Now I'd like to hear your side of the story."

Charlotte's gaze flicks to me, and I nod in encouragement. "Henry, I know this is going to sound absurd, but I found Casey Purcell's body under the Ukon Bridge and reported it."

"Okay. Did you have anything to do with her death?" he asks.

"No! I swear!" she rushes to assure him.

"Just tell him the truth. He'll believe you," I assure her, and she clenches her eyes closed. When she opens them, she glances at me so briefly my father wouldn't catch it, but the look was long enough to tell me she's already apologizing for not telling him the truth.

"I was driving through Charlottesville and my truck felt like it was pulling funny. So I pulled over near the bridge and got out to check my tire. When I got out, I took my flashlight but it was raining that night, and I slipped and my flashlight went down the bank. So I crawled down after it, but couldn't find it. That's when I found Casey's body." Charlotte finishes her lie and avoids eye contact with me. She knows I'll be upset she didn't tell him the truth.

"Why didn't you just go to the police?"

"Several reasons. I was scared. I didn't want to be named as a witness or anything. I have a lot of tickets from throughout the years, and I was worried I'd get in trouble for those. I didn't have any money to pay them."

"You know how stupid that sounds, don't you?" I say, and her lips flatten as if she's mad.

Pushing the notepad toward her, my father says, "Write up a statement, and we'll hand it over to the detective."

She nods and takes the pad and pen and begins writing. When she's done, my father hugs her tightly and assures her everything will be all right before he leaves to give it to the detective.

"I thought we agreed to tell him the truth."

"We did," she snaps. "But not right now. George is going through withdrawals. Let me get him through this and we'll tell them."

The room falls silent for a moment. She sits stiff as a board, her hands in her lap, staring straight ahead. "Are you all right, Charlotte?" I ask.

She smiles faintly. "What if they hate me for keeping the secret this long?"

"They won't," I promise. I know this without a doubt. They may be shocked at first, but they'll believe her.

"It's been so long since anyone has cared about me. I don't want to lose them, Ike. And I don't want to lose you."

"You won't," I assure her. "You may not be able to see me once I go, but Charlotte, I'll always be in your heart." I place my hand to my chest in emphasis. "My family won't turn you away either. You're a part of us now. They won't turn their backs on you. I swear it."

Her tear-filled eyes meet mine and she stifles a sob. "And once they know, if they accept it and find peace, you'll go. I feel like I'm going to lose no matter what I do, Ike. It's suffocating me."

"Charlotte," my voice cracks. Standing, I walk toward the mirror, fighting my own emotions. I hate seeing her cry, but I hate it even more that leaving her is going to tear me up inside just as much as it is her. But there's a pull, something invisible that I can't see, tugging at me, drawing me to another place. I'd be gone by now if not for George, but his hold, that weight he's had on my shoulders is lessening. When George finds peace, I'll have no choice but to go where that invisible tether leads me, and that will mean leaving this beautiful woman behind. I know on one hand it will be better for her, no matter how sad she'll be. Eventually she'll move on or her sadness will ebb and she will be happy. On the other hand, the selfish part of me needs her to need me.

"What if you're wrong? Then I'll be all alone again, Ike. I'll be exactly the way you found me. Alone and hopeless."

Flashing around the table, I lean over it so that her gaze meets mine. I won't let her be that way again. The memory of her standing on that bridge railing twists my insides. Life is full of color and magic and ups and downs, but Charlotte is the best parts of life. She's light and warmth and bliss. "You listen to me, Charlotte. I don't ever want to hear you say that again." My fists clench as my anger seizes me and her eyes dart away. "Look at me, goddamn it!" I shout. When her gaze flicks back to mine, she's holding her breath. "Never give up. Promise me," I demand in a steady voice edged with fury. "I can't find peace if I think for one second you'll turn back into that girl I found on the bridge that night, Charlotte. Promise me," I beg. My own eyes tear up as fear and anger seize me. She's so important to me. I have to know she'll be okay—that she'll be strong. It will be an eternity of hell if I'm forced to go and have to carry the worry of her possibly ending her life with me. I need to know she'll survive this; that she'll be okay.

Lowering my voice and staring deep into her eyes, I beg, "Please, baby girl. Promise me. I need . . . I need to know you'll be okay."

Tears stream down her face, but she nods slightly. "I promise."

"I'm sorry I can't take you in my arms right now and hold you. I'd sell my soul to the devil if I could, Charlotte." My words cause a sob to break free from her trembling lips.

"I know you would," she whispers as she wipes at her face and nose with shaky fingers. She takes a few deep breaths and after a few moments, she seems to calm a bit. After another hour, the detective enters with her statement typed and has her sign it in the presence of my father.

"You won't be leaving town anytime soon, will you, Charlotte?" Andrews asks.

"No, sir," she answers.

"Your vehicle was brought in for inspection. We'll be fingerprinting it. If we find any matches for whoever broke into your truck, we'll be in touch. We'll contact you when you can pick up the vehicle."

"Thank you," she says, and nods numbly before standing. My father leads her out of the interrogation room and down the corridor until they reach the lobby. George flies out of his chair and wraps his arms around her. "What in the hell took so long?" he growls. There are bags under his eyes and he's pale. It's not hard to see he's hurting.

"George, it's been a long day. Let's just get her home," my father encourages. He senses George's agitation, but doesn't realize it's in part due to his withdrawals.

"I'll drive them," Sniper volunteers.

Chapter 20

Charlotte

Sniper drops George and me off at his house, insisting he can handle things at the restaurant. George held me in the backseat the entire way to his house despite his own problems. His breathing was labored, and I know he's ill. I told him about finding Casey's body; of course, I left out the part about Casey's soul showing me where it was. He hugged me tighter and told me how strong I was after experiencing something like that. My insides twisted, knowing I was lying to him yet again.

Once we're inside, he leads me to the bathroom in the master bedroom and starts the faucet. "You take a warm bath and try to relax. I'll order a pizza."

"George, you aren't feeling well. You should take a hot shower and let me handle dinner."

"You've had a really shitty day. I'm going to feel like ass no matter what I do. At least one of us should feel a little better."

He gives me a T-shirt and some boxers and leaves me to bathe. I soak for a long time until I hear his doorbell ding and know it must be the pizza. I haven't eaten anything all day so I hurry out of the tub and dress.

By the time I reach the kitchen, George is in only a pair of basketball shorts, his skin coated in sweat. Shit. He doesn't look so well.

"I'm sorry to do this to you, Charlotte, but I need to lie down. Please help yourself to anything."

"Okay." I nod as he walks back to his bedroom. I switch on the television while I eat, trying to keep quiet so George can sleep. After a while I decide to go and check on him and find him curled up in the fetal position on his bed; sweat covering him. His body feels like it's on fire. I find a washcloth and a dry towel and attempt to wipe him off while applying the cool cloth to his forehead.

"You should go home, Charlotte," he moans in pain. "I don't want you to see me like this."

Taking his hand in mine, I kiss it. "I'm not going anywhere. The good, the bad, and the ugly . . . remember?"

And ugly it is. For the next few days I stay with George as his body punishes him for denying it the cocaine, pills, and booze it has become accustomed to. My heart aches for him; I'd do anything to take his pain away. At night, I've slept with him in case he's needed me, and by day, I try in vain to get him to eat something. Ike assures me as long as he keeps drinking water, he'll be okay; the body can survive days without food, but can't go longer than three days before dehydration sets in. The only times I've left is when Sniper comes between shifts and stays with George while I clean rooms for Ginger. At least I was able to use Georges' washing machine and clean my clothes.

The first twenty-four hours are the worst, but as time passes he starts coming to a bit more. Now, he's just really tired and wants to sleep. While he's been incapacitated, I've done some research trying to find him a therapist, or a facility that can help him keep clean. I hope he'll be open to it.

"He'll need rehab," Ike says, as I Google all of the information I can about drug addiction.

"He won't go," I answer. "Not at first, anyway."

"Who are you talking to?" George asks in a hoarse voice as he enters the living room. I nearly jump out of my skin. He's shirtless and I can't help staring at him for a moment, admiring his defined abs and bare, broad shoulders.

"Just talking to myself," I reply as I place George's laptop beside me and stand.

"You do that a lot?" he asks. "Misty said she saw you talking to yourself when you first started working at the bar."

I have to fight like hell not to scowl at the mention of her name. "Did she?" I ask, my tone not hiding my annoyance. "I'm sure she had all kinds of things to say about me."

"Easy, Charlotte," Ike interjects, and I roll my eyes.

Pushing past George, I enter the kitchen and start pulling out lunch meat and cheese to make sandwiches. "You hungry?"

I'm tossing the items on the counter to the right of the fridge while searching for the mayonnaise when I feel hands grab my hips and pull me back. George spins me around, shutting the fridge right after, before lifting me and sitting me on the kitchen island. My legs open to allow him to stand close to me without thought. In nothing but a pair of George's boxers and an old T-shirt, this position feels extremely . . . intimate. Running his hand up my thigh, he reaches the fabric of his boxers I'm wearing before he stops.

"Thank you, Charlotte," he says. "For taking care of me. I'm sorry you had to." His coffee eyes peer into mine and I reach up, threading my fingers through his shaggy hair.

"Thank you for letting me take care of you, George," I reply, letting my gaze fall to his lips.

When our mouths meet in a passionate, toe-curling kiss, I snake my arms around him and push my body forward so I'm as close to him as I can be. Before I know it, he's lifting me, my legs wrapped around his waist, our lips never leaving the other's as he carries me back to his bedroom. We're a tangle of madness and want as we fall to the bed and he presses his full weight on me. My body is riddled with a delicious ache and when his hand slides underneath my top and cups my breast, I nearly explode. He trails kisses down my neck to my chest and lifts the shirt so his beautiful mouth can suck on my pert nipple. A deep throaty moan escapes me, and I buck my hips up to meet his body, begging for anything and everything he'll give me.

"Charlotte," he whispers in between panting breaths, and my core clenches.

His hand leaves my breast and slides down my body, his fingers digging into my flesh as they tease at the waist of the boxer shorts. The fog of my lust begins to taper off as so many brutal truths bombard me all at once. For one, where is Ike? I completely forgot he was here when this all started. And having sex with George while Ike watched would be so wrong on so many levels, but even with that aside—I'm a virgin. And this has moved super-fast. And George is barely recovering from an addiction problem.

"George," I moan in an attempt to slow him, but it only seems to encourage him more as he tugs at the waist of the boxers and begins slipping them down my hips.

"God, Charlotte, you're so beautiful," he purrs as he slips the boxer shorts down my thighs. "I want you so fucking bad."

I want him just as badly. I'm the worst person in the world, but I do. How could I do this to Ike?

"George, we have to stop," I finally squeak out, and he freezes just as he pulls the boxer shorts down to my ankles. His eyes are wide with regret and embarrassment.

Pulling away as if I'm on fire, he apologizes, "I'm sorry, I thought you . . . never mind. I'm an asshole. I'm so sorry."

"It's not that, George, I do want you. Badly," I emphasize as I reach down and pull the shorts back up. Rolling over and moving to my knees in front of him, I let my gaze flicker to his rather sizable erection under his boxers. I want so badly to touch it; to run my hand down his hard length and feel what I do to him. "It's just, this is moving really fast and . . ."

"I know. I'm an addict loser," he says, morosely, and moves to climb off the bed.

"No!" I yell, and he stalls. "I'm a virgin, George," I admit before swallowing past the lump in my throat. His brows rise to his hairline.

"Really?" he questions in disbelief. I'm not sure if he doesn't believe me, or if he's just shocked.

"Really," I reply, waiting to read him further before deciding how to proceed. Silence hangs between us and heat begins to crawl up my neck and to my cheeks. Does he think I'm some kind of leper because I haven't lost it yet? With a sideways smirk, I add, "I just thought maybe you should know."

"How . . . just, how? You're so . . . everything," he mumbles, I think more to himself than to me. My heart expands five times its size, making my chest feel tight. *Everything*. He thinks I'm everything.

"I think you're amazing, too," I tell him, my gut twisting as I once again remember this man is falling in love with me and knows nothing real about me. At least not the most relevant truths.

His dark gaze meets mine just before he reaches up and brushes a strand of hair behind my ear. "I have no idea why you have such a high opinion of me, but I swear I want to be worthy of that opinion, and I want to be worthy of you, Charlotte." Swallowing hard, his gaze drops. "The man you met and have known, that's not me. Honestly, I know this is going to make me sound even more like an addict, but I don't want the drugs. I was just so lost, and I just wanted to be numb for a long time; not feel anything. But now, I want to feel . . . at least the good stuff. I want to feel things with you."

Tears threaten to spill from my eyes. I open my mouth to respond when there's a knock at the door. "You expecting someone?" I ask.

"No," he replies and stands and searches for a T-shirt to pull on, but I climb off the bed and stop him.

"I'll get it. I like you shirtless." I wink as I pass by him.

"I'll keep that in mind." He smirks as he pulls me back and kisses me tenderly. My body curves to his as his fingers gently thread through my hair. When he pulls away, he peers into my eyes and says, "I'll wait as long as it takes. I want to be with you. I know I have to prove myself to you first, but I will. I promise." Then he kisses me again as knocks hammer the front door, beckoning us.

As I make my way to the door, I commit to telling George the truth tonight. I have to. I can't keep this inside anymore. I only pray he doesn't hate me after he finds out the truth. But even I know, deep down, initially he won't take it well, and I need to be prepared for that. Maybe I should ask Sniper to be present.

The person at the door pounds harder this time and my brows furrow. "Hold your damn horses. I'm coming!" I shout just before whipping the door open. Only moments before, I had been walking on cloud nine, albeit a cloud riddled with doubt and uncertainty, but I was still swimming in the after effects of George's proclamation that he wants to be with me. I want to be with him, too. Now my heart has dropped into the deepest, darkest part of my stomach as a pair of familiar gray eyes stare back at me.

"Charlotte Anne," he says, with an obvious tone of frustration.

Licking my dry lips and knotting my hands together in front of me to hide my nerves, I reply, "Daddy."

chapter 21

Ike

The moment George pulled her away from the fridge and placed her on the counter, I morphed outside. This is the purest form of torture; to watch the woman I love with another man. It's not either of their faults, which makes it all the worse. I'm pushing her to George and because of that, she's fallen for both of us. This isn't fair to any of us; not her, not me, and not George, even though he has no idea this fucked up love triangle exists.

That invisible pull, that force, pulling me to what lies just beyond this world is strengthening as the weight of my worry for George lightens. I know he's still fragile, and not quite out of the water just yet, but I think it's time to tell him the truth. There will no doubt be some backlash on his part, and it may take him a few days to come to terms with all of this. But he needs to know the truth, and accept it. Speaking only for myself, this situation is tearing me apart. I want so badly for George to be better, to be happy, but his happiness involves him having something I would sell my soul to have. I'm an asshole for thinking this way. They're the two people I love most in the world, and I want them to have each other when I'm gone, but watching it happen is hard.

I'm pacing the driveway when a blue Sedan pulls up and an older man in slacks and a green dress shirt steps out. His face is hard, like he's pissed, and my body tenses. Who the hell is this guy, and why is he here? He pounds George's front door repeatedly until Charlotte whips the door open, and her face falls, all the blood draining from it.

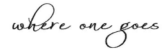

"Charlotte Anne," the man grumbles, and I'm on high alert. Who is he, and how does he know her?

I morph inside the house and behind her when she says, "Daddy."

My mouth drops open. So this is the asshole that treated her like a nut job and sent her away? I'd give my left nut to take a swing at this guy. Anyone who knows Charlotte, really knows her and her secrets, knows she's not crazy. She's beautiful and selfless. Look at what she's done to help me, and what about the others before me?

"How did you find me?" she manages.

"The police called me and informed me my truck was in their possession in an investigation for murder and a break-in. The sheriff gave me the address of your motel, but when you weren't there, they gave me this address." Charlotte remains frozen, staring at him.

"May I come in?" her father asks after a long pause, although he's not really asking. I can tell he's using his fatherly tone with her. His eyes dart over her, taking in her attire. She's wearing a shirt and George's boxers, rolled up so many times her ass is kind of hanging out. I think it looks hot, but I guess from a father's point of view, it wouldn't.

"Actually, now's not a good time," she finally answers. "Where are you staying? I'll come meet you there." The panic she's feeling is evident in her tone, at least it is to me. She's scared her father will expose her to George. She steps out and closes the door slightly, forcing her father to step back. There's enough of a crack that I can remain inside and still see both of them.

"I'm staying at Archer Valley Bed & Breakfast," he tells her, and I didn't think it was possible her face could get any paler, but it does. It's a small fucking world sometimes, and of course, of all the B&Bs in Bath County, her father would be staying at the one my parents own.

"It'll be okay, Charlotte," I tell her, like I always do, even though she never seems to believe me. Her hand is clenching the door knob, so when George whips it open, she almost falls, but he catches her. If her father was disapproving of her wardrobe already, George showing up shirtless isn't helping.

"Uh . . . can I help you?" George asks as he holds Charlotte against him. I wish I could hold her steady while she feels like the world is cracking beneath her, but if I can't, I'm glad George is here to do it. She needs someone to keep her grounded.

"I'm Wayne Acres, Charlotte's father," her father replies.

"Oh," George says, taken aback. "It's nice to meet you, sir." He immediately straightens himself and reaches out a hand to shake her father's, but Mr. Acres ignores it.

"I'm just here for my daughter. Charlotte, you have no vehicle. Why don't you get dressed and meet me in the car? Five minutes." With that, he turns and heads back to his vehicle.

George closes the door and turns to Charlotte. "I think he likes me," he tries to joke, but Charlotte misses the humor.

"It's not you. I have to go." She rushes back to his room and he follows. She's so frantic she doesn't notice either of us is in the room with her as she peels off her borrowed pajamas. And even though things are fucked at the moment, we are men, and we both stare at her. When she's fully dressed and turns, I expect her to glare and give George some quip about watching her, which would be meant for me as well, but she says nothing. She pushes past George and grabs her purse from the living room. When she moves to open the door, George places a flat palm against it, stopping her.

"You look like you're about to have a heart attack. Are you okay?"

"I'm fine," she says. "We don't get along very well, and it's been a long time since we've seen each other. I'm just shocked to see him is all."

"You don't have to go with him. I'll go out there right now and tell him to get the hell off of my property."

"I'll be okay. I'll call you later," she says, as she kisses his cheek.

"I'm going to work tonight. I've been gone too long. I need to check on things and start getting back in the groove of things."

"Okay," she says. "Are you sure you're ready?"

He smiles. "Ready as I'll ever be." He leans down and kisses her softly. She pulls away quickly, I'm unsure if it's because she's aware of my presence or her nerves. Maybe both.

"Bye." She slips out the door and I morph outside beside her. "I'm sorry you had to see that." She means what happened between her and

George.

"I know. But you have other things to worry about, baby girl. Just remember, you have nothing to be sorry for, Charlotte. Your father is the one in the wrong."

Somehow, she convinces her father to take her to her motel room so they can speak with more privacy. The silence outside of the very limited conversation they have on the way there is almost choking. Her father is brooding; it's obvious he's working out in his head exactly what he wants to say. Meanwhile, Charlotte sits rigid, her hands twisted together in her lap. I hate how scared she looks right now.

Once in her room, he sits in my chair, leaning forward, elbows to knees. "You've been gone five years," he tells her, and looks at her where she sits on the bed.

"I didn't think you'd be keeping count." Her gaze is fixed on the floor, but her voice is steady.

"How have you survived off of thirty thousand dollars for five years?"

"I've managed," she tells him.

"How?" he pushes, his voice stern; making her tense.

Her gaze moves to his and she straightens her back. "Be strong, Charlotte," I encourage.

"Well, I slept in the 4Runner a lot," she admits, and I close my eyes, detesting the thought of her sleeping in a cold truck. "Sometimes people gave me money, and a place to stay for a night or two."

"You became a beggar?" he asks with skepticism.

"No," she states firmly. "I know you might find this hard to believe, father, but there are people out there that believe in what I can do. Those people were given comfort by me helping them communicate with their lost loved one. In gratitude, they'd offer me shelter and sometimes a little bit of money."

"Oh, God, Charlotte. You're going around telling people you can talk to the dead? Honey, do you know how wrong that is?" Shaking his head, he leans back in his seat. Anger rushes through me at the image of my fist making contact with his face, consuming my thought process.

"I'm helping souls cross over. I'm giving them peace. Why is that wrong?"

"Honey," he sighs before running a hand through his hair. "You're sick, and you need to come home." Charlotte's mouth falls open slightly, but no words come out. "You need to come home and we'll get you back to the doctors—"

"And drug me again?" she snaps. "No, Daddy. I'm not coming with you."

Mr. Acres runs a palm down his face. "Charlotte Anne, I'm not asking. You've gotten yourself in trouble with the law . . . I can't leave you out here."

"I'm not in trouble with the law!" she yells. "I helped a soul cross over by finding her murdered body. I didn't tell the police she spoke to me . . . I made up a story, but that is what happened. Casey Purcell appeared and led me to her corpse!"

"And now you're mixed up in all of this," he argues, shaking his head. "It's time to come home," he says, again.

"*You* sent me away!" she cries. "And now you're saying I need to come home? That's not my home anymore."

"And this place is? You're living in a motel, for Christ's sake," he counters, his voice edging on angry.

Charlotte inhales a ragged breath as she attempts to rein in her emotions. "I haven't bothered you for anything. You wanted me gone, out of sight, out of mind, Daddy. That's what you wanted, and I gave it to you because I knew you would never accept who I am now. I can see the dead. I can. And you can't live with that. So *you* sent me away. And you expect me to come home with you?"

"I thought you'd take the money and take off for a month, maybe two. I thought, maybe you needed a break . . . maybe Axel's memory was messing you up in the head."

"No. *You* messed me up in the head, Daddy," she yells. She's standing now, but he remains seated, his expression calm, as if he refuses to encourage her rage any further, after all, she is *sick* according to him. God, I want to fucking punch this guy. "You've never believed me . . . I mean, do you think I wanted this? Don't you think waking up to discover my brother, my best friend, was dead was bad enough? But to top it off, seeing dead people was what I wanted?"

"No, baby, I know it's not what you wanted," he tells her softly. I can tell he's coming at her with gloved hands now, trying to calm her down by being gentle. "When you come home, we can work through this. Your mama misses you, Charlotte. She's dying to see you."

"No, Daddy. I'm not going. No."

Mr. Acres stands and bows his head as he slips both hands in his pockets and sighs heavily. When he raises his head, his expression is stern. "I'm leaving in two days, and you're coming with me. The police released the 4Runner and I sold it to the junkyard."

"What?" she gasps in disbelief, stumbling back to catch herself on the dresser. "Why would you do that without discussing it with me first?"

"Because it was on its last leg."

"Charlotte," I whisper. "It's okay. Sniper can help us get you another car," I try to assure her, but she doesn't seem to acknowledge what I'm saying.

"But . . . it was his." She's looking at her father like he's just stabbed her in the heart and the betrayal of it is so much worse than what he's actually done. "How could you?" she asks as her voice cracks, and my fists clench when I realize why she's so upset. It was Axel's 4Runner. This guy is a dick!

Mr. Acres' jaw sets in annoyance and the muscles tic, but he moves to the door. "Two days," he says, again, before opening the door and leaving. The moment the door closes behind him, Charlotte collapses to the floor and begins to sob.

"Charlotte." I kneel beside her, wishing I could scoop her up, and sit her in my lap and wipe her heavy tears from her face. "Baby girl, you have to calm down. Breathe."

"He sold it. He sold my brother's car," she sobs, her eyes clenched closed in pain. "How could he?"

"I don't know," I tell her. "He wants you to come home. Taking your transportation away seems like a good way to convince you."

After a few minutes, she calms down and sits up, leaning her back against the bed's headboard. "He's staying at your parents' place. Time has run out, Ike. I have to tell them everything before he does and spins some crazy story."

This is the moment we've both been building toward. We've known it was coming, but even I'm starting to dread the end of this. When she tells my family and George the truth, it will bring me one step closer to having to leave them—to leaving her. But we have no choice now. We can't have her dad spinning Charlotte as some kind of mental patient.

"Call Sniper to come get you," I tell her. "Then call my mother and explain you need everyone to meet at her home. Tell her it's really important and you need her to get George there, too." With a slight nod, she pulls herself up and stands frozen for a moment. "Are you okay?" I ask her, even though I know she's not.

"I'm scared," she whispers.

"I know. I am, too," I admit. "Just know they'll believe you."

"He'll hate me," she cries softly. "And you'll go, and I'll be alone again. I wish you could just take me with you."

My heart feels like it has officially combusted into a million tiny pieces of pain. In helping me, I've only made things worse for her. "Charlotte, please." My voice shakes as I speak. "It's going to be okay. We will make sure of it. I'm not going to leave until it is, okay?" But I know deep down it may not be a promise I can keep. That invisible pull has strengthened as George has gotten better, and I find myself digging my heels into this world to keep it from taking me. But I'll fight it with every bit of strength I have to make sure she's okay.

"Call Sniper," I tell her, and after wiping her nose with her forearm, she nods once and moves toward the phone. I give her the numbers and she calls Sniper and my mother and sets everything in motion.

"Go shower and get ready. Sniper will be here soon."

Nodding numbly, she heads into the bathroom, and just before she closes the door, she says, "Ike." I turn and meet her gaze, her eyes red and swollen from crying.

"Yes, baby girl?"

"I love you." And although the words are beautiful, the pain in her expression as she speaks them twists my insides. Then she closes the door and leaves me aching with her words.

Chapter 22

Charlotte

When Sniper picks me up I must look a fright because he immediately seizes me into a big bear hug. "What happened?" he asks as I cry into his shirt.

"My father found me. He wants me to come home, and I have to tell everyone the truth before he tries to convince them I'm crazy."

"It'll be okay, love. I'm here. I'll help you. I know you can see Ike. And I'll be beside you every step of the way." I hug him tighter for saying that; I need someone to be with me, to stand beside me. I know Ike is on my side, but that won't help unless I can convince them.

Sniper drives to the McDermotts' B&B while I try not to vomit. "Did Beverly call George?"

"Yes," he answers. "But she didn't tell him it was for you. So he has no idea what's going on."

"Good," I exhale. "George is going to be . . . upset."

"Maybe at first, but so was I. It only took a little convincing."

"Yeah, but he'll feel like I betrayed him."

Sniper pats my leg before returning his hand to the steering wheel. "He may surprise you."

When we arrive, I see George's motorcycle out front and know he's already here. The car my father drove earlier today is also parked out front and my stomach clenches. I was hoping he wouldn't be here.

When we climb out of the truck, Ike reminds me to breathe as we make our way to the porch. Before I take the first step, George comes flying out of the front door and straight to me.

"What's going on, Charlotte?" His brows are furrowed in confusion. "My mother calls me here saying it's an emergency, and I get here and she says we're waiting on you."

"Let's get inside, George," Sniper urges as he places a hand at the small of my back.

"Your dad's in there," he warns, and I nod in understanding.

Once we're inside, Beverly hugs me, her gaze riddled with concern when she sees my face. "He was so panicked when he arrived, we had to tell him you called. I tried to hold off as long as I could."

"It's okay, Beverly. Thank you for calling everyone."

"Did you come here to save me from the abuse?" Cameron approaches; joking. I smile as I hug him, grateful for the humor even though it's wasted on me.

"Afraid not," I tell him.

"I don't know what's going on, but my brother is all kinds of wound up about it," he whispers.

"I'm going to explain."

Beverly leads me into the living room and my heart stops. My father is sitting across from Henry speaking in a hushed voice. Henry's brows are furrowed as his gaze meets mine and I know without a shadow of a doubt my father has already told him I'm crazy.

"Charlotte," Henry says, and attempts to stand, but I hold my hand up, telling him not to.

"Hi, Henry," I greet him. "Thanks for letting me come here to explain things."

"Get to it," Ike urges me. "No time to waste."

"Everyone," I call out with a shaky voice, and everyone stops to look at me. "Please sit down. I have something really important to discuss with you."

"Now, Charlotte Anne," my father interrupts and stands, giving me a stern look. "You don't need to bother these nice people with your problems." Tears sting my eyes. He really is trying to make me look insane. How could he do this to me?

"With all due respect, Mr. Acres." Sniper steps toward him, standing to his full length. "This lass has something to say, and she's going to say it. Now, you can either sit down and listen, or I'll escort you out of this house." My eyes are bugging out of my head, as are my father's. Everyone else darts their eyes to one another as we all stand frozen in place.

"What the hell is going on?" George finally breaks the silence.

"Charlotte will explain as soon as her father sits down," Sniper says, calmly, as his eyes remained fixed on my father. Dad sits down with a 'humph,' and everyone else takes a seat except for George, Sniper, and me.

"Go ahead, love. I'm here," Sniper encourages gently, arms crossed, showing everyone they better shut the hell up and listen or they'll be dealing with him.

I glance at Ike and he nods. "I'm here, baby girl. Go on. You can do this. Tell them the truth . . . all of it. Even how we met."

Shame floods through me, causing the blood to drain from my face. How we met is an ugly story. But George said he wants to see all of me, even the ugly parts. Looking back at George, I see he's watching me, probably wondering what I'm staring at. I give him a slight smile and take a deep breath. "Most of you know, and if you didn't, I'm sure my father, Wayne, here explained I come from Oklahoma." Beverly hands me a box of tissues from the table beside where she sits, and I realize my eyes are watering. "Thank you," I tell her as I take a few tissues.

"Six years ago, there was an accident. My brother, Axel, and I were on a motorcycle when someone pulled out in front of us. He died." I swallow hard; meeting my father's gaze and find his eyes are tearing up as well. "When I woke up, I had an injured back, a broken leg, and had somehow made my way out of a coma brought on by my brain swelling from the accident, only to discover Axel was dead." I continue to tell them how I started seeing the dead, how scared I was, and how everyone thought I was crazy.

"My parents took me to doctors, who put me on all kinds of crazy medication, and of course, it didn't help. It made it worse because I couldn't think right, but I was still seeing and hearing the dead."

"We did what we thought was right, Charlotte," my father interrupts defensively.

"Not a word out of you," Sniper snaps at him.

"I guess it became too much for them, so my father gave me a large sum of money and sent me away. I've been traveling around the states for the last five years helping the dead."

"Helping them do what, dear?" Beverly asks timidly.

"I only see the souls caught in limbo—the ones that are caught between this world and what lies ahead." Everyone is silent for a moment and Ike steps toward me.

"Tell them. Tell them about me." Tears roll down my face because I know how emotional everyone is about to get. I know George will be upset, and Ike will be one step closer to leaving this world. Everything will be different, and I dread it won't be in a good way.

"Casey Purcell," I say her name and everyone almost leans forward. "I lied to you, Henry. I told you I found her by accident. The truth is Casey showed me where her body was. Her family was falling apart, and she couldn't cross over until she knew they'd be okay. They couldn't grieve for her because they were still holding on to that last shred of hope she was out there and alive somewhere."

The room is silent. No one really knows what to say. "Keep going," Ike urges.

"After I dropped that letter in the mail, I kept driving. I had no idea what I was doing, or where I was going. I had no money, and I realized how lonely I was. My life had become nothing but helping the dead. I hadn't even tried to settle anywhere. I mean, my own family didn't believe me, so why would anyone else?" I inhale slowly before moving on to the next part. It's not easy to admit how weak I was—and still am. "My truck ran out of gas by Anioch Bridge, and I made the decision I was going to end it. I didn't want to live anymore, not the way I was anyway. So I climbed onto the railing of the bridge, and I was going to jump in and let the river drag me under and away."

My father stands and gasps, "Charlotte," but immediately sits when Sniper steps toward him. "Honey, you should have come home. I know you think we're awful, that we treated you wrong, but we love you, Charlotte." I don't meet his eyes. I can't. It's still the same man that thinks I'm crazy . . . that I'm delusional.

"Why didn't you do it?" George asks, and everyone snaps their heads up and eyes him. His arms are crossed and he's looking at me like he doesn't trust me—like the way I've feared he'd look at me when he found out about everything.

Swallowing hard, I feel a firm hand squeeze my shoulder. Looking back, I find Sniper's warm eyes and he nods once. "Someone stopped me," I admit as my gaze moves to Ike.

"I'm so glad I was there," he tells me, closing his eyes, as if the thought of if he hadn't been there pains him.

"It was Ike," I say, quietly, and everyone except my father gasps in unison. Before anyone can speak, I continue to explain what Ike said, and how he led me to town and told me who to talk to and where to go.

"We made a deal," I explain. "He'd help me find a job and a place to stay, and I'd help him with his unfinished business."

"And what was his unfinished business?" George snarls.

Ike

The room is uncomfortably quiet; everyone's eagerly awaiting Charlotte's answer to George's question. With eyes shimmering with tears, she meets his hard, unforgiving gaze. Her lips tremble when she tells him, "You, George. You're his unfinished business." My brother's arms fall to his side and his expression becomes stoic. He has no idea what to think or say, so he goes blank. "You know you were in bad shape," she tells him, but doesn't elaborate on the drugs. She doesn't want to out him in front of our family. "He can't leave until he knows you're okay. He's been here the entire time, watching you—all of you." She stares nervously across the room. My father stands and moves to sit near my mother, taking her shaky hand in his. *Oh, Mom.*

"I know you're all thinking this is crazy and impossible. That's what I thought at first, too," Sniper steps in to defend her. "But she told me things only Ike would know . . . things we joked about or did in the army. She's telling the truth. She can communicate with Ike. He's here, right now."

"You knew she was . . ." George stops. He wants to say 'crazy,' but thinks better of it.

"That night you got beat up," Sniper tells him. "That's when I found out."

"You got beat up?" my mother squawks as she turns to look at George. "Honey, you said you fell down the stairs." I never wanted my mother to find out how bad things had become for George.

"So you're telling me you can speak with Ike? Right here, right now?" Cameron jumps in, and I think he believes her. Or at least he wants to. He's always been open-minded, and at this moment, I couldn't be more grateful for that.

"Tell Cameron I hid my porno magazines in my closet. There's a little cutout over the shelf. Tell him to go get them," I say, with a nervous chuckle. And she repeats it to him, but not before she gives me a pointed look that says, *Really?* Cameron jumps up and dashes up the stairs, eager to either prove Charlotte is the real deal, or to retrieve the porn for later. I'm not sure which he's more excited about.

Wanting the others to believe in Charlotte as well, I proceed to tell her things to share with my family in hopes they're as receptive as my little brother.

"Henry, you talk to him. Especially when you're fly-fishing alone because it was something the two of you did a lot. He says you tell him it was a privilege to be his father, and how you wish you'd taken more time off and done more with him. He wants you to know you are the best father ever. He couldn't have picked anyone better than you." The sob that breaks free from my father is my undoing, and hot tears fall down my face. *Jesus, Pop* . . . He and my mother hold each other close, working through the raw pain that my memory brings.

Charlotte tries to rip the Band-Aid off and continues, "Beverly, the lasagna and tiramisu? That's why I mentioned them. He was there the night we met, and I just repeated what he said." My mother nods as she places a trembling hand to her lips. "He wants you to know he hears you singing when you're thinking of him." The tears run freely down my mother's face and I feel like I'm choking. As hard as this is for all of us, I have to continue. Charlotte stares at me, her own eyes red with unshed tears. She pauses and listens as I explain what I want her to relay, then she stutters, "Y-y-you are my sunshine. You used to sing that to him when he was little. He hears you sing it now." My mother keels over and sobs violently.

"Oh, baby boy. I love you so much," she cries out, and my heart feels like it's breaking.

"Charlotte Anne!" Her father stands, and this time, he doesn't let Sniper intimidate him. "That's enough!"

"Can't you tell this guy to fuck off?" I growl. She has to finish. They have to know I can hear them. That I know how much pain they're in.

"No, Ike, I can't," she answers in a hushed tone, and everyone freezes.

"He's speaking to you?" my father asks quietly.

"Yes, sir."

"W-w-what did he say?" my mother questions.

"He wants me to tell my father to fuck off," she says, quietly, and then adds, "Sorry." Her father pinches his lips together; I'm guessing wanting to say something shitty, but won't do it in front of my folks.

The room goes silent again until we hear heavy footsteps coming down the stairs. A moment later, Cameron stomps in the room with a stack of pornos in his hands. "They were exactly where she said they would be," he announces.

All eyes move to Charlotte and she looks at me. "Keep going. They believe you," I tell her, with a small smile. Then we both look to George and realize he doesn't appear to be quite convinced. She walks toward him and takes his hand in hers.

"The song . . . the bet I won? He's the one that told me it was your favorite," she explains, but he refuses to look at her. "He loves you so much, George. He can't go until he knows you'll be okay."

George jerks his hand from hers and barrels out the front door. She chases after him and Sniper follows, too. She catches him just before he hits the front porch steps. "George, please," she pleads. "I'm so sorry I didn't tell you sooner, but you weren't ready. You'd barely speak to me at first. I needed to get to know you, and you needed to clean up."

He rips away from her, his eyes brimming with angry tears. "So it was all bullshit? You faked liking me to do this?" he snarls.

"What?" she gasps. "No. George, I've meant everything I said, I l—" She stops. She doesn't want to admit she loves him . . . and maybe it's because I'm here, or maybe she isn't sure how he'll take it.

"Are you the one that tipped Roger off about me and Misty?" he asks point-blank, and Charlotte's mouth drops open.

"Oh, shit," I breathe.

Charlotte remains quiet, eyes wide, until he asks again, "Did you? Misty told me someone wrote an anonymous letter. It was you, wasn't it?"

Charlotte looks to Sniper whose brows would be touching his hairline, if he had one. "I know that probably seems bad, but—" Before she can finish, he's halfway down the steps.

"Go after him! Make him understand," I insist, and she leaps over all four steps to the bottom to catch him, but loses her footing and trips, landing hard on her knee.

"Bloody hell," Sniper curses and follows after them.

"Are you okay, Charlotte?" I ask, but she ignores me.

George turns and rolls his eyes as he shakes his head in frustration. He yanks her up, steadying her on her feet. The way she can't stop staring at George tells me how much she loves him and how destroyed she feels by the look in his eyes. At least he cares enough not to just leave her. But as soon as she's steady, he whips around and storms off.

"George," she yells as she begins stumbling, the pain in her knee obvious. She limps quickly after him, but he doesn't stop. "She was giving you drugs! I had to get you clean so I could tell you the truth. I had to save you," she cries. She stumbles again, but catches herself and continues to limp after him.

"Goddamn it, George!" Sniper yells. "Stop!"

George turns and glares, which gives Charlotte just enough time to catch up to him again. She doesn't grab, more like slams in to him, and clings for dear life, burying her face in his chest. "Please don't go. Don't you see, George," she pleads. "He saved me so I could save you, which in a way means, you saved me, too." George's arms lay limp at his sides as she holds him tightly, his jaw set. He swallows hard, refusing to look at her. But the look in his eyes says it all. He's hurt. Mentioning me has affected him more than we thought, and I'm terrified he'll return to his destructive ways.

"Tell him I'm still here," I tell her. "Tell him to say or ask anything, I'll hear him."

Charlotte stands upright and wipes at her face with her soiled hands. "He wants you to know he's still here and you can ask him anything."

George shakes his head in disbelief, anger lacing his features. "George, man, she's telling you the truth," Sniper says. "This is your chance, brother, to tell Ike something. Don't miss your chance to say good-bye."

"You're a fucking asshole for not telling me how crazy she is," he spats. "And you," he adds, and points to Charlotte, who cowers away slightly, "you need to stay away from me." Spinning on his heel, he bolts and she follows. "Please don't leave," she begs, managing to snag him by the arm.

Whipping around, he bends so he can meet her gaze. "Leave me alone!" he growls in her face. "Do not follow me, don't come and see me, and do not come near me again!"

Sniper pushes him away from her. The rage in his eyes palpable on a scary level. "I hate to say it, mate, but you're a fucking idiot. Sod off!"

George watches as Sniper cocoons Charlotte in his arms as she cries, "I'm so sorry, Ike. I'm so sorry. I messed it all up."

I'm seeing red, I'm so angry. "No you didn't," I try to comfort her. "He's an idiot. I'm sorry he did this."

"George, you better go," Charlotte's father suggests before taking Charlotte from Sniper and leading her toward the house. Charlotte, so lost in her pain, doesn't seem to notice who has her. *God, I did this to her.* She's crushed. We both knew George would have a hard time accepting the truth, but he's acting like a fucking psycho.

Charlotte makes it up the stairs with the help of her father when George shouts, "Charlotte!" She turns and acknowledges him, her face puffy from crying. "I want to know if he got my last email."

He's testing her. He wants to see if she's the real deal. "You're a real dick for not asking her that first before freaking out on her," I tell him, even though he can't hear me. Charlotte's gaze moves to mine, waiting for me to answer, eager for a chance to prove herself to him.

I glare at George but stop when I see the pain on his face. "Damn it," I sigh. "He told me he missed me and said he couldn't wait to have me come home." She nods and repeats the words and everyone is silent as George stares back at her.

"I'm telling the truth, George. I can see him right now," she whispers. "You're both handsome, look a lot alike, but he's a little bigger. He has amazing brown eyes, very soft, but yours are darker. I know it's hard to believe, but it's true."

George doesn't respond. A single tear falls down his cheek and after a moment, he turns and heads for his bike. And Charlotte sobs uncontrollably as we all watch him take off.

Chapter 24

Charlotte

"Are you all right?" my father asks as he holds me tight. I can't help the way I lash out at him.

"Do you care? Looks like he believed I'm a nut job, just like you wanted," I cry.

My father's arms drop from around me just as Beverly approaches and pulls me back in the living room. "I'm sorry about George's reaction, dear. This is a little surprising to all of us," she states softly.

"I believe you, Char," Cameron pipes in as he thumbs through a Playboy. In a flash, Beverly snaps the magazine from his hands and smacks him upside the head with it. "Jesus, Ma," Cameron laughs as he scratches his head.

"Ike McDermott, I can't believe you had these," she says, and my heart stills. She believes me. She believes he's here. My eyes dart over to Ike and he smiles softly at me. "Is he here . . . right now, Charlotte?" Beverly asks, and when I meet her gaze, I see hope.

"He is," I answer in a husky voice.

I spend the next two hours communicating Ike's words to his family. By the end, we're all crying again. My father left at some point, which I'm highly grateful for. Henry and Beverly hug me tightly, both thanking me a hundred times over.

"Will he cross over now?" Henry asks; his eyes shiny with fresh tears.

"Soon. If he thinks George is okay . . . then probably very soon."

Chapter 25

Charlotte

Ike decided to stay with George last night to make sure he was okay. If there was a problem, he promised to let me know so I could tell Sniper. We all agreed I needed to let George have some space. My father never came to see me off when I left the McDermotts' house, and for that, I'm glad. I guess he knew I was a wreck, and pushing me wouldn't earn him any points. So when there's a knock at my door the next afternoon, I huff, just knowing it's him. And even though my father is the last person in the world I want to see right now, when I open my door and see who it is, I wish it was my father.

"Detective," I say, morosely. A tiny woman is standing next to him, and behind her, a short man with thin hair. I recognize them immediately. They're Casey's parents. I saw them the first night I met Casey at the restaurant in Vermont.

"Ahem." Someone clears their throat and I see Henry is behind them. "Forgive the intrusion, Charlotte. But may we come in?"

I look down at my sweatpants and Axel's old T-shirt, realizing I look like hell after crying all night, but I open the door, unsure of what else to do, and let them all in. Once we're all inside my small room, Henry and I sit on the end of the bed while the Purcells take a seat at the two chairs at the small table by the door. Detective Andrews stands rigidly next to them.

"Do you know who these people are?" Henry asks, jutting his chin toward the Purcells.

"Casey Purcell's parents," I answer.

"They've been in town since they discovered Casey's body," Henry explains. "I told them and the detective here, you may know more." Frantically, my gaze meets his, and I want to feel betrayed, but when I see the sadness in his eyes, I know he only wants to give these people peace like I gave to him and Beverly. "It's the right thing to do," he tells me.

Closing my eyes, I take a deep breath and then fix my gaze on Mrs. Purcell. "I met Casey in Vermont. You were having dinner with her sister. She was there . . . you just couldn't see her. But I could. I have the ability to speak with the dead . . . their souls, that is. They're caught in limbo with unfinished matters." The Purcells glance back and forth to one another, and it's not hard to tell they're not swallowing the pill I'm giving them.

"Mr. McDermott, you said she had more information. This is absurd," Detective Andrews intervenes.

"Just wait, Detective Andrews," Henry insists, holding a hand up to him, before looking back to me and nodding once, telling me to continue.

"She said you guys were falling apart and were all a mess. That you all needed to know she was dead so you could let go of the hope you were clinging on to. I drove here to Virginia because I had to see her body for myself before I could report it. I made an anonymous report. I can see you're having a hard time believing what I'm telling you, and that's exactly what I was afraid of."

"Do you know who killed her?" Mrs. Purcell asks timidly.

"Are you sure you want to know the details?"

The Purcells look to one another again before looking back to me. Mr. Purcell nods once.

"It was a Friday," I begin, my stomach clenching as I remember Casey's version of the events that transpired that night. "She was out with her roommate and her roommate's boyfriend. They'd left her; they were drunk and got caught up in each other. They knew other people there, so they figured she'd be okay if they left. Casey mentioned an older guy asked her to dance. She thought he was cute, so she agreed. They had a few drinks and she started feeling woozy so she told him she was leaving. She was going to try and walk back to her apartment."

Mr. Purcell shakes his head. "I told her never to walk alone at night."

"Not now, Leonard," Mrs. Purcell scolds. "Please, go on, dear," she encourages.

"She blacked out at some point on the way home and when she came to he was . . ." I can't say it. Not to them. It's too horrific to think, let alone say out loud. Casey woke up in the back of a van, her face plastered to the floor as he raped her. Even she couldn't finish without tearing up when she told me about it. My stomach is in knots but I know must continue. "He was . . . on top of her," I manage, and the Parcells immediately keel over; crying.

"I should stop," I say to Henry, who is rubbing circles on my back.

"No, we want to know," Mrs. Purcell pipes up; her voice shaky. "If she endured it, I can at least endure hearing it."

I nod once in understanding. "She screamed as loud as she could. She tried to fight him but he was too strong. She said her throat burned she screamed so loud, but he started bashing her in the head with something . . . she thought it was a flashlight. That was the last thing she remembered."

"Was it the man at the bar she danced with?" Detective Andrews asks, and I'm shocked he's entertaining the thought that he may actually believe me. "Another girl went missing a week ago," he informs me. "We think her disappearance could be connected to Casey's." My heart sinks. I should've gone to the police and tried to help. If it was the same guy, maybe I could've stopped it. The look of horror on the Purcells' faces is too much to bear and tears stream down my face as guilt slithers through me. I've been so busy running from my gift, only using it because I absolutely had to, when I could have been helping, really helping.

"His name is Jeremy. At least that's what he told her."

"Is she still here?" Mr. Purcell asks; his voice hopeful.

"No, sir. I'm sorry. But she rode with me from Vermont to here and told me some stories about you, both of you. You guys used to take a road trip to Montana once a year, right?" They both gasp, their eyes lighting with hope.

"She couldn't tell you where he went?" Andrews asks.

"It doesn't work like that. They're only tied to this world to the people they have to help. She needed to help her family. Nothing mattered more than that to her."

Mrs. Purcell sniffles. Taking her husband's hand, she gazes at him with tear-filled eyes. "It was killing us not knowing. Now, it hurts, but at least we know she's really gone."

We talk for a bit longer, and I give the Purcells all of the information I can. When they leave, they both hug me and Detective Andrews leads them out. "You're not leaving town anytime soon, are you?" he asks me.

"My father wants me to leave with him tomorrow."

"I may have more questions," he says, as if that will make me stay.

"He junked my truck, and I just lost my job at the restaurant. I'm not sure I have much of a choice at this point."

"We have plenty of room for you, Charlotte," Henry says. "You don't have to go anywhere. You can sleep in Ike's old room." My eyes clench closed as an ache forms in my chest. Ike will go soon.

"I'll be in touch first thing tomorrow," Detective Andrews says to Henry before leaving, noting my emotional state.

"Ike's a special man, isn't he?" Henry says, as he leads me back in and shuts the door.

"Yes, he is," I agree, wiping at my face with my arm. "One of the best men I've ever known."

"And George is pretty special, too, huh?" He gives me a knowing smirk. *Is it that obvious I love them both?*

"Ike saved me," I explain. "He came out of nowhere and changed my life. He's everything good in the world."

Henry smiles as he nods. "That's a good way to describe him."

"And George, there's a lot of love in there, ya know? He seems so . . . tough, but he has such a soft heart. I'm in love with both of your sons, Henry," I admit, and although I'm scared of what he'll say, it feels so good to say it to someone, and get it off my chest.

"So when Ike leaves, to you, it will feel like he's died," he says, grimly, with sympathy in his eyes.

"It'll feel like half of my heart is going with him," I weep, wiping at my face.

"Will you stay? I mean . . . after he goes?"

An image of George flickers through my mind, his dark eyes and easy smile—he's really beautiful when he shows the real him. When Ike leaves, if I leave George behind, I think I'll only be a shell of a person. But he's so angry with me, what else can I do? "I love George, Henry, but . . ."

"But he's acting like a jackass?"

I smile faintly. "Ike and I knew he might take it rough, but I didn't expect so much . . . anger."

Henry pats my shoulder. "I hope you won't give up on him. Give him a little time to come around. He's deeply hurt, is all."

"I'll try," I promise, but I'm not sure George will give me the time of day.

Ike

Mope. Mope. Mope. If you looked up the word 'mope' in the dictionary, George's picture would be right beside it. He's walked around in a daze, brooding for hours at a time. His dejected mood saddens me, but I will say this, he hasn't done drugs, and that is a very good thing. All he's done is sit around and be pissed off.

"George, I know you're hurting, brother. Stop being a douche and go talk to her," I tell him, and I'm filled with sorrow that he can't hear my words. It upsets me to see him like this. This is not how he normally is at all.

When there's a knock at the door, he sits frozen for a moment, debating on whether to ignore it or not. Maybe he thinks it's Charlotte. "George, I know you're in there," Sniper yells from outside, and George rolls his eyes. "Open the fucking door, ya wanker."

"Piss off!" George yells back, remaining seated on the couch.

The doorknob turns slightly, but it's locked. After it jiggles a bit, the lock pops and Sniper opens the door and enters, credit card in hand. "What the fuck, dude?" George snaps. "You're breaking in to my house now?"

"Oh, shut it," Sniper orders. "I'm not going to let you sit here and be pissed off. Do you even know why you're so angry?"

"Oh, let's see," George begins, his voice laced with sarcasm, as Sniper sits on the sofa chair next to the couch. "She lied about who she is and why she's here. I don't even know what to think about the crazy ramblings she's spewing; that she can see and speak to my dead brother. Oh, and let's not forget she ratted me out to Roger and I got my ass beat."

"You were fucking his girlfriend," Sniper says, dryly. "Kind of warranted an ass beating, if you ask me."

"Maybe, but she set that shit in motion," George snaps.

"She didn't mean for you to get hurt. She just wanted him to scare some sense into you."

"I'm not scared of that douche bag, and if it had been one-on-one, I would've taken him. They jumped me."

"I know," Sniper agrees, as do I. "She just wanted to get Misty away from you so you could get clean."

George shakes his head before leaning forward, resting his arms on his knees. "I really thought she might be the one. I mean, I didn't know what to think of her at first. I thought she was different."

"George," Sniper says, gruffly. "The girl is in love with you."

"I know, she started to tell me last night."

"And?"

"And how do I know she's being truthful, Sniper?" George asks as he stands and moves to the kitchen, grabbing a Coke out of the fridge.

"You really don't see it?" Sniper asks in disbelief, standing and walking over to the counter that separates the kitchen and living room. "The way she looks at you. Hell, even when she gives you shit, trying to piss you off, I can see how she feels."

George shakes his head. "She did it for Ike."

"No, shit head, she did it for both of you. Did you not see the look on her face when you told her you never wanted to see her again?"

George's face blanches with embarrassment and his eyes narrow as he remembers. "I was angry."

"You were a dick is what you were. She and Ike knew you would be upset and maybe have a hard time coming to terms with it all, but none of us thought you'd react like that."

"Look!" George shouts. "I'm just getting clean so I'm on edge. I fall for this strange drifter who keeps pushing me all the time, only to find out it was supposedly motivated by my brother's soul that's stuck in limbo because of me. Forgive me if I wasn't as rational as you would've liked."

"So you don't believe her?" Sniper asks point-blank.

"I don't know," he sighs. "She can be pretty damn convincing."

Sniper shakes his head and runs a hand over his shaved scalp. "I believe her."

"Her father says she's crazy. You heard the guy."

"Her father's a dipshit, and you know it," Sniper booms. "I know she's telling the truth, and if you had stayed yesterday and listened, you would've seen it for yourself."

"Man," George sighs as he places his Coke can on the counter. "I know everyone likes her, and even I was caught up in it. But no matter what, Sniper, I'm not good for her either. She needs to go home and be with her family so they can help her."

"You'd really let her leave?" Sniper's expression is sheer disappointment and shock.

"I think it would be best."

"Bullshit," Sniper snaps and stomps toward the door. "I can't see Ike or hear what he's saying unless she tells me, but I know him like the back of my hand, and so do you. I know he's here! And there is no fucking way he's not crazy about her. But he's dead, and he's crossing over soon. He has to leave her. You, on the other hand, are behaving like a fucking idiot. You could have her if you wanted, but instead you're choosing to sit here and be pissed off and miserable. Maybe you don't deserve her."

My eyes are wide as George silently watches Sniper exit, slamming the door behind him. A moment later, the door opens, and Sniper pokes his head back in. "And she's keeping her job at the restaurant if she wants it. If you make her leave, I'll be going elsewhere as well." Then he slams the door again.

George stumbles backward until he meets the fridge, his expression heavy with uncertainty. "Don't let her go, George." I wish I could shake some sense into him, but I can't. Here I am, wishing I could keep Charlotte for myself, but hoping against all odds that she and

George will end up together. *How fucked up is that?*

Chapter 27

Charlotte

Sniper arrives not long after Henry leaves. My tear ducts are on strike at the moment, dried up from overuse, but if they were working, I'd cry the moment I lay eyes on his somber face. He comes in, shutting the door behind him.

"I'm sorry, Charlotte," he says, quietly. I sit on my bed and hug my knees.

"For what?" I ask in a husky voice. I'm emotionally exhausted. "You've done nothing but try and help me." Just then, Ike appears, and I instantly feel worse because his expression is sad and worried. "Ike is here," I tell Sniper.

"How's he doing?" I ask both of them. They both release a snort.

"He's still processing," Ike says, gently.

"He's being an ass," Sniper mutters. "I know you're sad, but get dressed. I'm taking you out to dinner. Anna's going to meet us."

"Sniper, I'm really not in the mood."

"I know, and that's why I'm making you go."

"Who's running Ike and George's?"

"While George has been out the last week or so, we promoted Libby to temporary manager and Greg's been running the kitchen when I'm not there. We've hired a new bartender and two servers as well."

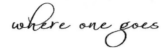

Letting out an exasperated breath, I stand. "I need to go and see my father."

"No problem. We'll go get dinner and then we'll head over to the McDermotts' place."

I refuse to go into Ike and George's, afraid George might be there, so Anna, Sniper, and I sit at the bar at Sam Snead's, which is a block away. I insisted we sit at the bar; I thought a table would provoke too much conversation, which I am not in the mood for. Ike stays with us, near me constantly, and although we can't speak, I find it comforting. I order a salad, but only pick at it; my stomach is knotted up with anxiety. Sniper keeps giving me worried looks, but mostly remains focused on speaking with Anna, to keep her from trying to talk to me too much. We told her my father was in town and we don't get along very well, so at least she has a reason as to why I'm acting standoffish.

After we eat, we have a few drinks, which help me relax a little, but when Sniper runs to the restroom, I tell Anna I'm going to step outside for a moment for some air. Once outside, I lean against the building, gulping in the cold night air. Fall has officially landed here in the mountains and the crisp air causes my breath to fog whenever I exhale.

"How're you holding up?" Ike asks.

"About as well as can be expected, I guess."

"He'll come around," he tells me.

"Every which way I look, there's pain, Ike."

"Hey there, Char." My head jerks up, and I see Roger standing about two feet from me. Where in the hell did he come from?

"Oh . . . uh . . . hi," I manage, wondering if he heard me talking to Ike, which would look like I was talking to myself. Misty probably told him I do that.

"What are you doing out here all by yourself?" he asks as he slides his hands into his jacket pockets.

"Just needed some air," I say. "You meeting someone?" It's a dumb question, and it's none of my business, but I don't know what else we have to talk about.

"Nope. All alone." His mouth curves slightly into a mischievous grin and my heart quickens. Is he going to hit on me?

"Walk away, Charlotte," Ike instructs me, and without thinking, I head toward Ike and George's. "No, back inside," Ike hisses, but Roger is already beside me, walking with me. I could turn and run back in to Sam Snead's, but I'm not sure if I have any reason to panic just yet. He hasn't been rude or aggressive.

"Where's Misty?" I ask, attempting to fill the awkward silence.

"Wouldn't know." He shrugs. "We're not together anymore."

"I'm sorry to hear that."

"Are you? I mean, you're the one that left me the letter about her and George." My stomach clenches. I did do that, and it led to George getting jumped. I decide not to lie. "I didn't mean for you to hurt him."

Roger snorts. "What did you think would happen? That we'd have a calm conversation about it over coffee?"

I pinch my lips together. I did want Roger to scare him; that is true. But I truly thought I could keep it from getting physical with Sniper's help. "I never meant for you and your brother to jump him."

Roger sighs and runs a hand over his dark hair. "I'm just curious, why'd you do it? Do you want McDermott that bad, or do you just hate Misty that much?"

"I had my reasons; although now, it seems like it was a horrible idea."

"Didn't get your happy ending with Georgey?" Roger mocks and Ike morphs in front of us. His eyes are narrowed as he glares at Roger.

"Get the fuck away from this guy! Now!"

Realizing we're now in front of Ike and George's, I stop. "I have friends waiting on me. I gotta go. Later, Roger," I say numbly.

"Sure," Roger nods. "But we have something to discuss first."

My brows rise to my hairline. "And what is that?"

"You and George aren't together, are you?" he asks as he steps toward me, causing me to step back.

"Tell him it's none of his business," Ike growls.

"Is there a reason you want to know?"

Roger steps closer and I back away again until my back hits the brick wall of the building. He's too close to me now, merely an inch or two away, and my heart is pounding in my chest. "I was just thinking, maybe you and I . . . ya know . . . could find some comfort in each other." He places his hands against the building on each side of my head and brings his face close enough to mine that I can feel his warm breath.

Licking my lips, I swallow past the nervous knot in my throat. It was only days ago I was basking in the feeling of him flirting with me, but that was before I knew who he was. Now, I'm freaking out. I try to hide the fear I'm feeling, but my voice trembles when I say, "I don't think so, Roger."

He grins, his mouth quirking to one side. "I can see how nervous you are. You don't have to be."

"You have me backed against a building," I point out as my chest heaves heavy breaths.

His dark eyes rove over me before meeting my gaze again. "You are a beautiful woman, Char," he says, quietly.

"Please back away from me, Roger," I ask calmly.

"Sure," he agrees after a brief pause. "But first . . ." he leans in and presses his lips to mine. His beard scratches my face and I pinch my mouth shut tightly as his tongue attempts to thrust in to my mouth. My hands are on his arms, pushing him as hard as I can, but he's not budging.

"Motherfucker!" Ike shouts, and Roger is torn away from me. *How the hell did that happen?* When I look down, Roger is quickly jumping to his feet and glaring. Then someone tackles him and they both tumble to the ground. My mind spins as I realize it wasn't Ike that yelled at him . . . it was George. He straddles Roger and begins pounding his fist to his face. Roger flails and tries to roll away but George is moving too fast.

"George," I yell, and move toward them, but Ike morphs in front of me.

"Don't go near them," he warns. Suddenly, Sniper is there peeling George off of Roger. Roger's face is covered in blood, but slowly, he manages to stand. Even though his face is mangled and bloody, he laughs as he wipes at his mouth.

"Doesn't feel so good when someone touches what you deem as yours, does it, McDermott?"

Both men are breathing heavily as they stare at one another and Sniper remains between them. George's shoulders are tensed, his arms hanging by his sides as if he's poised to attack again. His gaze flickers to mine briefly before returning to Roger's. "No. It doesn't," he finally says, some of the tension rolling off of him. Sniper holds a firm hand to George's chest as George steps toward Roger.

"I owe you an apology," he tells Roger, and my mouth drops open.

"Holy shit," Anna whispers, and I realize for the first time that she's there, and her arms are holding me. "Did he just apologize?"

"I was wrong to see her. I knew she was taken. I'm sorry," George says. Roger's mouth tightens, and the two stare at one another for a long moment.

"Well, I'd say we're pretty squared away now," Roger finally says. Reaching out a hand, the two shake. *Well I'll be damned.* Before he turns, he says, "She's a good girl." He juts his chin at me. "Make sure you give her plenty of attention. Don't make the same mistake I did." When he walks away, we all stare after him in silence.

"Why were you with him?" George asks, not looking at me, but there's a certain accusatory undertone in his voice. He's pissed.

"We were at Sam Snead's. I came out to get air," I snap, not appreciating his tone. "He was there."

"He did that shit on purpose, ya know?" Sniper says, and I snap my gaze to his.

"What?" I ask, confused.

"He wanted George to see you with him. Show him how it feels."

"Yeah, but I didn't want to kiss him. He forced that on me."

"He kissed you?" Anna shrieks.

"Yeah," George growls. "Had her pinned up against the building." His dark eyes meet mine again, briefly, almost glaring at me. *Does he think I wanted Roger to kiss me?*

"Yes, and I was trying to get him off of me when George showed up," I say to Anna, but I'm clearly saying it to George as well.

"Your knight in shining armor," Anna says, and smiles at George, but she's the only one. She has no idea what's transpired the last couple of days so her smile falters when she sees Sniper shake his head no, letting her know not to go there.

"Are you all right?" George asks, still not looking at me.

"Look at her, George!" Ike shouts from where he stands beside me.

"Stop shouting, Ike," I say to him calmly. His emotion is distracting.

"What's he saying?" Sniper asks.

"He's telling George to look at me," I reply quietly. George's gaze meets mine, his dark eyes swimming with so many emotions; hurt, anger, confusion, and guilt. We're all silent for a beat as George and I remain with our gazes locked, staring at one another. Silently, I'm pleading with him. *Don't walk away from me. Please believe me.* But I'm not sure he sees it. He's too caught up in his own thoughts.

"Does someone want to tell me what's going on?" Anna asks, breaking the moment.

"I'll explain later, lass," Sniper tells her. "Let's give them a few minutes."

After they've made it all the way back to Sam Snead's, I take a hesitant step toward George. "How are you feeling?"

"Like shit," he answers immediately, and my stomach clenches. He's been dealing with so much in the last few days, including fighting withdrawals. How could he not feel bad?

"Are you still experiencing withdrawals?"

"That's not the only reason why I feel like shit." Shoving his hands in his pockets, he looks up to the sky, his breath escaping his mouth in tiny bouts of fog.

"He feels bad for how he treated you," Ike says, as we both watch George. "He loves you, Charlotte." My gaze flicks to Ike's, my eyes brimming with tears. Ike's jaw is set, muscles tensed as he pleads his brother's case. He wants us to end up together even though he, too, is in love with me.

"Is he here?" George asks, bringing me back into the moment.

"He is," I say, as I clear my throat in an attempt to hide my brief moment of devastation at Ike's words. "George?"

"Yeah?"

"I know you're going through some stuff, you're angry with me and hurt, but . . . will you come somewhere with me?"

"Where?" he asks with uncertainty.

"To the Mercers' house. Their daughter, she speaks to me too. I haven't told them yet. We were waiting until we told you first."

He snorts and shakes his head as if he can't believe what I'm saying. "We?"

"Ike and I agreed you should be the first to know, and I promised Maggie Mercer as soon as you knew, I would help her."

"I don't think that's a good idea, Charlotte," George says, as he scratches the back of his neck.

Desperate for a chance to show him what I can do, and take him somewhere outside of his own grief, I seize his hand in mine. "If you'll come with me, let me show you something, I'll never ask anything of you again. I'll leave town with my father tomorrow and you'll never have to think of me again."

"Charlotte, you don't have to leave town," Ike says.

"If he doesn't believe me, I'll go, Ike," I tell him. George scowls at me, his brows furrowed. I won't ignore Ike anymore; he deserves better. If George chooses not to believe that I can see and communicate with his brother, that's his choice. But Ike is here, and I'll acknowledge him for as long I can see him. I'm not sure if it's my pleading gaze or the desperation in my voice but George nods once and follows me after I say, "Please, George. Please."

Sniper stays to keep an eye on the restaurant while George and I go on our little field trip. We take George's Bronco; he even helps me climb in, but his touch sends an ache rushing through me—unlike the last time. The ride is silent; neither of us knows what to say. There's nothing else I can say. Now I can only show him and hope it's enough.

The Mercers don't think twice about inviting us in when we show up unannounced after dark, even though Mrs. Mercer is already in her cotton nightgown and loose robe, ready to turn in for the night. They lead us in to the dining room and Mrs. Mercer sets about making us coffee, even though we insisted she didn't have to. While she busies herself, Mr. Mercer makes small talk with George, and George does his best to be polite, even though his mind is a wreck. Maggie is standing behind her father, quiet and patient, when she finally asks, "I know I'm not supposed to speak to you in front of them, but are you here for me?"

I nod once in response. When we all have our coffee and cookies—because bless Mrs. Mercer, she can't have a guest sit at her table without food and a drink—I clear my throat and begin to explain what I can do and tell them I can see Maggie. Mrs. Mercer immediately starts crying as I repeat what Maggie asks me to tell them, things only they would know. Mr. Mercer wraps an arm around her shoulder, his expression blank and unreadable.

George sits quietly, taking it all in, but when I stand, he stands, too. "May I go to her room? She's asking me to. She has something she wants me to find for you." Mr. Mercer nods once and as Maggie leads me, they all follow. Once in her room, Maggie indicates she'd like me to open the closet door. Inside, all of her clothes still hang—I'm guessing just the way she left them.

"I had been wearing a jacket the day before I passed. The necklace my mother told you about is in the pocket. The blue one there." And Maggie points.

Fishing my hand inside, I grasp the necklace and pull it out. Mrs. Mercer's eyes go wide and Mr. Mercer stumbles back. George catches him and helps him sit on the bed while he collects himself.

"She says the chain broke and she stuck it in her pocket, meaning to show it to you, but she wasn't feeling well, and she forgot." Gently, I place the cross and chain in Mrs. Mercer's hand as she weeps. Then, I tell them Maggie's good-bye. I repeat her words of gratefulness and love while the Mercers cry softly, hanging on my every word.

"She's going to wait until we leave and give you a few moments to say good-bye to her, and then she'll go."

"Where?" George asks. "Where will she go?"

I shrug sympathetically. It's a question I wish I could answer. "Where one goes when they cross over."

We say our good-byes to the Mercers, who hug me fiercely and thank me profusely. Before we leave, Mr. Mercer hands me my necklace and gazes down at me with red and swollen eyes. "This is yours, child," he tells me.

"No, sir. I still owe you money," I say, as I try and hand it back to him.

"No, you owe us nothing. You've given us peace, and we will forever be indebted to you."

"You owe me nothing, sir. You helped me on one of the coldest and darkest nights of my life. I could never repay you for that."

He smiles sadly. "I know a good way. Come have dinner with us again. We'd love your company." Then he looks to George. "You too, son. You're welcome any time."

"There's a strong possibility I may be heading home tomorrow," I confess, not even glancing at George to see his reaction. If he looks like he doesn't care, it'll only hurt me worse, and right now that's all I see and feel—hurt.

I promise the Mercers I won't leave town without saying good-bye, and then George and I leave. He drives me back to my motel in silence. I want to ask him what he's thinking; did he see the truth, did he feel it? But I don't. I'm going to let him process this, and when he's ready, if he ever is, he can ask me anything. When he parks in front of my room, he stares straight ahead, refusing to look at me. To my right, Sniper's truck is parked; he'd said he'd leave it and have Anna drive him home when he was done at the restaurant. He didn't want me to be without a vehicle, stating my father was a *shit head* for selling my truck. Can't say I disagree with him.

I realize this may be the last time I ever see George McDermott, the soul that so closely matches my own. My heart wants to keel over and die at the thought, but I've done all I can. The fact I can see the dead and his brother led me here to save him may seem impossible. I get that; it's hard for some people to accept. But if George loves me—really loves me—is it so wrong to hope he could operate on a little blind faith?

Moments come and go; quick flickers in time. Yet those moments can have the profoundest impact on our lives. Either we seize them, and wield them to our needs, or we let them go. It's the moments we let go that, I believe, remain with us strongest—because regret is something that never leaves us. And I know, in this moment, I must make one last attempt to reach George, or I'll regret it for the rest of my life.

Quickly, and without thought, I climb over and straddle him, seizing his face in my hands and forcing him to look at me. He's stunned, but doesn't push me off, placing his hands timidly on my hips. My mouth is dry as I stare down at him, willing him to see me, to see the truth. There are a million things I want to say, things I want to try and explain, but I fear I'll only be wasting my breath. Unhooking the necklace my brother gave me years ago, I place it around George's neck.

"Axel gave me this the last Christmas he was alive," I tell him as my fingers rub over the cross. "I've worn it every day since then until I gave it to Mr. Mercer the first night I arrived to hold until I could pay him back. I want you to have it."

"Charlotte, I can't—"

"Just keep it. Please. I want to give you something, one of my only treasures in this world." Then I lean in and gently press my lips to his. The kiss begins softly, but then it deepens as I do my best to convey my desperation, my need for him to accept this—to accept me. When he doesn't seem responsive at first, my insides wither, but after a moment, his fingers thread through my hair and his tongue sweeps inside my mouth, lighting me on fire. My insides burn with want and fear, but I push it all aside, and when I know I can't kiss him any longer without completely destroying myself, I pull back, meeting his dark gaze.

"I love you, George McDermott," I whisper, my voice cracking as I struggle to keep from crying. "And if that's not enough, if you think I'm crazy or a con artist or whatever it is you're thinking, I hope you'll try and remember how I feel about you when I'm gone. That I love you, and I think you're a great man. Maybe you're broken, but so am I. Broken doesn't mean we're valued any less, it just means we've loved someone so much and so fiercely that losing them feels like we've lost part of ourselves. I don't want to lose you, too. Ike will go soon," I say, with great emphasis, hoping to express how important it is that he realizes this. "Even if you think I'm a sham, I hope you'll talk to him and say good-bye. He'll hear you." I kiss him softly once more, allowing my lips to linger against his for a long moment, then climb off him and hop out of his truck. He waits until I'm inside my room before he pulls away. I crawl in to bed and cry as Ike sits beside me and tries to console me.

"Please don't leave me tonight," I beg him.

I drift off to sleep as he tells me, "I'm here, baby girl. I'm right here." But it only reinforces the pain, because I know he won't be around much longer.

Ike

Before Charlotte awakes, I go to George's to check on him, and I'm surprised when I find him wide-awake, sitting on the couch, staring numbly at the television when I morph into the living room. He's showered, and at least that's an improvement. His chin lifts and his eyes scan the room almost as if he senses me.

"Ike?" he questions and my brows rise.

"I'm here, George," I tell him.

His head lowers and he stares at a notepad in his lap, the first page covered in writing. He tears the sheet off and folds it, setting it on the table beside where he's seated. When he lifts his head again, he says, "I don't know if you're here, but I feel like maybe you are." He's silent for a long moment before continuing. "I've felt that way a lot since you died, like maybe you were watching over me."

I move toward him and kneel down at his side. "I have been, George."

His eyes tear up a little, but he takes a deep breath and keeps the tears at bay. "I'm sorry I let you down, that I wasn't better or . . . stronger, but I'm okay now, Ike. I don't want you to be trapped here because of me. I promise I won't go back to the drugs. I swear it. I'm going to rehab."

As he speaks, the remainder of the weight I've carried slips away. He's telling the truth. He will be okay. But, what about Charlotte? Will he be foolish enough to let her go?

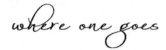

"I'm in love with her," he says, as if he's just read my mind. My gaze jerks to his, my brows narrowed in shock. "I know you're worried about her. I know you have to be in love with her, too. How could you not be?" he snorts.

My chest tightens with his words. Is he guessing all of this or does he sense me? Now that he knows I've been here, is he allowing our bond, that bond between not only siblings, but twins, to speak to him?

"I fucked up. I was angry at myself, and I took it out on her."

"Yeah, you're an ass," I mumble as I stand.

"I'm an ass," he says, shaking his head.

"I'm going to do my best to make things right with her. If she'll wait for me, I'll try my hardest, for her. So . . . don't worry about that, if you are. I'll take good care of her. I promise." Rubbing his eyes with the heels of his hands, he says, "I love you, Ike. Thank you for loving me enough to stay and watch out for me, but I want you to find peace, brother. I need to know you're okay, too." A tear trickles down his cheek before he stands and wipes it. Heading back to his bedroom, he quickly dresses for work.

When he comes out he's holding my dog tags. *Why is he taking those with him?* Grabbing his keys and the folded piece of paper on the table by the door, he takes a deep breath and says, "Good-bye, Ike. I love you, man." Then he walks out the door.

"Good-bye, George. I love you, too." I nod sadly and morph away.

Ike

When I return to the room Charlotte is just waking up. "Come on," I tell her. "Let's go to our place." I manage to encourage her to get up and force her to shower and dress. She is definitely not a morning person. The intention is to meet with her father first thing, but I think I need to take her somewhere peaceful.

"Our place?" she asks.

"Yeah, under the tree by the water. Bring a blanket."

We climb in Sniper's truck and drive up the mountain. Neither of us says a word the entire drive. The pull that was annoying before is now something I have to literally fight or it will drag me away. But I can't go yet. The truth is George is okay. He's let me go and Charlotte helped him do that. He knows I'm okay and now, my business is done. The problem now is he doesn't feel worthy of her. He hasn't admitted that to anyone, let alone himself, but sometimes others can know someone better than they know themselves. I only pray he'll pull his head out of his ass before it's too late and he loses her forever.

The day is warm, and the sun is shining brightly, enhancing the elaborate colors of early fall. Charlotte grabs the blanket from the back of the truck, and we head down to the water. After she spreads it out, we sit side by side and stare at the river; the surface ablaze with the light from the sun.

My throat is tight. There are things I must say to her because I don't know how much longer I can fight the pull.

"It's almost time, isn't it?" she asks, her gaze fixed on the water.

"Yes. It will be soon."

"Are you scared?" she asks. She's asked this before, and the answer is still the same. I'm not scared. I'm sad. I'm sad to leave her and everyone I love, but this is part of the cycle; something that must be done. I know I need to put on a brave face for her; after all, she's the one being left behind now. I'll be gone and if George doesn't get his shit together, she won't have him either. I do know if she stays here in Warm Springs, the Mercers will watch out for her. And if she's ready to forgive her family, she could go home, but I know that's not what she wants. She loves it here . . . or she did. She loved the feeling of home, the people, the magic of a small town filled with tranquility and beauty.

"No. I'm not scared. But . . . I will miss you. I'm in love with you, ya know."

A sob breaks free from her that tears at my insides. "I feel like I shouldn't tell you these things, but I don't know how I can't. You, you gave me peace, Charlotte . . . in so many ways. I can never thank you enough for that." Tears form in my eyes as she sobs, pulling her knees up and hugging them, hiding her face from me.

I'm desperate for a way to ease her pain, so I tell her, "Lie down."

She looks up at me, eyes red and swollen, and her lip trembling. "What?"

"I want to try something. Will you lie down?" She does as I ask, tears streaming down her cheeks onto her neck. "Close your eyes, please." After a long glance that tells me she doesn't want to but says she will do as I've asked because she trusts me, and she closes her eyes. I have no idea if what I'm about to do will work, or help in any way, but I have to try. "Remember when we talked about our first date?"

Her mouth curves slightly. "And our first kiss," she adds.

"And the first time we made love."

"It would've been right here."

"And I would carve *I & C* in a heart on that big tree back there." Her smile falters as the *what could have been* thought hits her. "Live those thoughts with me now." Her brows furrow and she's about to open her eyes, but I tell her not to. "From the beginning, imagine it with me. It's as close as we'll ever get to the real thing, but I swear I'll take it all with me. It'll be real to me."

Tears break free from her closed eyes and she nods twice to let me know she's ready to begin. "You start."

I stand and move beside her. She's beautiful. Her dark hair is fanned out around her head, the tips reaching over the blanket and resting on the brittle, fallen leaves surrounding her perfect form. "You'd be at work and I'd show up with flowers," I begin as I lie down beside her, joining my hand with hers. It's the closest I'll ever be to touching her. But as I continue speaking, something miraculous happens. I see myself through her eyes. And I feel as though our souls are connected. Staring across at her, I smile, my heart full with tranquility. A part of me will always be present, through her.

Chapter 30

Charlotte

I have no idea how he's doing it, but somehow as I imagine what he says, the visual feels so real and has so much more depth to it than I could create on my own. His soft voice smoothly guides me through every event. We're in the restaurant and he approaches me with lilies; my favorite. His smile is polite. Warm and genuine.

The way he asks me out plays out exactly the way we discussed. "Date by ambush," I chuckle as we imagine having dinner and laughing in a back corner booth at Ike and George's. "You could have at least let me go back to the room to change."

"Nah," he disagrees. "You look beautiful no matter what you're wearing."

I smile sadly. As lovely as this is—imagining this with him—it hurts.

"Don't," he warns softly. "I need you right here with me, baby girl. We don't have long. There's plenty of time to be sad later."

Before I can argue, he continues narrating. We're standing before each other in front of my motel room. The night is chilly and I'm wearing his jacket. I tug it around me and pull the shoulder to my face. It smells exactly how I imagine he'd smell. "Your scent is amazing," I say.

"It's the cologne I used to wear," he tells me. And I bask in the delicious fragrance of his manly, warm scent.

My gaze meets his, his soft brown eyes looking at me like I'm a jewel. And in that moment, I don't feel strange at all. I feel treasured. "You're beautiful," he whispers. Then he gently places his hands on my face, his long fingers splayed across each of my cheeks, before our lips meet in a tender kiss. The night breeze causes goose bumps on my arms and back, and I cherish his warm mouth. He has given me a rare gift, something I never thought I'd have. The kiss is soft and sweet and it goes on and on until our surroundings seem to swirl and we're sitting hand in hand in the dining room of his parents' house. We're seated side by side as we laugh with his family. Cameron is telling a joke that has us all in stitches.

"Of course, you'd meet my parents . . . ," he tells me and smiles.

"Of course," I agree.

As we sit completely still and he narrates, images flash and the sounds of his family fade away. The first image is of us singing to the radio as he drives us around, and we're laughing at how awful we sound. The next image follows immediately after the first and it's of us hiking up the mountain through the park while I whine about how far we've gone. I can't seem to keep up with the athletic abilities of a solider. The next picture shows me on Ike's back as he carries me back down the mountain because I'm a klutz and sprained my ankle.

"You carried me the entire way back down, huh?" I ask quietly.

"Yep. Happily." Warmth blankets me.

Throughout every image what I notice most are the smiles on our faces. And that causes my chest to ache.

As he speaks, more images appear of us cooking spaghetti together, me straddling him on the couch as we make out while he cops a feel. Heat radiates through my body as I watch how his hands fist my hair and how our mouths press to the others, achingly hard, as if we just can't get close enough. The passion in that moment, hits me hard.

"I love your breasts," Ike says, breathless.

"Perv," I jest and he grins.

"By now I have a serious case of blue balls, but you're making me wait."

In the image, he's just taken off my shirt. Even though I'm wearing a bra, he stares at me, his brown eyes fixed on me as if I'm the most beautiful thing he's ever seen. I watch myself stare back, and the want and need in that moment is palpable; it's a living and breathing thing. I need to see this moment with Ike. "Maybe I'm ready by now."

In this beautiful daydream, our surroundings swirl and we're by the river under the large tree staring at one another. Ike's soft gaze meets mine and while I see want and need, I see pain. This will be every bit brutal as it will beautiful. We're giving ourselves to one another the only way we can, but afterwards, we must face the inevitable. We must let each other go.

"Take your shirt off," I order him. He's not wearing his normal Army uniform. He's in a dark button up shirt and jeans. Our gazes remain locked as his fingers slowly undo each button while I slip off my jacket and kick my shoes off. When his shirt falls from his body, my mouth goes dry. He's perfect. His large broad shoulders and arms are smooth, his dog tags resting against his firm chest. His abs are ripped and peppered with the faintest dusting of hair that trails down into the waist his pants.

"Now you," he urges.

Ike

She's nervous. And it's beautiful. Her arms cross as she reaches down for the hem of her shirt and pulls it over her head, her long hair moving up with her shirt, but tumbling back down her shoulders and back as she tosses it aside. Even though I'm only imagining this, the image is so clear and feels so real. Stepping toward me, her hands move to my belt and begin undoing it, before she works on the button of my pants. Before she pulls them down, my hands graze her shoulders as I reach around and unhook her bra. It falls to the ground and I step back and admire her, memorizing every detail of her body that I can. Quickly I pick her up and lay her on the blanket. The day is warm, but there's a slight chill in the air causing her skin to pebble with goose bumps. I pull her jeans and panties off and quickly remove my own. Before kneeling down and pressing my body to hers, I stare at her, naked and waiting for me. *Fuck,* she's exquisite. My insides ache with want for her, but there's a pain there, too. This is it. This is all there is for us. But it's more than I thought I'd get so I'll seize it. Once I feel her under me, her breasts against my chest, I tug the side of the blanket over us, keeping as much warmth around us and between us as I can.

"Are you ready?"

She licks her lips and nods yes. "I've never been more ready for anything in my entire life."

Time stands still as we become one. Sadness lingers in her eyes as our gazes remain locked. She knows I'll be gone soon. I've never experienced anything so agonizingly beautiful. I pray I'll get to remember this on the other side, that whatever higher being there is will allow me to hold tightly to this memory. This is only a dream; the two of us imagining what could have been in another time or another life. Her breath on my neck, her hands and fingers pushing into the flesh of my back; all tragically beautiful memories I need because I'm not sure I can endure eternity without them. Grabbing my face, she slams her mouth to mine, kissing me fiercely. I push back, cursing the world that I can't get closer. My thrusts quicken as she claws at me, catching my lips between her teeth, driving me fucking crazy. I pull my lips from hers as she cries out, her body tensing.

"I love you, Ike," she cries as a tear drifts down her cheek. With the tip of my tongue, I collect it before joining my mouth to hers again. It's only moments later when she cries out in pleasure, and I finish seconds after, resting my forehead to hers as we both fight to catch our breath. I kiss her neck, her jawline, and her lips once more as she whimpers. Sitting up, I pull her to my side and tug the blanket over us. Her head rests on my shoulder as we watch the water glisten. I'd give anything to do this for real, not just imagine it.

"How do I let you go, Ike?" she whispers.

I have no answer for that. So I retreat back into our dream where I squeeze her tighter. The background changes and we're at the bank of the river, and together we take turns narrating the life we'll never have together. We watch a million memories play out before us, just over the water's surface. Some of my favorites are our wedding day, the way she smiles at me when she reaches the altar. Another is her asleep on the sofa, her belly swollen and round with our child. And of course, the day our daughter is born, cradled in Charlotte's arms as Charlotte smiles lovingly at me.

The images play on in beautiful and chaotic order. They're not all perfect, in some we fight, but those are followed by the ones where we make up.

"I guess you never figured out I'm always right," she jests as we watch an image of her throwing a pillow at me as she shouts.

"No," I say as the image shows me grabbing her and kissing her fiercely causing all her anger to melt away. "I just like to stir you up so we can have epic makeup sex." She chuckles softly and nuzzles her head into the crook of my neck. "What are we missing?" I ask her.

This," she says just before she describes the image of an old man and woman sitting side by side in rocking chairs. It's us after a lifetime together. She slips her wrinkled hand in mine as we stare out into the mountains from our front porch, watching the splendor of fall.

In this fantasy, I kiss her temple, closing my eyes and praying she will have this one day. And I pray it's with George. She loves him just as she loves me; fiercely. She's crying quietly, tears softly seeping down her beautiful face. Leaning toward her, I say, "When you miss me, come here and talk to me. This will always be our place."

"Will you be here?" she weeps.

"A part of me will always live here . . ." Looking back at the tree behind us, I sigh. "I'm sorry I couldn't carve that *I & C* in the tree for you."

"I'm sorry for a lot of things, Ike," she whimpers as she attempts to stifle a soft cry. The moment feels tragically painful, reaching in the deepest part of my soul. And although I hate to leave her, I need a few minutes to sort myself out before I unravel.

"Charlotte," I say, and squeeze her hand tightly. "I need a bit of time alone. I'm sorry, I just . . . Will you be okay here?"

"Sure," she says, quietly. "I'll go back to the motel. You will come back and see me, won't you?" Her gray eyes linger on mine, hope and sadness etched across her face.

Brushing my knuckles against her cheek, I reply, "I promise, baby girl." Then I morph away.

Chapter 32

Charlotte

When I open my eyes, Ike is gone, so I remain still, lying on the blanket and staring at the sky. Everything we just imagined together felt so real; so content. But real or not, he's leaving soon. There are no words to describe the pain I feel inside right now. The ache is endless, reaching from my toes to the tips of my hair. It is a relentless, gaping hole of torture. When he goes, he will take a part of me with him; a part that can never be replaced because it is his—he owns it. He was the first person in a long time that offered me comfort and friendship. And I realize the agonizing pain of letting him go is exactly how George has felt for a long time.

The other half of my heart belongs to George. And that pain is altogether different. Against my initial better judgment, I fell for him. And boy, did I fall hard. George could own his part of me, take it and love it, treasure it even, but he's choosing not to. And in that, I feel hopeless and lost. How do I move on without a complete heart? How do I navigate through life with nothing but an empty chest of what-ifs? It bothers me to go back into that dark place, but the pain is becoming too much to bear. I had a plan. To end it, and as sad as it may sound, a part of me believes that would've been better than this. Losing the McDermott brothers will be my undoing. Ike saved me, but what for? To go back to the life I've lived for the last five years, but this time carrying the pain of having loved and lost? I have no idea if George will ever speak to me again, and I don't want to say good-bye to my best friend. I did it once with Axel, and I almost didn't survive. How can I possibly do it again? Am I really destined to be all alone?

I shake my head at my darker thoughts. I could never regret it; not one moment of it. Meeting and loving each of them has been my life's greatest accomplishment. I didn't know what life was until death came to my door. And I had no clue what love was until Ike forced me to live. He gave me a second chance at life when he brought me to this town and showed me the beauty of it. 'Where one goes to rejuvenate,' he had joked. I lived in a consuming darkness—barely getting by—and he brought me to the light. And although the pain is unyielding, I won't forget my brief time in the warmth, and I refuse to let it go.

I let out a snort when the magnitude of how fucked up our situation is hits me. I just imagined a lifetime of love with Ike. We laughed and loved and fought, and it was beautiful. Our situation is so complex. I love them both, equally and for very different reasons. And while a tiny little voice inside of me whispers that it was wrong to share that with Ike—even though it was a dream—when my hopes are for George to come to his senses and make me his, I'll never regret it. If George had been the soul that found me on the bridge that night instead if Ike, I would have imagined that beautiful life with him. But he didn't. It was Ike that found me. And it is Ike who loves me enough to understand that he shares my heart with his brother.

Hopping up, I shake the blanket off and I make my way back to Sniper's truck. Once inside, I pop open the large toolbox in the backseat and remove a large hunting knife.

Walking back down toward the shore and gripping the knife tightly, I decide there's only one thing left to do where Ike is concerned; show him what he means to me.

By the time Ike appears back at the motel, I've already showered and put on my pajamas. I'm lying in bed when suddenly he's there beside me. He rolls on his side so his eyes are level with mine. "Hey, beautiful," he whispers.

"Hi," I reply and muster up the best smile I can. "Did you go see George?"

"This morning before you woke up."

"How is he?"

"He's going to be okay. He said good-bye to me."

My eyes widen. "So he believes you were there?"

"I think so," he answers and nods. "I don't feel that weight anymore."

I want to cry—because I'm not at all ready for him to go—but I feel like that's all I've done for days and days. "When, Ike? When will you go?"

Ike closes his eyes and swallows hard. He doesn't have to say it; I know it will be soon. "We should say our good-byes now, Charlotte."

The finality of it all hits me. This is it. How am I supposed to sum up how much he means to me? There aren't enough words meaningful or poetic enough to show how I feel or that would do him justice. Lamely, I say, "I'm going to miss you so much."

Ike gives me his signature sly grin. "What will you miss most? My amazing sense of humor, or this hot body?" He motions a hand down from his head to his toes.

I can't help but chuckle through the tears I refused to shed only moments before. "Your ass. That's my final answer. Mostly that hot ass of yours," I laugh.

Ike laughs out loud, his eyes twinkling. "I knew you only liked me for my epic ass. You're so cliché," he jests.

We both grow quiet and I take another stab at expressing my feelings for him. "I'll miss your laugh, your killer smile, and Ike, you do have a killer smile. Sometimes it hurts, it's so beautiful. I'll miss how you always find a way to make me laugh. I'll miss the sound of your dog tags jingling under your shirt as you move around." His soft brown eyes stare into mine as I speak, soaking up every word.

"I'll miss your potty mouth," he tells me, and we both grin. "I'll miss how calm and peaceful you look while you're sleeping. You have no idea how badly I've wished I could touch you when you're sleeping, your skin so soft and smooth. And I'll miss your courage and kindness."

"Thank you, Ike," I say, as my lip trembles. "I've never thanked you for saving me."

"Oh, baby girl, you saved me," he says, softly, as he nervously rubs the back of his neck. "I'm dead and I still got to fall in love with my best friend. I'm a lucky bastard."

"D-do you think we'll see each other again? On the other side, I mean?"

He takes a deep breath. "I do. But not for a long time," he insists. "You're going to grow old, Charlotte. You're going to live a long and beautiful life. The happy life you deserve."

"But when it's time, if you can, will you try to find me? Will it be you who welcomes me to the other side? I want to know that you're okay."

"Come hell or high water," he promises. "And I mean it. If I can be the one to bring you over to . . . wherever it is, I will. But I need something from you."

"Anything," I weep softly.

"Wait for George. He has a plan. Give him some time, he'll come around."

I wipe my face on the pillow my head is resting on and nod. "I want to, but what if he doesn't come around?"

"He will," he assures me. "I know he will. And don't feel guilty for loving him, Charlotte. Maybe a lot of people wouldn't understand it, but I do. I know what's in your heart. I know how much you love us both. You just love us in a different way. Don't ever feel bad for that."

We talk for hours, saying our good-byes. And I pray for vigor the entire time. I promise him I won't ever be that girl he found on the bridge the night we met. That much I'm sure of. He's changed my outlook on life, and I'm a stronger person because he believed in me. He promises his heart will remain here with me. And I know that even when I can't hear or see him, his memory will always give me strength. He tells me stories about his childhood, beautiful and simple stories to keep my mind from unraveling. He's always had the gift to distract me so I don't breakdown. And I don't know what time it is, but my eyes have grown so heavy, I can barely stand it.

"Go to sleep, baby girl," he whispers.

"Will you be here when I wake?"

His warm eyes meet mine and he smiles softly. "I'll always be with you, Charlotte. Always. Right here." And he points to his chest.

That means no. This is it. I want to protest. Beg him not to go, but I have no energy left. As my eyelids close, refusing to stay open, even though I desperately want them to, I tell him the truest and most pure thing I can. "I love you, Ike McDermott."

"I love you, too, baby girl," he whispers. "Here, there, forever."

And come morning, I know that this is the last time I'll ever see or speak to the beautiful and wondrous soul that is Ike McDermott.

Chapter 33

Ike

I watch her sleep until the early rays of the morning sun begin to stream in to the room. She slept restless, crying softly in her sleep and calling out for me, begging me not to go.

I want to be angry and hateful about how unfair this is. But I can't. For I feel truly at peace. I was given a gift. This beautiful woman not only saved my brother, but she loves me. In that, I can only rejoice. I think back to how George was. I feared he'd waste away to a shadow of his former self. She is the beacon of light that my brother needed. I can rest easy now.

After using all of my will and strength, I finally stand, allowing my eyes to slowly graze over her; getting my last visual fill before I leave. I have to go before she awakes or it'll only drag out the emotional hell we're both going through. She needs to begin the healing process and she can't do that while I'm still here. In these last few seconds, I commit to memory every physical detail of her that I can; her long, dark hair, soft, pink lips, and smooth skin. But the best thing about her is her newfound joyous and spunky personality. I imagine her laugh, how light and beautiful it is. And that makes me grin. These memories are what will hold me through what lies ahead. The remembrance of her and what she has done for me and my family will be what gives me the courage to move on.

I smile as I stare at her for the last time.

"Good-bye, Charlotte," I whisper, and morph away.

I'm at our place by the water, watching the sun glisten on the water's surface. Fall is in full effect and I smile slightly. This is my favorite time of year. The pull is so strong, I know if I don't focus, it will take me at any moment. But I want one more minute. Just one. Turning, I walk back to the giant tree, wishing I could leave Charlotte a little piece of me; a tangible memory she could see and touch. When I look up, I stand frozen in shock. Carved in the tree, in bold letters is ***I & C*** inside of a big heart. For a moment I just stare, wishing I could go back to tell her what it means to me. But that's not an option now.

"It's time," I remind myself as I step closer to the tree and rest my hand over our initials. With one last look at the water, and my hand on the tree, I close my eyes and let the pull take me.

I finally just let go.

Chapter 34

Charlotte

Grief. What a horrid thing it is, yet I hold tightly to it. The agony I feel is how I remember he was here, that he existed. Sweet, beautiful Ike—he always had a smile on his face. The morning Ike leaves me, my father shows up. When I refuse to leave, he takes pity on me or decides it's not worth arguing with me, and pays my motel bill for the remainder of the month, shocking the hell out of me. For a brief and beautiful moment, I think maybe he's come to terms and realized my gift is real, but he obliterates that notion when he informs me Detective Andrews had requested I stay, even though, technically, I didn't have to. Then, to really hammer the nail in my coffin, he tells me he'll return with my mother in a few weeks.

Later that day, Sniper shows up and holds me as I sob. I'm a wicked mess, but he doesn't mention it. He simply tells me Ike would want me to be happy, and I know he's right.

When he finally stands to leave, he says, "I'm not sure if this is the best timing or not, but George asked me to give this to you." He lays an envelope on the bed beside where I'm sitting. I don't remember saying good-bye to him or him leaving, but when I look up, Sniper is gone. It must be a good-bye letter from George is all I can think. Maybe it was too hard for him to face me. Maybe he's worried I'll go crazy if he says it to my face. I'm not sure what he has to say to me, but I hope he's at least kind. My feelings for him haven't changed, and if his letter is a full rejection, I fear I won't be able to handle it.

It's an hour or so before I can bring myself to open the letter. The envelope is thick and I can tell there's more inside of it than just a letter. My hands are trembling as I tear the envelope open and see what's inside. In addition to the letter are dog tags. Something feels as if it's lodged in my throat as I gently pull out the chain with the two small tags attached.

Clutching the tags to my chest, I fall back on my bed and wail. I'll never forget the sound of his tags jingling under his shirt as he moved around. Is George giving these to me? I weep for what seems an endless amount of time before I'm able to sit up again. Finally, I manage to unfold the piece of paper that was also in the envelope, and hold my breath, bracing myself for the worst.

Dear Charlotte,

Forgive me for writing you this letter instead of talking to you face-to-face, but to be honest, I'm not exactly proud of how I've behaved around you the last few times we've seen each other. I told you the man you met when you first came here isn't really me. And that's true. The real me isn't the kind of man to get hooked on drugs and sleep with loose women, and I hate that that's your first impression of me.

I also told you I want to be the kind of man you

deserve and is worthy of your high opinion. That's also true. But telling you who I really am and showing you are very different things. So I'm going to rehab, Charlotte. I'm going to get clean and get my head straight. I know I haven't given you much reason to have faith in me, but I hope you'll wait for me. I hope you'll stay and give me the chance to prove myself to you.

If not, I understand. I've given you plenty of reasons to leave. But know this, Charlotte . . . When you told me you loved me the other night, something changed inside me. You marked me, and I'll never be able to let that go or forget it. Please know I'll do anything to be deserving of that love if you'll give me the chance.

I'll be back in thirty days. You still have a job, too. I've worked it out with Sniper. Please be safe and no matter what you decide, Charlotte, please be happy.

Enclosed you'll find Ike's dog tags. Since you gave me something treasured from your brother, it's only fair I do the same. I know he would've wanted you to have them.

~George

Returning the letter to its envelope, I lie back down and cry.

chapter 35

George

I've been gone thirty days. Not a lot of time, but it felt like an eternity. Now, I finally get to go home and face the real world again. I'm fucking nervous as hell. Anxiety has taken over because I know I have to look everyone I love in the eye and face what I've done. I know my family will forgive me; Sniper, too. But it's *her* I'm most worried about. Can she really forgive me for the way I've behaved? I've been a colossal dick, a sentiment confirmed by Sniper more times than I care to count. I've spent the last month digging up the bones of my past and facing them, but behind all of the shit, I had to figure out the millions of things I had to learn to forgive myself for. The one thing I know for sure is I need her. Hell, I love her. I've just been too much of a chickenshit to tell her. I crave Charlotte like if she were my next breath. She's been there in spirit the entire time, telling me, *I don't want to lose you, too.* Rehab was a bitch to get through. The shakes and night sweats I wouldn't wish on my worst enemy. But I'd made a promise to my brother, and damn it, I intend to keep it. He deserves that much from me. I'm lucky I made it out of my self-deprecating hell. It's a damn shame my anger has kept me away from her for this long—from accepting her for who she is. But through it all, I never stopped wanting her.

The last night I saw her, after leaving the Mercers,' I'd been impressed. The way she restored their sense of calm was nothing short of a miracle. As if their pain was healed instantaneously. Later that night, when she'd climbed in my lap and kissed me, I knew there was no way I could ever let her go. But in that moment, there was no way I could keep her either. I was a fucking mess; barely clean and just coming out of a quasi-relationship with a woman I had no fucking business seeing. Charlotte deserves better than that, but for some reason, she loves me. She wants to be with me, or at least she did. And to give her the best, my very best anyway, I had to go and fix me before I started anything with her.

My father has just picked me up and is driving me home from rehab, making mindless small talk along the way, but my mind is stuck on her. *How is she? Where is she?*

"How's Charlotte?" I interrupt him; unable to hold it in any longer. My father smiles, but never takes his eyes off the road.

"She's well, I believe. Why do you ask?" And the way he's smirking I know he knows why I'm asking.

"You know why, Dad," I mumble.

Picking up his stainless steel travel mug, he takes a long sip before saying, "She's a great girl, George. I hope you can convince her to stay."

My fingers instantly intertwine, full of tension as I squeeze them until the tips turn white. "Is she talking about leaving?" I ask tentatively, my throat growing tight at the thought. I couldn't blame her if she is. It's not like I've given her much of a reason to stay. And fuck me if I don't want her to.

"Her mother and father were just down here for a week or so. Word was they begged her to go, but she refused." I let out an audible breath, full of relief. *She stayed.* Maybe, just maybe, I have a chance. My father continues talking, and I have to fight to pay attention. "The trial for Casey Purcell's killer is in a week or two. She said she'd at least stay until after the trial."

"Where is she now?" My nerves are on edge, and I shake my right leg, the anticipation burning a hole inside me.

He cuts me a sideways glance and smirks, his eyes twinkling with mirth at my expense. "She's at our house, waiting to welcome you home."

Rubbing my chin as I grin briefly, I quickly wipe my sweaty palms on my pants. I take a deep breath and prepare myself.

Don't fuck this up, George.

Chapter 36

Charlotte

"Cameron, if you eat one more of those ham biscuits I will strangle you!" Beverly yells as Cameron flees the dining room, where a meal fit for kings is spread out on the McDermotts' large table.

Sniper, Anna, and I chuckle as Cameron shoves another biscuit in his mouth as he rushes by us.

"I'll be back for the cookies," he mumbles around the food in his mouth, although it's barely audible.

"They are bloody good," Sniper says. "Beverly used to send Ike care packages with them. Greedy bastard would only give me one or two."

"Are you nervous?" Anna whispers as she loops her arm with mine. Since the night Roger and George fought, Sniper has kept her abreast of my gift and all the events that transpired between Ike, George, and I. She accepted it rather easily, and we've become very close since.

"Extremely," I answer honestly as she leads me onto the front porch. I've waited for George for the past month knowing my feelings for him have not changed. I'm just not sure how he'll react to me being here. What if he changed his mind about us while in rehab? Regardless of the butterflies in my stomach, I'm so proud of him for going to rehab, for wanting to get better. And if I'm being honest, it gave me a chance to get myself together, too. I was devastated after Ike left, and I needed some time to cope. My heart still hurts every day for Ike, but slowly, it's getting better. My hope is George and I can move on from here. But deep inside there's a fear that maybe he won't feel the same. Maybe he won't want me anymore.

"Well you look fabulous," she says, as she bumps my shoulder with hers; bringing me out of my thoughts. Of course I do; Anna dressed me. I'm wearing a burgundy dress with three-quarter sleeves and tights with boots. Anna put my hair in a high ponytail and I'm wearing a little more makeup than I usually do. But even the cutest outfit and makeup can't cover the dread I'm feeling inside.

"They're pulling in," Cameron announces as he steps out on the porch and nods his head in the direction of the driveway. And my heart skips a beat. Beverly and Sniper join us on the porch, and Cameron wraps an arm around Beverly's shoulders and kisses her temple when she becomes teary-eyed. Sniper takes my hand and squeezes it, giving me a wink; letting me know everything will be all right. *Breathe, Charlotte.*

When Henry parks his car, I once again have to remind myself to breathe. I'm so damn nervous my legs are shaking. Having my legs give out on me would not be good right now. Sniper, Anna, Cameron, and Beverly fly off the porch and surround George the moment he steps foot out of the car. I can barely see him as he's lost in the tiny crowd surrounding him. After a few moments, they seem to break and his gorgeous, dark eyes meet mine, sucking the breath right out of me. They're clearer now, and not so foreboding. As the others chitchat amongst themselves, he slips away and walks toward me. My heart hammers in my chest as he watches me with every step he takes. He looks amazing, so much better than when I last saw him. He's put on a little weight, filled out a little more, and his hair is trimmed. Light panting breaths release from my mouth as I will myself to stand still. When he finally reaches me, he takes my hand and runs his thumb over the back of it. Caressing it lightly.

He worries his bottom lip for a few seconds as he stares down at me. "How are you?" he asks, his voice deep and husky, making my insides curl.

"I'm good," I manage after a beat. "How are you?" I add. "Y-you look really good, George," I finish in a nervous stutter.

He smiles and nods in agreement. "That's because I'm clean."

The others sidle by us, quietly, all of them giving quick, knowing glances. It's no secret to anyone George and I have some things to work out, and it makes my heart burst with happiness that they're all rooting for us. It's nice to know I finally feel at home here, and they want to see us happy and together.

Once they're all inside, George remains steady and continues to hold my hand. He pulls me toward him and slams my body to his. I tense for a moment from shock, but quickly mold to him as I tentatively wrap my arms around his neck. He holds me to him, tightly, breathing into my neck. And it feels amazing. My chest presses firmly against his. The electricity between us is palpable. A long minute passes where neither of us says a word. When his mouth finally finds my ear he whispers, "I've missed you like crazy. I gotta spend some time here with everyone, but I'd like it if we could leave together afterwards. I need to tell you some things. Is that okay?"

"Of course," I whisper, still holding onto him for dear life. He doesn't let me go, and I'm not sure how long we'd remain standing here if not for Cameron popping his head out and clearing his throat.

"I hate to break up this lovers' moment, or whatever this is," he motions his hand wildly in our direction, "but Mom says we can't eat until you two come in. And I'm a growing boy," he adds. "I need to eat."

George snorts as he pulls away from me and turns his head to Cameron. "We'll be right in." Cameron, satisfied with this, leaves us and George's gaze finds mine. "Just in case I forget to tell you later, you look beautiful tonight, Charlotte."

Warmth crawls up my neck and covers my cheeks as his heated stare stays focused on mine. Before I respond, I look down and realize he's wearing my brother's necklace. My fingers brush over it softly as I smile. "You're wearing it."

Swallowing hard, he takes my hand and presses it to his chest. "I have your brother's necklace, and you have my brother's tags." Then he tilts his face down and presses a soft kiss to my forehead before pulling me inside to join the others for dinner.

Dinner went great. Everyone laughed and reminisced, and when the subject of Ike came up, George asked me questions about my time with him, and I take that as a good sign. When I became teary-eyed, he'd handed me his napkin to wipe my face and squeezed my leg under the table to comfort me. George told us about his struggles with addiction, how and why he thinks he came to be in that bad spot in his life, and he apologized to all of us for any hurtful things he may have said or done.

When the evening ends, we all collect our coats and before I step outside, Beverly pulls me into her arms and hugs me tightly. "Thank you for saving my son," she whispers before kissing my cheek. I smile at her but I know George decided to go to rehab on his own; that's something I can't take credit for.

"You two be safe tonight," Cameron winks as he gives George a one-shouldered hug. "And by safe I mean—"

"Cameron," Beverly warns.

"What?" Cameron feigns ignorance. "I was going to say wear your seatbelts—by safe I meant wear your seatbelts. What did you . . . ? Oh, Mom, come on. Dad, we've gotta do something about this woman's gutter mind. She's a bad influence on me."

Beverly's face turns bright red as we all laugh. Even Henry can't help chuckling, even when Beverly smacks his chest.

We hug Sniper and Anna good-bye and climb in the Ford Focus my mother made my father buy me when they were in town. She was appalled he'd sold my 4Runner, knowing what it meant to me because it had been Axel's.

The ride to George's house is silent. I can sense he's as nervous as me, but when we pull in to his driveway and I park, he turns toward me. I stiffen when I notice the pain in his eyes. He rubs the back of his neck as he stares at me. "Charlotte, I'm sorry for everything I've put you through," he whispers, making a strangled noise before looking down. His hands tremble as I reach out to touch him. He takes my hand in his and traces a circle on it with his finger, finally looking back up at me. "I want to take things slow, but I'm fucking dying over here," he adds as he leans in closer. "I've spent the last month terrified you'd be gone when I came back or might have changed your mind about me," he says, sadly. He tilts his head to the side as he reaches out his hand and runs his thumb down my right cheek. "I need to know . .

. do we still have a shot?"

Swallowing hard, I nod, but quickly turn away from him and open my car door. Slipping out, I walk up the steps to his door and wait. After a moment, I hear the car door open and slam shut, then he's right behind me. I take a few quick breaths; anxiousness and excitement coursing through my body. Licking my lips, I step closer to his door. Not meeting his gaze, I stare ahead at the door and say, "I'd like to spend the night with you. Is that okay?"

He doesn't say a word as he steps closer behind me. His body is so close, for a second I forget to breathe. My chest pounds at warp speed when his arm grazes my waist. Then he unlocks the door and pushes it open, motioning for me to enter first. Once inside, he flicks on some lights and takes a look around. "Your mom and I came over yesterday and cleaned. We wanted it to be nice for you when you returned."

"You didn't have to do that, but I really appreciate it," he manages. Deciding to put him out of his misery, I finally meet his gaze. Stepping toward him, I reach one hand out and thread my fingers through his hair.

"I've really missed you, too," I whisper as his hands rest on my hips. "I do want to be with you . . . but I need to know something."

My heart thunders as I remind myself to breathe again. "What do you need to know?" he asks after swallowing hard, his Adam's apple bobbing as he does.

"I need to know you believe me," I squeak. My mouth is suddenly dry, but I dart my tongue out and lick my lips. "You didn't believe me before. And that's okay, not everyone does at first. Hell, my father still doesn't believe it. But George, I'm not crazy," I add as I look him square in the eye. "I never asked for this . . . gift, but it's mine now. There was a time when I hated it with every fiber of my being, but I don't anymore, because without it, I wouldn't be here right now. I was in such a dark place I would've killed myself that night . . . I know it." I give him a once-over, but I can't read his reaction, so I decide to continue. "And because I can see the dead, I'm alive. Ike saved me and brought me here. Without my ability I would've never met you." I remember to get to the point as I nervously push some of my hair behind my ear. "It's not going away. I will most likely always see the dead, and if we're going to be together, that may make our relationship difficult at times, especially if you don't believe me."

George pulls away and my heart drops to the pit of my stomach.

He doesn't believe me.

George

"If I could go back and redo the night you told me that, I swear I would do it differently. My head was so fucked up and . . ." I'm doing a horrible job explaining this. "It was a lot to take in."

"I know it was," she tells me, her gaze on the floor.

"Charlotte. Look at me, please." Her gaze is riddled with sadness when she lifts her head. "I've had a lot of time to think about it. I did believe you that night."

"You did?" she asks, surprised.

"I was mad. Unreasonably so, but I was," I admit with shame as I run a hand through my hair.

"But, why?"

This is the hard part. This is the part where I have to try to explain why I was such a dick. "I was jealous."

"What?"

"I was jealous you could see him and I couldn't. And I was envious the two of you spent so much time together. I was a clusterfuck of emotions all the way around." Her brows narrow as she listens to me. "Charlotte . . . since the day he died, all I've felt is guilt. It's suffocated me. He was the good one, the brave one that died in war. If one of us were going to go, it should've been me, Charlotte. When I found out you could see him . . . communicate with him . . . that he was still here, I don't know, it just reinforced all of those feelings. He should be the one here, not me. And to top it off, because I couldn't get my shit together, he'd been stuck here."

"George . . ." She says my name quietly. "I miss Ike," she whispers, and her eyes close briefly, the pain in her heart evident. "And I'll miss him every day of my life, but I would never trade you for him. Ike was all of those wonderful things you just said, but you're selling yourself short." She steps toward me, her gray eyes gazing upon me softly. "You are such an amazing brother and person; he couldn't leave you behind until he knew you'd pull through. George, his love for you saved us both. Don't you see how beautiful that is?"

My chest tightens and dread runs through me. I hate the thought of her trying to kill herself. I don't like when she brings it up. *Where the hell would I be without her?* I swallow hard as I shake my head. "I just didn't think I deserved you . . ."

"And now?"

I run a wide palm down my face and exhale loudly. "Now . . . well, now I hope I was wrong. Now I realize all I did was hurt you, myself, and even Ike." Her understanding gaze tilts my world on its axis. All I want is to bury my face into her neck and brush my lips across her smooth skin. Stepping toward her, I seize her face in my hands and stare deeply into her eyes. "So to answer your question, I do believe you, and I believe in you. And no matter how intense your gift may make life sometimes, I want to be a part of it. Charlotte . . . I want you. All of you. The good, the bad, and the ugly. I love you."

And now, all I want is to get lost in her. Lifting her, she squeaks in surprise as I set her on the kitchen island. No more words are needed as her lips meet mine. Biting back a growl, I settle closer between her legs. I know I should slow down, but I can't help it. She's driving me out of my mind, and I wouldn't want it any other fucking way. If she keeps making all those little noises, I'm going to lose all self-control. I hold on to her delicate hips, craving the warmth of her body. "Baby," I breathe against her lips. "Do you know how much I love you?"

Her body trembles beneath my touch and I want to devour every inch of her. "Mmm-hmm," she moans in reply. And she brings her lips back to mine. Her kiss says everything I've been hoping to hear. It says she wants me as much as I want her . . . that she's mine.

I reach around her and firmly take hold of her bottom. "Wrap your legs around me, Charlotte," I whisper against her neck. Immediately doing as I asked, our bodies meld together in want and need.

Tangling my fingers in her hair, I bring her head back and kiss my way down to her jaw, and then her shoulder. When I bite softly across her flesh, she squirms against me.

"George, please," she whimpers, her tone begging. I bring my mouth over hers, needing to taste her. She suckles my tongue, and I let out a groan, sucking her bottom lip between my teeth.

"Are you ready?" I pant, and she nods, her desire prevalent in her eyes. I walk us back to my bedroom, her chest pressed eagerly against mine the entire way.

Making love to Charlotte, her giving herself to me like she's never given herself to anyone is the most beautiful gift I'll ever receive. We spend hours exploring each other, tasting the other, and now, I lie awake as she rests peacefully curled up beside me.

I'm mesmerized by her beautiful soul, and I'm losing what little control I have left. She's a part of me now. Since the day we found out Ike died, I've felt adrift; like I was simply floating through life, unable to anchor myself. But here, right now, with Charlotte in my arms, I feel grounded. There will always be a part of me that feels empty. Ike was my twin, and his absence is palpable. I feel it with every breath I take. But I know now I can survive it. And instead of letting the memory of him and the loss of him hinder me, I'll let it strengthen me. My brother saved me. My brother gave me her; the woman he loved.

She's never told me what went on between them, the feelings they shared for one another, but I know deep down they loved each other. The way she speaks about him tells me so. And if I'm honest, I'm a little jealous of that, but I know she loves me too. And if she were to share her heart with another man, my brother is the first and only man I'd allow.

After all the grief and pain I've caused her, she's still here.

And she wants me.

"She loves me, Ike," I murmur. I stare at her slumbering form and smile. I'm so damn happy. There are questions I want to ask, things I want to know about their time together, but I won't. All that matters is she's here in my arms and she loves me.

"I'll love her for both of us, Ike," I whisper.

Pressing a soft kiss on her forehead, I take in her sweet scent. Inhaling the soft fragrance of perfume, I let out a sigh of contentment. She is my forever. And I close my eyes with a sense of peace I haven't felt in a long time.

Charlotte

"They'll be here in five minutes," George calls from our bedroom where he's dressing.

"I know, babe," I laugh. "I think you're more nervous than I am."

When he enters the living room, I bite my lip. He's gorgeous, dressed in a black T-shirt and jeans. God, I love him. "Don't look at me like that, you," he says. "Or they'll be outside waiting a while when they get here."

"Do you think this was a good idea?" I ask for the hundredth time.

Pulling me to him, he kisses my forehead. "I think using your gift for such a good cause is beautiful, Charlotte. We only signed for one season. If it doesn't go well, we won't sign again."

After Casey Purcells' trial and her murderer was brought to justice, word spread like wild fire about me. It wasn't long until I was contacted by Lifetime and they offered me a television show. After much thought, George and I decided to give it a shot. Lifetime will send us state-to-state with cameras following us everywhere and capture me using my gift. With most of the money we make, we're going to donate it to Virginia colleges to provide free transportation for students at night. While this will be offered to male students as well, my true hope is female students will take full advantage of this. Maybe we can stop what happened to Casey from happening to someone else. We're calling it, Casey's Ride. The Purcells were truly touched and even agreed to do an interview for the show telling the world about how I was a huge help in bringing Casey's murderer to justice.

Looking up into George's dark eyes, I tell him, "I love you. Thank you for doing this with me."

He kisses my mouth gently and smiles. "Thank you for loving me."

My life with George has been wonderful. After so much time in the dark, I can't explain what it is to live in the light. My gift, which was once a curse, something I hated, is now treasured. It brought me to Warm Springs. It led me to Ike McDermott. It introduced me to George, my husband.

We have dinner with the Mercers once a week. They keep asking when George and I will have children; they want to babysit. I could never replace their daughter Maggie, but I think, in a way, we help fill a void for each other. I'm like a daughter to them; they're like the mother and father I've needed.

I still visit 'our spot' as Ike called it, often. And when I do, I talk to him. I imagine him in the water with a fly rod and that stellar smile of his on his face. And I pray his hopes came true; that it's a place just like it that he went to.

I tell him about George and how well he's doing, and I try to let him know how well I'm doing, too. And I thank him. For his love, for saving me, and for George.

George and I love so fiercely. Because when Ike went, he not only took a part of me with him, he took a part of George, too. In this way, among many ways, we are bonded. And I know, one day, we'll all be together again, and George and I will be whole. But for now, George and I live every day to the fullest, loving and laughing.

Just the way Ike wanted us to.

Thank you to Kari, with Cover to Cover Designs, for the awesome cover. I know I was a pain on this one, but I love the result.

Thank you to Marilyn, from Eagle Eye Reads. I am truly grateful for your hard work and help molding this story.

Thank you Rae, from 77peaches, for your thorough proof read. I appreciate all of your hard work.

Tami, from Integrity Formatting, thank you for always going above and beyond. You are amazing.

Thank you to my amazing Smitten Kittens. You ladies rock my world. I love you all.

Author Kim Holden . . . you are epic. Thank you so much for beta reading this and for your awesome notes. I am so glad I met you and we've become friends. You are probably the nicest person I have ever met.

Dreama Boo, I love you. Thanks for being the best beta ever!

Meg Collett . . . you know. You're awesome. Thanks for telling me what a narcissist I am and setting me straight when I freak out over my work. I truly love you and your brutal honesty.

Leah, thank you for always encouraging me and always being excited for me. I know I can always count on you, and I love you so much for it. I also love you for teaching me the word 'meh.' It feels good.

Thank you to my friends and family who constantly support and encourage me. I love you all.

Thank you to my children who I owe a ton of playtime to. You guys have really been patient, and I'm so grateful. I know I owe you lots of Mommy time and cuddles.

And, as always, Toler. I love you. Thanks for being you.

Warm Springs does exist and I strongly encourage everyone to visit Bath County in the fall. It is truly, breathtakingly beautiful. There are tons of Bed & Breakfasts, the Jefferson pools, the Homestead Resort, and miles and miles of scenic mountain views.

For more information, please use the link below.

http://www.bathcountyva.org/

about the author

B N Toler lives in central Virginia with her husband and three children.

For more information on B N Toler, please visit her social media sites.

Web: http://www.bntoler.com/

Facebook: http://www.facebook.com/pages/B-N-Toler-Author/279007692235640

Twitter: http://twitter.com/BNTOLER

27299170R00150

Made in the USA
Middletown, DE
15 December 2015